9.40

The School-Marm Tree

The School-Marm Tree

a novel by
Howard O'Hagan

Vancouver, Talonbooks, 1977

published with assistance from the Canada Council

Talonbooks
201 1019 East Cordova
Vancouver
British Columbia V6A 1M8
Canada

This book was typeset by Linda Gilbert of B.C. Monthly
Typesetting Service, designed by David Robinson and
printed by Hemlock Printers for Talonbooks.

First printing: November 1977

Canadian Cataloguing in Publication Data

O'Hagan, Howard, 1902–
    The school-marm tree
      ISBN 0-88922-129-4 pa.

     I. Title.
    PS8529.H33S36   C813'.5'4   C77-002214-6
    PR9199.3.0

To
J. Douglas Bulgin

introduction

"I know it sounds silly, damn silly, but I used to feel, oh, I don't know, a presence in the mountains. Some kind of a presence."

Howard O'Hagan

Despite its title, its plot, its portrait of the past, *The School-Marm Tree* is really a novel about that mountain presence and the quality of heart capable of discerning it. From first to last — inspiring or threatening — the omnipresent mountains dominate. And Selva, dreaming girl, is the delicate instrument through which we sense and respond to the presence they conjure up.

"Selva dreamed. Selva was awake, wide, wide awake — and still she dreamed. She dreamed beyond the window by which she sat, waiting for Slim Conroy to come up the street, and beyond the street and beyond the town and far beyond the mountains rising above the town."

In this, the opening paragraph, where the mountains make an unobtrusive first appearance, we taste the subtle flavor of O'Hagan's prose: *beyond*, what a world of yearning is evoked by those syllables — repeated no less than four times in as many lines. And what is it in the words — does Slim's name lack sufficient weight? — that already we half suspect he will

7

not answer Selva's dreams? The mere sight of him "trailing his shadow behind him ... with the orange bow-tie like an angry blossom at his throat," strengthens our suspicions. In a matter of pages, we are convinced. Selva sees "through a jagged hole in the brim of his hat ... a star glitter and then disappear as he (turns) his head." Though Selva is unaware, O'Hagan is letting us know Slim will never do.

Then, like a visitor from another planet, Peter Wrogg appears, tissue and bone of Selva's fantasies. On their initial walk together she takes him to the cemetery the better to see 'her' mountains, "some of them a hundred miles away, blue and glistening in the sun, ribbed with ice and snow, silent in tumult, frozen in great waves of immobility." And this, O'Hagan tells us "was her country. Those were its ponderous barriers." So he delineates her world.

Like the good mountain guide he once was, O'Hagan leads us through the ranges of his story, pointing there, drawing attention here and, if we have a mind for it, letting us in on their secrets.

The book is a steady climb, sombre and slow — violence and yearning jostling each other — from the small but brutal violence of the beating of the porcupine on the trestle near the beaver meadow, to the greater violence that lies in wait under Mount Erebus — the principals moving implacably towards the climax in what feels like a kind of silence. Parallel to the mounting tension of the tale is Selva's rise from the role of domestic in the valley town to that of hostess at the lodge in the High Valley, where in their threatening proximity, she no longer sees the mountains as height but as "angry depth — the depth that she might fall." Finally their protean presence weighs so obdurately upon her that she feels she is never alone: "When I look up at that mountain, I feel that something is going to happen, something awful, I don't know what it is. It's as though someone were up there looking down."

That mountain is Mount Erebus. (Erebus — son of Chaos, darkness, the subterranean region through which departed shades enter Hades.) The final typescript read Pinnacle Peak but O'Hagan stroked out Pinnacle and wrote Erebus. With his sensitivity to the relationship between name and mood, it was invitable that he should do so.

Yet in conversation he had a dozen rationalizations. "There is no Pinnacle in that particular range," he said, as if his left and logical lobe had no understanding of what his creative right lobe had done.

How did he invent Branchflower — so perfect a name for an alpinist? "I knew a Branchflower," he recalled. "Good looking fellow. Came into the stables behind Jasper wanting a job."

What more fitting than Prior for an elderly couple who live entirely in the past? Change one letter of Wrogg and you have Wrong. With the introduction of Clay Mulloy, we recognize the good earth. And so it goes, with a kind of absolute pitch.

Marvellous too, his 'similarity in dissimiliars:' "A shower was coming down the valley, hanging like shaggy goat hair from the belly of the laden sky." Surely only a seamstress who had sewn pink fabric with red thread could understand at first reading: "her new pink tinged silk dress, which fitted her like flesh, appeared to be bleeding at the seams."

Time and again, minute observation of people is compacted into a single exact image: "He . . . was tall, erect and reserved as a grandfather's clock . . . (and) made a whirring sound in his throat, as though, instead of speaking, he would strike twelve o'clock."

O'Hagan's sense of the fragility of man and the immanence of death are repeatedly reflected in metaphor and image: "This little man, sparkling and brittle as an icicle — were she to touch him roughly, he would shatter, fall in gleaming pieces at her feet . . ."; "His eyes seem to float in their own luminosity. Selva remembered a man taken from the Athabaska river . . . his body . . . was floating on its back just under the surface of the water and people said the eyes were open, staring at the sky."

Curious, complex, the image of the school-marm — lumberman's term for a forked tree. O'Hagan's school-marm is a "pine . . . whose upper trunk has been broken off by the wind. Two great branches had grown up to usurp the place of the trunk so that the tree now resembled a gigantic human figure upflung against the twilight of the sky, enfolding the wind in its arms."

In this image we see Selva, the supplicant, but it is one

aspect of her only. From her name we know she is not one tree, but many — and the forest continually regenerates itself.

The School-Marm Tree originally appeared as a short story in *Story*. During the nineteen-fifties, while summering at Cowichan Bay in what O'Hagan describes as the most beautiful room he has ever written in, where the light and shadows flickered on the blue wall, he turned the short story into a novel. The result, a piercing look at the Jasper of the nineteen-twenties.

O'Hagan's extraordinary eye for detail records time and place with great vividness. But to read at this level only would be like drinking a fine, full brandy from a small glass. For this book has an aroma, a bouquet, another 'body,' which will reveal itself to the reader who savors it slowly and allows its breathing presence to fill the air.

P.K. Page
Victoria, B.C.
July, 1977.

The time of this in its beginning
is the year 1925:
the era of the steam locomotive,
the open observation car platform,
the flapper and the fox-trot.

one

Selva dreamed. Selva was awake, wide, wide awake — and still she dreamed. She dreamed beyond the window by which she sat, waiting for Slim Conway to come up the street, and beyond the street and beyond the town and far beyond the mountains rising above the town.

Having washed and put away the supper dishes, Selva now at close to eight o'clock on a Friday evening, wore a frilled white blouse, a grey tweed skirt, a brown suede jacket and the brown low-heeled walking shoes she had bought on her recent trip into Edmonton where she had gone on a two day holiday. When Slim Conway came up the street she would go out to meet him and they would take their usual walk down by the river.

Waiting for him, she had been reading a fashion magazine opened on the white-topped kitchen table before her. The magazine belonged to Mrs. Wamboldt in whose house she worked. In the magazine dreams were advertised in bright colours. The dreams, of course, were for those who had money to buy them. In the glossy pages where they were displayed, Selva sat with dapper men and women at tables in exotic climes. She stood in a one-piece swimsuit on a sandy shore as green waves broke and washed at her feet. On the desert, wearing jodhpurs, she galloped on a painted horse through the sagebrush. Again, as she posed in doorways in a new blue frock or ascended an unending series of marble steps, the sun of California shone upon her tawny hair and laid the black velvet of a shadow for her to tread upon.

Selva sighed. A moment's shadow touched her cheek. She looked up from the magazine and through the cream coloured lace curtains of the window, saw Slim Conway, in riding gaiters and a tall Stetson hat, approaching up the street. She sighed again, more deeply, and shut the magazine upon the tanned features of a young woman who had recently returned to her Long Island home from the Bahamas. Selva rose from the table and went out the back door and passed by the side of the Wamboldts' house in which, as maid, she cooked and served and washed and swept and dusted. She walked as far as the corner of the lawn, by the two stone steps, and stood beneath the young pine tree growing by the squat tight hedge of spruce.

She had heard that afternoon that Slim was in town. Yellowhead was a small town of not quite a thousand people and arrivals and departures were its constant gossip. The clerk in the general store had told her about him. He had come in to buy a shirt, the clerk said, having seen the one he wanted in the store window draped over a headless bust and tied with a blue bow-tie. Selva saw it, still in the window, a pink shirt close to the colour of a sunrise.

The clerk had tried to show Slim another of much the same colour but with a grey pattern. Slim had been firm. It was the pink shirt he wanted and none other. The shirt when taken from the window, temporarily spoiling the display, was too small in the neck. Selva remembered that Slim usually had trouble finding a shirt large enough in the neck. In addition, the clerk explained to her, the selection was limited because there had been a run on pink shirts. It always happened that way during the month of May. As a result, there was not a pink shirt in the store whose collar would have permitted Slim to swallow as much as his conscience. Slim had departed with a blue shirt and an orange coloured necktie bundled in paper under his arm.

Now as he came up the street into the sunset trailing his shadow behind him, Selva saw that he wore the new blue shirt with the orange bow-tie like an angry blossom at his

16

throat. He also wore with his tall, black Stetson hat, the rim curled into a funnel over his right eye, and his high heeled riding gaiters, his old blue serge suit. The blue suit would be shiny and it would be wrinkled from being in his valise as though he had passed the day leaning against a picket fence. While he was away at the horse ranch over the divide in the foothills, he left a change of clothes at the hotel where he stayed while he was in town. Nowadays, with spring well on its way and riding to do on the range, as later in the summer when he would be out on the trail, he could make the trip into town but seldom. In the winter, he came more often, tramping in on snowshoes and staying until his pockets were slack and his face lined and drawn from drink as though sudden age had fallen upon him.

Selva supposed that this evening, as usual, he would have had a drink or two before leaving the hotel to meet her. He liked to take a drink before the mirror he once told her and watch his thirsty Adam's apple reach up and pull it down. She could see him standing tall, dark and lean as a bull pine before the mirror putting the brown whiskey bottle to his lips, tilting back his head, then baring his white teeth, coughing and wiping the back of his hand across his mouth. Perhaps he would have a second drink before setting the bottle down and stepping out into the corridor, shutting the door and descending the creaking stairs carefully, sideways, one hand on the wall, as if he still wore spurs. He would pass the lonely palm in the lobby to the porch and out of doors and the late May smell of pine buds and wild roses.

Slim had braved the hazard of the pool hall with its inviting clink of ivory balls and rounded the corner of the drugstore to appear before her and approach within half a block, when two men walking down the street in the opposite direction stopped and held him in talk. Selva recognized them as Red Carstairs and Shorty Burnap. Red and Slim shook hands — Red's staring blue eyes, flushed face and wiry red hair signifying surprise and consternation at each incident the day might throw across his path. Shorty Burnap merely rubbed his hands slowly down his thighs. Selva noticed that Burnap, who worked as a dude wrangler in the summer if he could land the job, or on the spare-board of the railroad if he failed, wore a pink shirt and a blue bow-tie, the combination which Slim had tried unsuccessfully to buy at the store.

They stood, the three of them, heads down in discourse. They would be talking of weather and horses and the new spring grass on the range or Burnap or Carstairs would be suggesting to Slim that he meet them later for a game of poker. Selva grew uneasy waiting for him to break away.

Overhead, above the town and across the valley, she saw the sun flush red on Mount Tekarra's snow and from a locomotive idling in the railroad yard, saw white steam rise straight and high, remarking it as a sign of good weather. From the roundhouse she heard an occasional groan or roar, the ring of steel on steel, as if there a metallic giant were being tortured. In later years electricity would replace steam as power. The town of Yellowhead was a divisional point on the railroad and its life centered on the railroad yard, and when the two passenger trains, east and west, came in, the town went down to meet them. The town, indeed, was no more than a street set down in the wilderness beside the tracks. On one side was the railroad with its green painted station, its roundhouse, its coal tipple, its rows of freight cars and beyond it, the river and mountains. On the other, western side were the stores, hitching rails in front of them, the bank, the pool-hall, the drugstore and behind them, the people's houses. Farther back beneath the hill were log cabins and corrals, some of them built before steel had been laid in the valley. There guides and outfitters kept horses and equipment. North of the town, their peaks towering and frozen, their lower slopes covered with pine and spruce, the Rocky Mountains rolled, range after range, across northern Alberta to the barren lands. Westward over Yellowhead Pass, the waters emptied to the Pacific. Here by Yellowhead town, melting snow and glacier flowed through the Athabaska into the Mackenzie and the Arctic.

It was an austere and lonely land, it sometimes seemed to Selva, whose home had been in the foothills where creeks flowed gently through the poplars and the Rockies were only a low white wall that a dog might jump across, distant in the west. It was Slim's country more than it was hers. He belonged here. She had merely come in from outside.

She and Slim had been walking out together now for

nearly a year. He had met her at the station restaurant where, before coming to the Wamboldts' house, she had worked and where he frequently ate. He had watched her as she came in through the swinging doors carrying a tray and her eyes met his over steaming bowls of porridge and plates of ham and eggs and fried potatoes. They smiled at each other through the steam of puddings and shot a few quick words through the clatter of dishes and the grumbling and crackle of determined mastication around the half circle of the lunch counter. He saw her leave and disappear again through the ever-swinging doors, tall and lithe, with copper hued hair and brown eyes as expectant as a doll's. When she was gone and lost in the loud harangue of angry dishes in the kitchen the image of her erect aproned body remained, its breasts, pouched in white so that it seemed she was holding up a timid offering before him, and returning, she felt his broad hands, accustomed to the smooth reaches of a horse's flank, were restless to reach out and touch her. Their courtship, such as it was, smelling of boiled onions and carrots, freshly made tea and coffee staled in saucers, had been largely an adventure in peripatetics and uninspired gastronomy.

A rider on a lean grey mare rode down the street past Selva and the Wamboldts' house. Another who had ridden in from the prairies or the foothills. The buffalo, the Indians, and the horsemen all made their last stand in the mountains. He rode on down the street, pulled up his mare and bent over his saddle pommel to talk to Slim and Carstairs and Burnap. The group dispersed, the horseman trotting away, his shoulders shaking as with laughter, and Slim turned to grin and wave an arm to a remark which Burnap had made.

A girl with black hair wearing a green dress and black high heeled shoes coming out of the side street passed close to him, her feet hurrying her away, but her body lingering, and it appeared to Selva that he looked after her with longing. Selva wished that she had worn high heels and pointed toes instead of the walking shoes she had chosen.

Slim came towards her along the gravelled sidewalk, stiff-legged in his riding gaiters as though he walked on tiny stilts, his knees, each used to solitary life on its own side of a horse, strangers to one another. He touched his hat, said

"Hello!" Selva stepped through the gate in the hedge and on to the sidewalk. She pressed her fingers against the shimmering mass of her hair. She had full, thick hair, strongly rooted. People often admired it. More than once she had thought that that was why Slim went out with her at all — because people spoke about and admired her hair.

Now beside him, she fluttered her eyelids. A few freckles were upon them as though she had lately fallen asleep in the sun. "I didn't know you were in town," she said. He would know it was a lie. He would know that she would have seen him, that someone would have told her and that, as always, after her work in the Wamboldts' house was done, she would be waiting for him behind the window, under the tree or at the gate.

"I came right along," he replied. "I figured we might take a walk . . . unless you're busy."

She did not answer, but looked back at the house, so he asked again, "Are you busy?" She stuck her tongue out at him and laughed. He knew she would not be "busy."

They walked together up the street. Slim coughed once or twice because his voice was husky when he began to speak. Selva trotted at his side, her attention divided between him and the heavy new shoes which had cost her ten dollars on her trip into Edmonton. She was half running to stay abreast while he apparently took a step just once in a while. She reached her hand up to his elbow to tuck it in against her side. Slim shrugged her off.

Men and women sat on porches listening to the piping calls of children, the drowsy notes of robins, the chattering of a high placed squirrel, sounds that men are most aware of in the twilight when the day is ended and before the night has come. Slim spoke to some of the porch dwellers, lifted his hand to others and the response was a muttered assent to his and Selva's progress up the wide clean street lined with freshly leafed poplars to the dark pines at its end.

In the welcome gloom of the pines, he stepped ahead onto the trail that led down to the Miette river and across it by the railroad trestle to the green park-like flats below the mountain where the spring's first green grass grew and where Selva sometimes came to find an early crocus to put in the blue bowl on her dresser top. Down there, beaver had dammed small streams into pools fringed with tense and quivering poplars. Once, with Slim, she had seen a pair of wild swans floating on the dark waters.

When they had climbed up to the tracks and reached the railroad trestle, Slim took her arm, paused. "Stop! Wait a minute," he said.

A porcupine waddled across the trestle in front of them, quills rising and falling, rimmed with the fire of the western sky. "Watch," Slim said. He took a rock the size of his fist and threw it. He missed. The rock passed on harmlessly into the water below. "Damn!" said Slim. The porcupine hesitated, lifted its clawed front paws, swung its long, blunt nose in the air, then put its head against the steel rail and waited with fearful, rising quills. Slim went closer with a handful of stones and pelted it. Selva saw quills broken off like splinters and the white skin beneath them slowly redden when the blood began to flow. She put her hand on Slim's arm and asked him to stop. Instead, he went back, found a stout piece of wood, returned and pried the porcupine loose from its hold on the timbers and tipped it into the stream. He was intent, his lips pulled back from his teeth, and forgetting Selva, stood watching as the riled, rushing waters seized the bundle of thrashing tail and angered quills, quietened it slowly in their embrace until, at a point where willows grew, it floated finally inert and helpless as a bunch of sodden brush beyond his view.

For a time he had become another man and a stranger.

"Why did you do that?" Selva asked, stamping her foot on a tie of the trestle.

"If you'd seen a horse with his muzzle full of quills," he said, "or a dog and had to shoot him . . ."

"I know. But you didn't just kill it. You hurt it. And it wasn't the same one anyway."

Slim did not explain to her how he felt. Now that it was over, he said it did not matter. There was one porcupine less. That was important. And in the manner of its death, Slim implied, he had been indulgent. It was a hard thing to do, to have to shoot a horse. He told her he had once been sick at his stomach from shooting a horse.

They continued carefully across the trestle, stepping from tie to tie, and Selva, staring up the valley and at the hard blue rails speeding on to the sunset until they merged to a burning white point as though they had fused and melted, thought again of the pictures in the fashion magazine, and looking beyond the summer, of a train going west and herself with a man at her side sitting in the club car. She was not sure whether the man was Slim dressed in city clothes or another man entirely, someone with a moustache and a ticket to California in his pocket. She was nearly twenty-three. She could not wait too long . . .

As she slid with Slim down the gravel bank at the trestle's far end toward the deep and shadowed trees they were to enter, he moistened his lips and slipped his arm around her. His hand reached up and grabbed her hair from behind, pulled back her head, tilted her face to his own. He pressed his lips on hers until her lips opened and her body throbbed against his leg. Then she pushed him away, ran her hand across her mouth, drew back a pace.

"Oh! . . . Are you trying to kill me?" she asked as she backed farther away, closer to the trees. Then quickly she stopped and raised her tight grey skirt until he saw the close pressed knobs of her knees and the spread of tan stockings on her widening thighs. She leaned forward to see them too, and dropping her skirt, whirled and ran up the trail into the waiting poplars.

She fled through the trees, showing the white insteps of her shoes. She was panting as she rounded the corner of the trail where the mottled birch trees grew, and stumbled when she left the trail and turned downhill by the big fir. Then, below in the beaver meadow she stood and listened and heard nothing but the flow of the creek and far away, as though it were yesterday, a coyote exulting on a hill side. In a moment she heard Slim hoot as he pursued her shadow though the white boled ranks of the poplars and she turned to look around the little meadow of grass half circled by willows and poplars, topped by a school-marm tree and, at its foot, gleaming water pooled behind the beaver dam. She opened her jacket and lay in the grass and fallen needles beneath the school-marm tree, eyes closed as if she slept, hands at her side and the toes of her shoes pointed hopefully at the sky.

In the dusk, before they left to turn homeward, Slim

waited while she tidied her hair, powdered her nose from a compact taken from her jacket pocket. He rolled a cigarette and Selva knew that he was already wondering if he would be back at the hotel in time for a glass of beer with the boys before he went to bed.

"Come on, let's get going," he said.

He tossed his half smoked cigarette into the pool, stretched out on the gravel, lowered his head to the water and drank. Selva was at his side when he regained his feet.

"I'd like a drink too."

"All right. There's lots of water," he told her.

She laid her face down to the water, trying to hold her body rigid as he had done, flexing her arms and lowering her shoulders, knees not touching the ground. Her arms collapsed beneath her weight.

"Oh!" she gasped. She reached out flat on her belly now, dipped her lips to the pool. As she commenced to drink, the toes of her shoes straightened and tightened in the grass and the frail shaft of her neck obedient to her impulse held her face and forehead just at water level.

For a moment, she recalled the tense, hungry expression of Slim's face as, earlier, he had tipped the porcupine from the bridge into the river. She had an urge now to glance up at him quickly, observe him when he was unaware. He stood above her. She was helpless at his feet. If her face should sink lower, she thought, if he should bend over and close his fingers on her neck, press his shin across her legs behind her knees, she then could not move, nor see him, nor utter a word nor sound. And he would go away and leave her on her belly by the pool as though her thirst were beyond all quenching, and her eyes beneath the water transfixed forever. She would lie for days in the small beaver meadow, deep down in the willows. And pursuit — she saw him as a man pursued. She saw him a bearded man on horseback beyond the Jackpine, beyond the head of the Wapiti, or knocking at a log-house door in some wind and snow beleaguered settlement.

He was close to her now, so silent that he did not seem to breathe and yet she thought she felt his breath upon her and imagined the tentative touch of his fingers upon her neck. She jumped up with a cry so quickly that her head bumped his chin.

"Let's get away from here. I'm frightened," she whispered, hands weaving to brush the twigs from her skirt.

Slim touched her arm. She looked up, startled at his touch and at soft-footed darkness moving nearer to the clearing. Through a jagged hole in the brim of his hat, she saw a star glitter and then disappear as he turned his head. Stars were out in the pale sky and she started when a night hawk, two wings with a shadow between, zoomed low above the tree tops. She was glad Slim was there, that she was not alone in the strange, troubled stillness of coming night.

She slipped her hand under his arm. His arm trembled. She looked up at him again and touched his face and felt slow cold sweat on his brow. He shoved her from him, then took her to him and held her.

He released her, pushed her back on her heels so that she staggered. "Sure," he said, "let's get going. It's getting late."

two

The next night, that of Saturday, May the twenty-fourth, Empire Day, and the date of the annual town dance over the pool-hall, Selva stepped from the backdoor of the Wamboldt house. She had tidied the dining-room, washed the dishes and opened for their night's repose, Mr. and Mrs. Wamboldt's bed. She was to meet Slim at the corner drugstore. He was taking her to the dance and she was proud to go with him. He was a good dancer, assured, balanced and unhesitating. Other girls liked to dance with him, while men accorded him the off-hand respect due to a first rate rider and an accomplished horseman on the trail. If he stayed sober, they would have a happy time. If he took drunk, the dance would end in a blur of faces, of hands and feet, and the shouted echoes of profanity.

It was after ten o'clock, but twilight lingered in the valley. To the south, the high ice fields glowed green and pink and warm like a sudden garden against the sky. From a fir tree on the hill a drowsy robin chirped and sought the night beneath his wing. Wind blew down Yellowhead Pass from the west. On leaving the house, Selva turned to face it. She lifted her head, smelling the sweet smell of wild roses, the sharp scent of spruce buds, the rank, tingling odours of willows tangled by the river. She parted her lips and drank the wind, drank it full and deep. It blew through her, around her, cleaved the light blue crepe dress between her legs.

She turned again to walk down the path and by the garage to the street, holding a shawl tightly about her head and shoulders. A gust of wind caught her from behind, billowed her skirt above her knees. She ran her hand carrying her black bag between her knees to hold it down. The wind pushed her hips forward and loosed a tassle of tawny hair which spurted like sullen flame from under the dark blue shawl. The wind propelled her, shoved her with masculine force, held her with the intimacy of possession. Going with it, she struggled against it walking stiff-legged, high hipped, in black suede pumps, gasping, flushed and with tears in her eyes. The wind's cool draught touched her with a gentle ecstasy and its breath against her neck and humming in her ears was an urgent counsel of fulfillment.

Far down the Athabaska valley an engineer pulled the cord above his head and a locomotive uttered into the night its fragment of nostalgia. Selva for a few steps shut her eyes, leaned back against the wind and wished that it would take her where it blew — down the valley where the whistle sounded, beyond the foothills, far across the prairies where she had never been, to the eastern cities and their stores with draped windows and the big hotels with fountains in their lobbies and rooms apart where, unhurried and secure, people sat on white satin couches. Men in black coats and grey striped trousers stood and women held their voices at the moment of her entry. She wore a long black dress sheened by shaded lights. Jade and pendant earrings gleamed from beneath her hair which, loosely combed, touched her shoulders. She moved with grace and confidence across the polished floor. A tall man, sharp featured, moustached, his temples flecked with grey, came forward, offered her his arm . . .

A rough hand caught her elbow, swung her about. "Where you going?" Slim asked. "You're walking with your eyes shut."

"Oh!" she cried. "The wind! It's blowing me to pieces!"

She was at the drugstore corner and Slim stood before her, hat cocked over one eye, a dingy, hand-rolled cigarette hanging from his lip. He had discarded the bow-tie and instead with his blue suit, wore a red neckerchief, its knot held by a leather ring, its silken ends blown by the wind against his shoulder. For an instant she was shocked, roused so abruptly from her musing, to find him beside her, and at the neckerchief which blew and snapped, reaching out for her and drew her back, streaming from his throat, red as blood, into the wind.

As they walked with others behind the station and towards the pool hall, she took his arm as was her habit when he would let her and pulled it tightly to her. Slim, she knew, was not the man, but he was all the man she had. She remembered the night before in the beaver meadow under the school-marm tree, how strangely and how forebodingly he had stood beside her when she rose up from drinking at the pool and the recollection served only to bring her more closely to him until her hip was neighbour to his own. As with the wind, she fought against him and still yielded herself to him. He came riding vagrant into town from over the passes, from the heads of mountain rivers and from the foothills where the horses ranged. Like the wind, he seemed to come and go for no apparent reason. He smelled of horses and of leather and of campfire smoke and tonight, he smelled of whiskey too. His hands urged her, searched her, knew her. All of him was in those hands, slow and gentle and always moving around a horse and on her body, forming the inevitable pattern of his desire. Slim was the only man she had ever known well and the beaver meadow had become their accepted trysting place. Stars or slanting sunlight seen through a shifting canopy of boughs — this and the creaking forest, the moaning wind and the soft flow of the nearby river had been constant with them in their communions.

She knew no more of Slim than he knew of her, yet men such as Slim had been by her for as long as memory served. When she was a little girl playing on the kitchen floor of the homestead in the Alberta foothills, they had come stamping in from the rain and the sunshine, spurs jingling, jarring the floor with their heels and shaking the walls with their laughter. Once in a while one of them stooped, patted her head and called her "sorrel top." Later, when she had grown and stood in the doorway in the morning wearing a print dress with a blue ribbon in her hair, they seemed to be forever riding away into the poplars by the creek, up the draw, into the forest towards the mountains. In the winter they walked off on webbed feet and their voices faded into the white stillness of the land. Sometimes from far away she would hear a rifle shot where, beyond her vision, man and wilderness contended. They would return with meat, with pelts of wolf, marten, fox and fisher, into whose fur she would sink her nose.

Men were apart and in a world of their own. They always returned, but they never stayed. They talked and they seldom listened. Slim at her side was one of them, going and coming, his arrival but the promise that soon he would be leaving her again. They knew one another only through their flesh and behind that wall of flesh they were strangers.

They moved now with the throng of other strangers to the dance above the pool-hall where flesh would touch and bodies grapple in the pain of each one's loneliness. Faces passed in the crowd, borne along in the dusk like pale autumn leaves floating on a river. Selva held to Slim's arm as they left the street and went up the narrow up-ended valley of the stairway to the dance-hall floor. On the landing halfway up, men stood furtive, filching swallows from whiskey flasks. Looking at her from out of the shadows, she saw Hank Barton, the lean faced son of the bank — somehow she thought of him more as the son of the bank than as the progeny of its manager. Like the sons of the grocery store, who travelled together as though they were hitched, and the freckle-faced son of the liquor store, he would dance too closely to her and try again to arrange to pick her up on the edge of town tomorrow night in his car. He would not ask her out tonight because he would be afraid of Slim. Men such as these would only go out with her at night and would not call for her where she worked. She had accepted none of their invitations, disdaining their fears and their snobbery. Their very presence affected her with discomfort, made her conscious of her hands, red and chapped from washing dishes and the clothes. Others whose hands, like those of Slim, bore the marks of labour, would call for her and sit in the kitchen or walk with her on the street. Occasionally, when Slim was away with the horses, one of them would take her to the movie show. Beyond that she had not gone. Loyalty, vague and undefined, never spoken of between them, bound her for the present at least to Slim. Not once in the months of their acquaintance had she failed to give her time to him when he came to town.

They climbed the final steps and stood before the table where plump, red-cheeked Mrs. Otley, the town's general charwoman, was taking in the tickets. It was a draughty spot, but Mrs. Otley, in her second-hand coat of muskrat fur, accustomed to hardship, regarded as a tribute the opportunity afforded her — an opportunity declined by others, and though this one paid little, it was a job and jobs were hard to come by. Slim groped through his pockets and cursed under his breath because he could not find the tickets he had bought at the drugstore earlier in the evening. Selva looked past the entrance to the couples in the hall dancing an uneven fox-trot to the four-piece orchestra, whose players, set above the dancers on a platform, resembled fervid and perspiring priests intoning over the heads of their followers measured and redundant magic against an ever-threatening silence. "Hurry!" she said to Slim. "Hurry! I want to dance. I've never wanted to dance so much before." She was impatient to be on the floor in her blue dress with its narrow trimming of lace, heart shaped upon her throat and breast, and to feel the music thrumming in her veins.

Slim at last found the tickets tucked in the inside band of his hat. "Come on," she said to him, "wait for me inside. I have to go to the ladies' room."

There, before a mirror so cracked in its upper portion that it seemed to frown, after Miss Winters, the old-maid school teacher, dressed in a flouncy purple, had sniffed and shrugged herself out of the door, Selva turned her head, looked from the corner of her eye to catch, if she could, her face unaware and in profile. It was an old trick — an attempt to discover how she appeared to others. She posed again and remained unsatisfied with what she saw. Brown and sulking eyes rimmed by the glow of her hair stared back at her in wonder, in reproach, in sadness. She fluffed her hair and felt her body tingle as it lightly brushed her shoulders. She put rouge on her lips, set like a bud of hope in the paleness of her cheeks. She folded over her arm the shawl she had been wearing, put her wrist through the strap of her purse and walked out, tall, tense and eager to the dance.

Slim was waiting for her, and to the old tune of "Tea for Two," she offered herself to the decision of his arms. When the music ceased and before it had struck up for the encore, they joined the other dancers walking arm-in-arm in a circle around the room. At the dance's end, Slim took her to the bench by the south wall where, according to custom, women and girls sat out the intermissions. He crossed to the men's side. There, while the orchestra fiddled with strings, struck chords, wiped brows, scraped its collective feet, the members of the two teams, male and female, glared or stole quick glances at one another across the empty floor, ready to rise again to battle when the music began once more. Islands of respectability, neutrals in the conflict, formed in the corners of the hall. In one corner was the bank manager talking to Mr. Ogelthorpe, the town lawyer and insurance broker. In another corner, between his wife and her sister from out of town, was Mr. Peckarin, owner of Yellowhead's leading grocery store. Selva often shopped at his store. She liked him. He was a little man with stooped shoulders, wizened as the raisins he sold. She knew that he was worried about his boys. Even now, she supposed, they would be downstairs well on the way to being drunk. They got drunk together and sobered up together, and together had even tried to take her out. They were twins, short and squat, wide-mouthed and eager-faced.

Across the floor walked the western divisional manager of the railroad who had come from down the valley in his private car. He was going over to talk to the doctor, grey moustached, red cheeked, lifting his knee to slap it as he laughed at a joke told to him by Bill Wilkins who ran the outfit for which Slim worked as guide, packer and horse-breaker. These, and others like them, were older people, established people who did not work for wages, nor have one job today and another one tomorrow. They had made their compromises and stood by them. They sometimes addressed one another as "Mr." and "Mrs." and met with reserve and, on occasion, when unprepared, with dignity. Among them, of course, were the Wamboldts, in whose house Selva worked. They had nodded coolly to her when she had been dancing with Slim. Mr. Wamboldt had money. He owned the movie house, the main garage and the only apartment house — it had two storeys — of which the town could boast. Mrs. Wamboldt, at the moment, sat alone, chin tilted as though she were waiting for someone to come by and scratch it. She was a dark, big-boned, stout woman and her new pink tinted silk dress, which fitted her like flesh, appeared to be bleeding at the seams.

Selva got up to dance with Slim's friend, Shorty Burnap, and gazed down upon the cinders caught in the roots of his sparse, fair hair. He was now firing on the railroad and she feared that his hand would leave a black smudge on her shoulders or the back of her dress — this though she knew he was scrubbed and washed. Shorty surrendered her to Red Carstairs, and for two hours she was passed along from hand to hand, thrown from one pair of shoulders to another, jolted, swung, shaken, hugged, squeezed, breathed and trod upon by men from the roundhouse, from the train's head-end and from the caboose, by men smelling of soap, in red shirts from the foothills, by men fresh from the moss of high valleys, by a logger from the Whirlpool and by a trapper from Calling river, who took her out to the porch and gave her two stiff drinks of whiskey and brought her back in to the dance. She danced until the music became no more than a distant wail and until she was conscious only of the frenzy and the sudden calls and stamping of those about her and of the dust in the air and the tremor of the floor. Men had come into Yellowhead for the dance from lonely camps and cabins and ranch houses. They had climbed to it out of the shafts of mines, and come down to it from mountain sides. Girls in town had altered their dresses and then marked the day on the calendar. Nothing would keep them from having the time they had planned, from wringing joy from each soggy minute — nothing, not God nor high water — if determination and energy, a shot of whiskey and the music's laying waste of silence would bring them to it. This was Empire Day, cele-brated in the dominions and colonies around the world, wherever the British flag shadowed foreign soil. It was the birthday of dead Queen Victoria. In their forgetfulness they paid her homage.

Selva, seized by the spirit of the crowd, pressed against her partner's arm, white teeth glistening, eyes half-lidded.

Sweat ran down the runnel of her back. It was beaded on her nose and along her eyebrows and under the hairline above her brow. The music's high pitched and wavering exaltation gripped her until she felt she was no longer herself, but merely a portion of what was around her, that she had handed herself over and was being carried, carried . . . The lights grew dim and voices came to her faintly, in snatches, as from across a wide and rushing river.

Selva first noticed the man she was to remember as Peter Wrogg while he was dancing with Nancy, the sister of Slim's friend, Red Carstairs. She noticed him because he was a stranger, someone from out of town, a man who did not belong to the valley, and one who was set apart by the cut and quality of his clothes and the casual air with which he wore them. Seeing him with Nancy, she wondered again what men saw in the girl – a flimsy blonde with small buttocks which appeared to gleam through her tight fitting black silk dress. Nancy had wide open blue eyes and a habit of calling everyone, man, woman or child, "Darling." She did not know what it was to work. The Carstairs – the father was a conductor on the railroad – had "gone without" to send her to a private school on the Coast. Selva did not like Nancy, whose pliable white hands fluttered like dove's wings about her hair, her snowy throat, her breasts, small as plums. At times, especially seeing her at dances, she felt her stomach hot with hate.

She saw Peter Wrogg later, during an intermission, standing in the centre of the floor. He was a younger man than Slim. She took him to be in his late twenties. His black hair was full and curly and as she regarded him, he nervously pushed it back from his forehead. His eyebrows too were dark and formed a heavy straight line above his eyes, while his cheeks bloomed like apples from the Okanagan valley. His grey flannel suit was out of press – in contrast to the neatly pressed blue serge suits favoured by the businessmen of the town. But it was not his hair, his flushed cheeks, nor his flannel suit which attracted her. What drew her attention was the impression he gave of being alone in a sense that no one else at the dance was alone, not so much a part of the dance as he was on his guard against it. When he caught her eye, his forehead furrowed, his nostrils, small and narrow, twitched.

She smiled at him ever so slightly. His face, already flushed, grew redder, as if in guilt of his solitary and conspicuous stance. He moved from the centre of the floor, not towards her, but away, and for a few seconds lost himself in the group by the stairway. Then as the music for the next dance began, she saw him making his way to her through the crowd, head averted to avoid her glance. Standing before the bench where she was seated, he said, in a precise, clipped voice, with a touch of English accent to it, "I was wondering . . . that is, would it be . . . ?"

"Sure," Selva said, "let's dance."

His hand, which helped her up, was small for a man's hand, slim, not much larger than her own. Its nails were neatly trimmed, its palm soft as velvet. Dancing with him, she was surprised at the lightness of his feet. He danced as though he had air in his bones, guiding her with skill among the others on the floor, anticipating, as it were, their every motion, so that no one stepped upon her heel or ran an elbow into her back. The dance to him was scheme and plan, and not, as with Slim, a headlong, if controlled, gallop over broken country.

She smelt tobacco from the flannel of his suit and through the cloth felt warmth and wiry strength in his body. He said he had been watching her during the evening and hoped she would forgive him for asking her to dance without having been introduced.

"You were dancing with Nancy Carstairs," Selva reminded him. "Were you introduced to her?"

"Nancy Carstairs?" he asked.

"Yes, you were. I saw you."

"The little blonde girl in the black dress? Quite a different matter."

"How different?"

"Well, you see," he said, "as a matter of fact, I was standing beside her and she asked *me* to dance."

"Oh!" Selva said.

He told her that he had stopped off in town on his way to the Coast from the East. He had come in to the dance when he heard its music as he was walking down the street from the hotel. He spoke in a voice that was abrupt, nervous, but at the same time vibrant and therefore pleasing to her.

"Then," he said, "I noticed your hair. It's like a Titian."

"What's Titian?" she asked, tossing her head, bending back to look into his eyes. She did not have to look up. His eyes were on a level with her own. They were blue, dark blue, full and brimming as with tears, and their lashes long and straight as a buffalo's. She wondered who he was and where he came from, what sort of a house he lived in. Somehow it seemed to her that it would be a white, square house, with green space around it. Its windows would be very clean, gleaming against the sun.

Titian, he explained to her, was an Italian painter. He added, "Liked to paint women with the colour of gold in their hair — buxom women, had hair that was golden, but not exactly blonde, and rather red, all at the same time."

Selva did not like the word "buxom" nor did she like her hair to be called "red," even by implication. Indeed, she was weary of having her hair mentioned at all. Men constantly referred to her hair as though she were no more than a head of hair. After all, she had eyes, ears, lips and she knew she had a figure to be proud of, even if her hands and feet were, as a girl friend once told her, "somewhat large for their size." A while before meeting Peter Wrogg, she had heard in a movie or read in a magazine of a similar situation. There the man said to the woman, "You know, you have really splendid eyes." The woman turning away from him, replied, "You remark upon the obvious. Someone once praised my ears — but then, of course, he was a man who understood women." Selva wished that she could command such a retort as that. It remained, and probably always would remain, beyond her capacity.

The dance, a waltz, came to its end when they were near the open door leading out to the porch. Before they went out, Selva glanced over her shoulder for Slim. She did not see him. Probably he would be down with the boys in the pool-hall or in the alley by the woodshed where a bottle of whiskey was perpetually cached.

Peter Wrogg's hand guided her elbow. No one else was on the porch and they walked down to its far, dark corner. The wind had fallen and an old moon wearily climbed a rack of clouds beyond the eastern mountains.

Peter Wrogg turned her so that she had her back to the

railing. With both hands he took her hair and tucked it under her chin making a frame for her face, lifting it gently upwards.

Peter Wrogg did not attempt to kiss her, though she felt his breath warm upon her cheek. Having gone so far, he went no further. He was hesitant, lost. His hands fell to his side. He postponed the issue. He said, "Maybe tomorrow, it's Sunday, we might go for a walk, take a lunch, or I could rent a motor car . . ."

"Not a motor car," she said. "And anyway, I couldn't."

She shoved him away from her because in the open door-way which she had been watching, a man's form had broken the shaft of yellow light emerging from the dance hall. She ran towards it, took Slim's arm, tried to turn him back indoors, and when he stood in refusal, tugged at him until he took the step down to the porch.

"Slim," she said as Peter Wrogg came up from behind her, "I want you to meet . . ." She stopped. She did not know his name.

"Wrogg," he said. "Peter Wrogg . . . Montreal."

He held out his hand. Slim did not accept it. He shrugged himself free of Selva, tossed his cigarette over the railing. He hooked his thumbs in his belt and stood with legs straddled.

Selva went up to him again, touched the hard muscle of his arm, whispered, "Don't! Don't! We were just talking. See . . . I didn't even know his name." She had once seen Slim in a general and drunken rough house after a dance, but she had never seen him in a stand-up fight. She had heard stories. When with another girl, she had been told, he had kicked a man in the groin, hurt him so seriously that he had been hospitalized. Peter Wrogg, she thought, with his soft hands, his slight, grey clad figure, his questing and uncertain blue eyes, needed her protection. Protecting him, she also protected herself.

Peter Wrogg studied his own outstretched hand, pulled it back, put it in his jacket pocket. His eyes moved slowly from Slim to Selva, from Selva to Slim. "Well," he said, "if that's the way . . ."

Slim made a step forward, hunched his shoulders. He seemed to speak, thought better of it, turned his head and spat into the night. He seized Selva by the upper arm, his fingers biting into the flesh so that she clenched her teeth with the pain. "Come on. Let's get going. I'm taking you home," he said.

Leaving, she captured a final glimpse of Peter Wrogg. He stood in the glow sifting through a curtained window. Only his chest, shoulders and head showed, as though he had waded waist-deep into darkness. His chin was tucked against his shoulder so that he looked at her from the corner of his eye. In the moment of her leaving, he raised his head. He smiled. It was the first time she had seen him smile. His teeth showed, even and white, like a light that glimmered and was gone. His lips rounded as if to shape the word "tomorrow."

Later, standing in front of the mirror in her little room, combing her hair before she got into bed, Selva felt a tingle in the middle finger of her right hand. She looked at the finger. A porcupine quill held by its barb hung from the skin in its tip. She pinched it loose. A bead of blood welled from he finger. She sucked it then took the quill into the kitchen and put it in the stove. How it had come to be lying loose in her hair she did not know. Perhaps it had been in Slim's clothes. She remembered the previous evening when he had tipped the porcupine off the bridge into the river. It might have been in the sleeve of one of the other men with whom she had danced. It was a mysterious thing to have discovered in her hair in the quietness of her room, an intruder from the wilderness which on all sides bounded the mountain town. Certainly, she thought, climbing into bed, it had not come to her from the young Englishman with the rosy cheeks whose lips, as she left him, had shaped the word "tomorrow."

three

Tomorrow being Sunday, when she had washed the noon-day dishes and put them away, Selva had the afternoon and evening to herself. If Slim were in town they took it for granted that she would keep the day for him. They might go walking or riding, he on his big bay and she on a dappled roan mare with a light grey mane. If alone, and the sun were shining, she would often go for a walk, perhaps up to the cemetery. The cemetery was on a hill a mile away and offered a sweeping view of the peaks and glaciers at the head of the Athabaska valley. It was one of the finest views for miles around. Selva occasionally had asked herself why the cemetery, whose people could not see, was set on a hill, while the town was down on the flat. She felt sorry for those under the ground because they could not see the mountains, nor hear the wind, nor the voices of children rising up on it from the town. She was not lonely among the graves. People in their graves, their given names and brief histories above them, were friendly people. They were tired and side by side had gone to rest. Over their little mounds hung the collective sigh that they had uttered.

Today Selva would not go riding, nor had she gone for a walk. She sat at the table in the kitchen, her hands folded on its enamelled top and looked out of the window through the cotton lace curtain. She did not smoke, nor did she need to sew or read. Hard work had taught her the simple gladness of sitting still. In the morning she had lifted up her white face with its red lips and brown eyes and sung in the choir of the United Church, and there had met Rosie, the dining-room maid from the Chaba Hotel who told her that Slim and the boys had begun a poker game when the dance broke up and that they were now down in "The Shack." The shack was in the north end of town. At one time an artist had lived in it, a Dutchman with long up-turned shoes and a red beard. He had stayed for two years and painted the mountains and gone away to Toronto and New York to sell a number of paintings and have his name in the papers — much to the surprise and discomfort of the people of Yellowhead who had rarely asked him into their homes and who had not liked the blue mountains and the slanting outhouses which appeared on his canvases. The showing of outhouses, they felt, was unjust when most of the people in town had bath-rooms with modern appurtenances. Besides, tourists would not be attracted by outhouses, and the summer's business might suffer.

When the Dutchman left, his shack was for a time unused. Then it was taken over by one of Slim's friends and became an informal meeting place for "the boys." The poker game that was now going on within its walls would probably continue all day and into the night. Once Selva had passed close to the shack when a game was in progress. Grey, twist-ing smoke rose from its chimney, voices muttered and, as she walked away, she heard a burst of laughter.

The game, its necessities and its ritual, were as removed from her and as foreign as the flame-centered, shadowy pow-wows of the Blackfoot Indians to which, as a child, she had been witness. Men moved in tribes, in packs. Slim on his visits to town would escape and be with her for an afternoon or an evening only to be called back to the group he referred to as "the boys" where his deeper allegiance seemed to belong. Selva tried to imagine him at the table, studying his cards from the slits of his eyes. At times she was not sure whether his eyes were brown or dark blue. She knew best the piercing black of their pupils. The skin about them was puckered and drawn, seamed with fine lines where weather and sun had stitched them in. Even in town Slim appeared to be straining, intent on distance through narrowed lids. His eyes were like windows with the blinds pulled almost to the bottom. He could crouch and look out through them. She could not see in. Even though she stood on tiptoe she could not see in.

And this Sunday afternoon, she did not wish to see in. If he came by, she would not go out with him. She was tired of him, angry with him. What right had he to treat her as he had the night before? To grab her arm with his big hand so that now her skin was black and blue? He used her when he needed her and forgot her when the need was gone. He was the teapot. She was merely the cup. When they met, she had some things to tell him that he would not easily forget.

Although she had danced with him only once and barely knew his name, she sensed in Peter Wrogg the qualities lacking in Slim. He was gentle. He was easy to talk to. More than that, she recalled his smile on the instant of her leaving. He had smiled so quickly that he was no longer smiling when she realized that he had smiled. It was as though some part of him, of which she had been unaware, had for a moment looked out at her. It was a conspiracy and signal of a word still to be spoken between them.

She had not told him where she worked. There had been no time. She supposed, thinking of his suggestion of a walk or a drive, that he could easily find out. She did not believe that it would affect him one way or the other that she was maid and cook in someone's house. He would have to come by the house. The town had no telephones as yet. The storekeepers had objected. People bought more goods, they said, when they came in and saw what was for sale on the shelves.

The clock's eager face above the cupboard where the breakfast dishes were kept showed fifteen minutes to four when, with a pang that was gladness and yet regret, she saw him approaching up the street. He wore no hat. He took short, quick steps and walked back on his heels, toes pointed out, face held up to the sun. He frowned. He was serious. Selva smiled. He came up the street until he was abreast of the house. She lost sight of him, then the dark smudge of his head, a pink ear pressed against it, and his grey shoulder passed beneath the window. She rose, opened the kitchen door and waited for him on the stoop.

"Didn't try to get a car," he said. "If you aren't too busy . . . might go for a walk. Like to see a bit of the country." He spoke without a drawl. Speech to him was a knife that trimmed each phrase, pared each word.

His upheld forehead was furrowed against the sun and one eyebrow rode higher than the other. His eyes seemed to float in their own luminosity. Selva remembered a man taken from the Athabaska river earlier in the spring. The Mounted Police decided that he had been a tramp riding the freight trains west to the milder climate of the Coast. His body had been caught in a log jam below the town. It was floating on its back just under the surface of the water and people said the eyes were open, staring at the sky.

"Come in," she said to Peter Wrogg. "Come in and sit down for a minute." She was ready to go. She wore her new walking shoes, the grey skirt, white blouse and the leather jacket, but she did not wish to appear anxious for the outing.

"How did you know where to find me?" she asked as he stood awkwardly in the doorway, looking over the kitchen.

"Told me at the dance after you left. Fellow with fair hair asked me for a match. Been drinking. He told me I would probably find you here. Described the place. You see, you didn't give me your name."

"Selva. Selva Williams."

"Yes, I know." He nodded.

The short fellow with fair hair might be Shorty Burnap and he would likely tell Slim. Selva considered and determined that it did not matter. "Let him know," she thought. "It will do him good." She rubbed her arm where it was bruised.

She sat down and Peter Wrogg took the chair across from here. He opened his grey jacket, tightened the knot of his black, knitted tie. His white shirt was darned just below the collar.

She asked if he had seen Slim again.

"I stayed only a few minutes after you left," he said. "I went back to the hotel. Went to bed."

He began once more to inspect the kitchen. She was pleased that he should see it. She wanted him to see the well polished stove with its enamel front, the kettle simmering

40

back against the flue. She wanted him to see the kindling she had made, neatly piled behind the coal scuttle, preparation for tomorrow, and the dishes gleaming on the cupboard shelves, the sink that shone, the white woodwork of the walls and the floor's green linoleum reflecting the window's light. It was her kitchen. Here she spent her days.

His eyes rested on the closed door which led from the kitchen to her bedroom. They hesitated, then moved on.

She stood up, beckoned to him and went towards the swinging door opening into the dining room. "They've gone out," she whispered. "No one's at home." The Wamboldts had taken their car and gone for a drive down the highway to visit friends at Entrance in the foothills. They would be away until Tuesday.

Walking on tiptoe, as if those who were absent still could hear, she showed him the dining room with its polished mahogany table, tall candlesticks and silver, and then the living room with its thick carpet where, across from the fireplace, the great fern stood in the bay window. The Wamboldts owned it all, but it was she who kept it as it was. "Think I like the kitchen better," Peter Wrogg said, pushing his hair back from his brow.

Selva was disappointed that he was not impressed by the furnishing of the front room. It was said to be the most expensively furnished room in all of Yellowhead. After all, Mr. Wamboldt, with his movie theatre, garage and apartment house, made a lot of money. She wondered if, in his house in Montreal, the man beside her had anything better to show. She supposed he had.

A moment before she had been tempted to let him look into her bedroom off the kitchen where a cluster of blue bells sat on the dresser and a blue counterpane covered the bed. She was partial to blue because it favoured her hair. Returning to the kitchen, she refrained, though her hand touched the panel of the door and pondered on the impulse. She had never thought of opening her bedroom to Slim, who, nevertheless, on his own had one afternoon put his head inside and sniffed and said, "Ugh!"

In the kitchen, Peter Wrogg said, "They've put up a lunch for us at the hotel. We can pick it up on our way. Didn't bring it because you might have had something else to do."

"They don't know how to put up lunches at that hotel," Selva said. "I baked on Friday. I'll make one here." On another day, she might have been happy to walk down the street with a stranger who wore brogues and a flannel suit, or even to have made a display of him in a motor car, but with Slim in town she was not willing to take the risk.

"You sit down and wait," she told him. "It will be only a minute."

He lit a cigarette, while she went into the pantry and made sandwiches of cold roast beef and prairie cheese, rolled them in wax paper, added two whole tomatoes, a piece of angel cake, a pinch of tea and wrapped it all in a white napkin. She descended to the basement for the tea-billy and two tin cups hanging in a canvas bag from a nail. She found a haversack and in the kitchen put the lunch and billy in it. She set the haversack upon the table and went into her room. She shut the door and bound back her hair with a blue bandanna and put two blue bells in her jacket buttonhole. She came back to the kitchen, picked up the haversack and slipped its strap over her shoulder.

"Here, I'll take that," Peter Wrogg said, rising, dousing his cigarette on the saucer she had put beside him. He reached for the haversack, his arms tentatively around her. They were standing before the little mirror above the flour bin. In it she saw his dark head and her own, golden beside it. With one hand he took the haversack, but his other arm did not leave her. She braced both her hands against his shoulder.

"Please, Mr. Wrogg!" she said.

He stood back. "Sorry," he said. "Didn't intend ... Anyway, can't you call me Peter instead of Mr. Wrogg?"

She laughed a little, lifted the mass of hair at the nape of her neck between thumb and forefinger. "Peter," she repeated. "It's a nice name. It's like a boy's name."

When they were outside and gone around to the front of the house and passed through the gate in the close cropped hedge of spruce, she glanced quickly at him and again she smiled at the seriousness with which he alternately raised his brows and drew them together in a frown. Only once, the night before, had she seen him smile. His eyes looked forward now, along the road. They were glazed as though his thoughts were miles away.

42

"You don't wear a hat," she said to him. "No one here ever goes without a hat. Anyway, none of the riders — and most of them, like Slim, are half bald when they're past thirty."

He wore a hat in the city, he said, but he liked the sun. In his work, and especially in Montreal during the winter, a man could enjoy the sun all too seldom.

"What work do you do?" Selva asked. She realized that she should not ask any one what they did for a living, but after all he knew what she did. She had shown him over the house where she worked.

He said, "I am on my father's business." He laughed lightly. Selva looked questioningly at him. She did not understand the allusion.

"My people export woollens," he explained, "in Leeds. That's in Yorkshire. I was sent out to take charge of the Montreal office and now I'm on my way to the Pacific Coast to open a branch in Vancouver."

He told her it was his first trip to the West. He had stopped off in Yellowhead because he had heard of the lakes and mountains nearby. A bit like Switzerland, he thought. He had climbed in Switzerland. Now in Yellowhead, if he had had time, he would like to have hired a man and ascend one of the peaks. "Perhaps, on my way back east from the Coast, I will be able to," he said. "At any rate now is too early in the season. Meanwhile, just where are *we* going?"

"Over there, up that hill. I want to show you the view up the valley from the cemetery," Selva answered. Yet what she said was not quite the truth. What she should have said was "my view up the valley." She was taking him up to the cemetery for the same reason that she had shown him through the Wamboldts' house. She had a pride of possession in the little point of land which, beyond the wire fence enclosing the graves, looked up towards the ice fields.

They walked along the street past the doctor's red brick house and the Catholic Church and crossed over into the pines growing by the school, now wrapped in sun and sabbath quiet. There they followed a path to the old log houses and corrals at the back of town, built against the hill in the years before steel was laid in the valley. It was here that Slim stabled his horse when he was in from the ranch and here that she rented the roan mare when she went riding with him.

The path crossed a road and they waited while two early tourists rode by — they would be American by their uncompromising khaki dress — man and wife, maintaining the diligent silence of marital middle age. The woman's lips were firmly set. The man had rosy cheeks and, as if one stomach were not enough, he had two small ones, one above and one below the tightly drawn belt. His cheeks, his stomachs rippled with his horse's walk. He slouched in the saddle, head bent forward, eyes staring ahead, like Napoleon on his retreat from Moscow in the picture above the Wamboldt's bed. Selva looked after them down the road. Their horses' plodding hooves raised small spirals of dust. Then at the turn of the road the riders disappeared beyond a group of pines.

When they had crossed the road and climbed the hill, Selva and Peter Wrogg sat down against a rock, town, river and valley spread like a varied carpet at their feet. She gave the names to him of mountains and of rivers.

"Know this country well, don't you?" he said to her.

"I've been raised in it, here and in the foothills. I've never been anywhere else, except on trips to Edmonton."

"Never been East?"

She shook her head.

"That's odd," he said.

"What's odd about it?" she enquired.

"Just that you've never been East."

"Lots of people have never been East. You just said you'd never been West before."

Before replying, he offered her a cigarette. When she refused, he lit one for himself, blowing the smoke from his lips in a grey gust. He held the cigarette between his fingers and tapped his fist upon the ground to shed the ashes from it. Although his hands were small, the fingers were long and spatulate. Again she noticed the carefully kept pink nails with their white half moons. They were hands formed to select and not to grasp.

"Yes, but I've come West," he said. "You could probably go East if you wanted to."

"Who said I wanted to go East?" Selva demanded stoutly. She was annoyed, not so much at the direction the conversation had taken, as at his assumed knowledge of her wishes.

"No one told me," he said to her. "No one, I assure you. I daresay, it was just a fancy. Somehow I got the idea on my way back to the hotel from the dance last night." He spoke more slowly now, with greater ease and without elision. He snuffed his cigarette against the ground, and as he glanced down to the task, the sun cast the shadow of his thick lashes on his cheek. He turned, regarded Selva for a long moment.

"Yes, last night, Selva," he said, "I was thinking about you. After our dance together, you know. I thought — Oh, it seemed to me that a girl with your colouring, your bearing, your blue dress . . . Put it this way — I hardly expected to meet someone like you in a dance above a billiard hall."

"Why not?" she held her face in profile to him — the smooth forehead, the little nose, the pursed lips, the clean sweep of chin and throat. She picked a piece of grass from beside her knee, let it fall.

"Why not?" he echoed. "That's a hard question to answer. Perhaps because you reminded me of someone I know. A man's always looking for and finding the same woman, you know. She comes from a small town too. A place called Granby in the Eastern Townships in Quebec. She now works as a model in one of the women's shops in Montreal."

Selva said, "A model?" He nodded, ran his fingers through his curly, black hair.

"Yes," he continued, "I suppose it was impertinent of me, but that was the idea at the back of my head that, if you cared to, you could go East and get a job as a model." He raised his hand. "Don't misunderstand me. Probably no reason why you should go East. You may be quite happy where you are. But in my business, one is interested in such things, in clothes and how they are worn."

Selva had studied pictures of models in fashion magazines. They lived in a far and different world. She had never considered their vocation as one which she might make her own.

"And, of course," Peter Wrogg continued, "I have connections. I daresay I could be of use to you when I return to the East. That's, if you were at all interested. The work, mind you, is not easy. It is very tiring. I know that because . . ."

Selva interrupted him. "What's her name . . . Is she pretty?" she asked.

His lips parted. He had not expected the question.

He replied, after a pause, "She's French-Canadian. Her name is Genelle Trudeau and I believe you would say that she is a girl to be noticed. She is quite tall, about your height, but grey eyes. Somewhat your colour of hair too."

"Why did you ask me to dance last night . . . and come up here with me now?" Selva wanted to know.

He stretched his legs, rolled over on his elbow, lowered his head, smoothed with his hand a bunch of grass. "I might have guessed you would ask me that," he said. "I have already given you the answer. There was something about you, as though we had met long, long ago."

"Are you very fond of her?" Selva asked him.

"Fond of whom?" He sat up, rubbed his brow.

"Of this girl you told me about just now who works as a model."

"Of Genelle, you mean?" He shook his head, laughed gently. "Genelle and I are friends, good friends . . ." But Selva, impatient with Genelle, no longer listened. Instead, she stared at a mountain top, faintly heard a locomotive's whistle. It would be the through freight travelling east from Yellowhead Pass. She did not see the mountain across the valley, the snow upon it, nor the white cumulous cloud rising on the south wind from behind it. She saw again beyond it the salon in an eastern city, the polished floor and the well dressed men and women in soft light. This was a slightly different room. A giant chandelier hung from its ceiling and she heard musicians hidden by the palm trees. Once more, as she entered from a darkened doorway, a man rose to greet her. He was not the same man she had imagined before. He was more like Peter Wrogg. He wore tails with a stiff white shirt, his hair was curly and carefully combed.

She drew in her breath and was back again on the hillside. "Do you think there would be any chance?" she asked Peter Wrogg.

"Chance of what?" He sighed. His thoughts too seemed to have strayed.

"Of what you were saying . . . of my getting to work as a model in a big store?" She sat on her hands, shook back her hair, drew herself up straight.

"Oh, that!" he said, looking away. "Of course, of course . . . always a chance. No more than a chance, but still a

46

chance. I'll be back in Montreal. I'll write and let you know, if you would like me to."

Selva ripped a strand of grass savagely from its roots, sucked it, leaned against the hill and looked up into the blue sky. Nothing would come of the chance. She knew it. She would not cease to be a hired girl in Yellowhead and overnight find herself a model wearing expensive clothes in Montreal. Even if she had the money to make the gamble, she would lack the courage so to test her destiny. At the moment, however, that was not significant. What was significant was that Peter Wrogg, a man whom she had known for less than twenty-four hours, was the first person who had seen into her and followed where her longings led. In Yellowhead she was "the girl who worked for the Wamboldts." Someday she might marry a railroader or become a storekeeper's wife. Peter Wrogg saw more and what he saw, others might see too. He saw her not only as she was, but as what she might become, a model, appearing before people with money and with influence, invited to fine houses, taken to the theatre and to the cabarets.

She gathered her grey skirt beneath her thigs, hugged her knees under her chin, wiggled the toes of her brown walking shoes. "Come on, Peter, kind Peter," she said, straightening her legs, doubling them again, rising to her feet and dusting twigs and grass from the folds of her skirt. "I was going to show you the view up the valley from the cemetery. Remember?"

She ran ahead along the trail upon the hill top. She pulled the blue bandanna from her head, waving it in her hand, letting her hair low free. "Hurry up!" she called back to Peter, her voice high and light as the trilling of a bird.

"No hurry. They'll wait," he replied, rising to his feet, hoisting the haversack to his shoulder.

She looked back. "Who'll wait?"

"They . . . the people we're going to see."

Selva's pace slackened to a walk. Yes, they would be waiting, she thought, as she and Peter dropped out of sight of the town into a draw and met the road's more leisurely progress up the hill and pursued it across a creek and through a grove of birch trees to the cemetery's gate. They would be waiting, all of them, the old and the young, their eyes sealed with their own dust against the sun. They would wait forever, through all the seasons, through the rain and the snow and the sunshine. Lucinda, the little girl with the shining name, the section foreman's daughter from up the line, she would be waiting too in her neat crib of earth with the bright pink and yellow flowers above her head. They were artificial flowers protected from the weather by an inverted bowl of glass. There they bloomed all year through. Even in the winter when the snow flew and the withered wreathes on the other graves were mere white shapes, Lucinda's flowers bloomed like springtime, their roots warmed by a child's gentle breath.

"She was such a little thing," Selva said to Peter as they stood by the grave.

They walked slowly, side by side, through the cemetery of monuments and tilted crosses, of graves tended and untended, of people remembered and forgotten, to the other gate opening out to the rocky bluff which looked up the valley. The gate creaked as they closed it behind them.

"Funny thing, gate on a cemetery," Peter observed. "They all have 'em. No one can get out. No one wants to get in."

Selva did not respond. The remark she thought was in bad taste. She stood facing up the valley towards the southern mountains, some of them a hundred miles away, blue and glistening in the sun, ribbed with ice and snow, silent in tumult, frozen in great waves of immobility. This was her country. Those were its ponderous borders. She might one day cross them, but she would never leave them behind. They were part of her and she was part of them. They were Slim and the pool hall and the town and the Wamboldts' house and the beaver meadow and the school-marm tree. Peter Wrogg was not of them. He was alien, from another part. She would not escape the mountains unless she became an alien too, yet she knew that at the end of the farthest journey she would only find herself. But she would never cease from the effort to escape. Those who held her where she was were her enemies. Those who helped her to see beyond that ring of rock and ice would be her friends.

"This is what I wanted to show you," she said to Peter. "The mountains, the river, the trees. Look, they're so far away they look like grass. I often come here on my free afternoon and sit and look."

"And wish you were somewhere else?" he suggested.

She laughed. "And suppose I do? I never remember afterwards what I've been thinking."

"Nothing like this in Montreal," he assured her.

"Pouff! Who said I was going to Montreal? And if I did, I'd likely finish up working in someone's kitchen. Still . . . you will write me, won't you?"

"Of course, I'll write you. Tell you all about it." He patted her shoulder, stepping closer to her.

She turned from the valley, looking down upon the town. They were now above its northern end. Because it was Sunday, few people were on the streets. She thought she saw the priest crawling like a black beetle across the dusty road to the station carrying with him dreams of torment and eternal fire. He would be going down to meet the incoming passenger train from the West. Beyond the green frame station the freight train she had heard earlier was pulling into a siding.

Closer in to the bottom of the hill, she saw sheets behind the Chinese laundry already hung out to dry. It made her think of her own washing waiting for her tomorrow and she saw the town below in another way, as a town of front doors, all of them shut against her. She was a servant girl and those who came to visit her called at the back door. When she went to visit the girls who worked at the hotel she also went to the back door.

On a field hidden by a stand of pines, boys were shouting in the lengthening shadows as they played lacrosse.

"How about our lunch . . . or is it supper now?" Peter asked.

Selva nodded slowly. "Yes, we should," she said.

She looked again at the town, at the station, the store, the Wamboldts' house, the bank, the Catholic church, the red-roofed houses and the newly green poplar trees, and then to the left in a clump of second-growth pine, she saw the yellow painted shack where Slim was playing poker with the boys. She had forgotten Slim. Smoke rose from the shack's chimney and a group of men was clotted at its door. She saw the group break up and its members begin to go their separate paths. The poker game, apparently, had finished. She could not, at the distance, distinguish Slim from among the others, but she knew that he would be with them — unless he had already left — going now to the hotel, or more probably, to the Wamboldts' house, expecting to find her there. He would be unshaven. The skin around his eyes would be more deeply tanned. His breath would be stale with smoke and whiskey and flecks of dry saliva would be caught in the corners of his mouth.

Her upper lip puckered, her cheek winced. She stepped back and her hand, as though of itself, reached out and touched the soft flannel of Peter's sleeve. He started, raised his eyebrows.

With the feel of the flannel in her fingers, a great hunger came upon her, for the cloth itself, for the way of life it represented, for the man within it. He was pink and clean. He stood secure above the town, removed from its necessities. Tomorrow, the day after, he would be gone. She would see him no more. He was a man of business and affairs, his roots in the East, in England. He moved in the world at large. In Vancouver on the Coast, in Montreal, other people would be waiting for him, other girls, other afternoons . . . And even now Slim might be knocking on the backdoor of the Wamboldts' house.

She looked again towards the town. The sun shone from behind her and when, for a moment, her shadow down the hillside merged with Peter's, she felt a slow delight, as though their bodies had touched. Glancing at him, she noticed again the darn in his shirt, just by the point of his collar. It brought her closer to him and she knew she could have made a better darn.

She grasped his elbow firmly. "Let's make tea and have supper," she said.

"That's what I was saying," he replied. "How about back up there, underneath that tree?" He shifted his shoulder under the strap of the haversack, gestured with his head to a lone-growing fir.

"No, no, not here," Selva cried, her voice shrill and rising. "Not here. There's no water anyway. I know a place. It's just a little walk, back over the way we came and down the hill on the other side. It's across the railroad trestle. It's a beaver meadow down among the trees."

four

Selva twirled on her toes, ran before Peter to the cemetery gate. "Come along!" she cried, "It's getting late." She led him through the cemetery, by the birch trees, down the road and up the rise to the rock where, earlier, they had rested.

From there she followed the crest of the ridge. To her left was the town, bound by the covenant of its hills, to her right, the shadowed forest of fir trees. She broke again into a run, then slowed herself to a walk. The blue bandanna trailing from her jacket pocket, her tawny hair bounding upon her shoulders, she walked quickly, taking long strides, with a haste which she justified by the approach of the eastbound passenger train.

"We want to cross the trestle," she called back to Peter, "before the passenger pulls in." She could not bear the need of waiting, looking up, while the train went by. She had to put the trestle between herself and the houses of the town.

Grass wrapped itself around her ankles. A soft bough of fir brushed her shoulder. She pushed it angrily aside. A young spruce tree appeared in her path. She skirted it. A tall growing willow slapped and stung her cheek. She hurried on, unheeding, to the trestle and the beaver meadow beyond the river.

When the trail dropped down the hill, she paused, turned

to Peter. "Did you hear anything?" she asked.

He took a green silk handkerchief from his breast pocket, wiped his brow. "Too busy trying to keep up," he said. "Why the hurry?"

She found a further reason. Pointing to the clouds in the western sky, she said, "It's going to rain . . . but just now I thought I heard a horse's shoe strike against a stone."

She hesitated, looking down the hill, past an old corral, to the railroad tracks and bridge and to the Miette river, flowing green and reluctant between spruce and alder to the Athabaska. It might be another horseman, she thought, or possibly the American tourists, riding out of sight along the wagon road close in under the hill. Slim would hardly have had time to go to the stables, saddle his horse and set out to look for her. Nor could she be sure that, finding her absent from the Wamboldts' house, he would follow, nor know where to follow, nor yet that, in the event, he would be riding. At any rate, she comforted herself, it was her affair and none of his that she and Peter Wrogg were having supper in the beaver meadow.

Down on the flat, passing the corral, forsaken by its owner years before, they crossed the wagon road below the railroad embankment. She stooped, pointed to its dust. "See," she said in relief, "I was right. It was a horse, but going in the other direction. See, two of them just went by, going back to town. Likely they were the tourists we saw this afternoon."

"Does it matter?" Peter asked squinting at the tracks. "Sunday afternoon. Probably lots of people out riding. I might have rented horses myself. I like to ride."

Selva did not reply and, leaving the wagon road which led to a ford half a mile up the river, they scrambled up the soft earth of the embankment to the railroad track. She listened for a coming train before they walked out on to the trestle. "I guess the passenger's late tonight," she said.

They stepped carefully over the swirl of water glimpsed between the ties. Halfway across the trestle, Selva saw the splintered quills lodged in the side timbers where Slim, two evenings before, had tipped the porcupine into the stream. She grimaced, drew back from them. Then her eyes, as always, swept the westward stretch of track, blue now and not tinged with the sunset for the sun was behind a bank of clouds. A shower was coming down the valley, hanging like shaggy goat hair from the belly of the laden sky. Below it they heard the rumble of the eastbound passenger emerging from a cut.

"Better hurry," Peter said, taking her arm, pushing her along beside him. She stumbled on a tie. He hoisted her to her feet, urged her on.

Reaching the end of the bridge, his hand supporting her elbow, they slid on their heels down the shoulder of the road-bed as the black muzzle of the locomotive, trailing a white mane of steam, appeared around the curve. At the bottom, they turned, looked up to watch the train go by. Selva held her hands to her ears to shield them from the sizzle and roar of the locomotive, its great wheels interlocked and spun by urgent piston arms. She recognized the engineer, white haired Tom Bascom who lived in a single house at the back of town. She had often seen him working in his garden. From his narrow outlook, secure in eminence, speed as his mission, "orders" in his pocket, left hand on the throttle, power at his fingertips, he lifted a glove in lazy salute. Selva's vision coursed the line of coach windows, each with its white face, until her eyes blurred and were bruised as troubled as knuckles on Monday morning's washing board. The train passed on and she stared at a man and woman framed in the rear window of the observation car. The man wore a dark suit. He smoked a cigar. The young woman had a nodding white feather in her tipped, black hat. What did they speak of, where were they bound? They retreated, hauled backward into space and time, were lost to view, like dolls taken in from a store window, when the locomotive whistled at the mile post and the track curved beyond the bridge. In the sudden silence, a few pebbles, dislodged by the train's passage, rolled down the embankment and came to rest at Selva's feet.

"Well!" Peter said, grasping her arm more tightly.

"Well!" she repeated after him.

"There's your train," he said. "Three nights from now it will be in Montreal."

"And what if it is . . . I'm not going to Montreal."

He ran a thumb over his shoulder under the strap of the haversack. "We'll have to see about that," he said hugging her arm.

Selva wheeled from him. She saw again the darn in his white shirt. "Maybe you'll need someone to darn your shirts," she called to him, backing away.

"My shirt?" He frowned. His hand went uneasily to his collar. He did not comprehend.

Selva laughed, the tip of her tongue between her teeth. She swung away, grey pleated woollen skirt curling above her knees, and ran up the trail into the poplars and along it to where the big fir tree grew. There she dropped down from it and a minute later, stood panting, lips moist and parted, in the beaver meadow by the school-marm tree. A red squirrel, head down on the lower tree trunk, twitched its tail and scoldingly chattered at her.

Waiting, Selva turned on her heel and looked around the beaver meadow. She thought she saw it more clearly, more in detail than she had ever seen it before. It was no larger than the Wamboldts' backyard. On her left and to the west as she faced the pool was the school-marm tree. It was a pine tree whose upper trunk had been broken off by the wind. Two great branches had grown up to usurp the place of the trunk so that the tree now resembled a gigantic human figure upflung against the twilight of the sky, enfolding the wind in its arms.

Along the margin of the pool, grass grew green and among it, like pickets, were the rounded stumps of poplar trees, grey and weathered, where the beaver had cut food and wood to build their dam. Across the water she saw the grey mud mound of their house and below it, the low wall of the dam laced with willow and poplar branches. The beaver had long ago departed. They had migrated to another stream or been trapped by poachers, or going farther and farther from their pool for food, had become prey to coyote and lynx. Their house was abandoned and a few feet out from her, water flowed with a low murmur through a break in the untended dam.

A drop of rain touched her cheek. Rain pattered on poplar and alder and willow. It dimpled the surface of the pool. It was a gentle rain, a spring shower. It would fall over all the valley and wash the roofs of houses in the town and lay the dust upon the roads. She remembered the sheets behind the Chinese laundry. There would be little time now to bring them in.

The rain renewed the earth beneath her feet and brought its odours fresh and pungent to her nostrils. She closed her eyes and held her face up to it.

She opened her eyes and turned when she heard branches crackling on the slope that led up to the trail and the mountainside.

"Damn it! I say, damn it!" Peter shouted. "Why are there so many trees in this country and why are they so close together!"

"It's not far," she called back to him, seeing that he had missed the path down from the fir tree. "Just come straight down." She heard his deep breathing and watched as trembling leaves marked his approach.

He appeared on the edge of the clearing, stared about him, eyes squinting, head tilted. The sides of his sharp nose flexed, as though he smelled rather than saw. He mopped his face.

Selva walked over to the school-marm tree. He followed. "We can keep dry here," she said, "until the rain passes over. It's already brightening in the west."

A dry twig of spruce was caught in Peter's hair. She reached up and brushed it off. His hair was cool as silk against her palm. She and Peter were so close together that she was aware of the slow, strong pounding of his heart. His hand came up behind her shoulder, stroked her head with a gentle and even stroke. His cheek was against her own. She moved against him and her body warmed waiting for his arm. That was what she yearned for — the security of his arms around her. In the next instant she pushed herself from him, stood back alone, beyond the shelter of the pine and in the rain.

"Hark!" she commanded. It was a word barely remembered, that her mother had used, lifting herself up in bed in the dark of a winter night. "Listen!" Selva said to Peter.

Peter's mouth opened in surprise. His arms hung loosely. His eyes blinked. Selva listened to the rain up on the leaves, saw its high-kneed dance upon the pool and from the town heard a church bell peal. Then she heard what she had heard before, a tinkle, as though a man up there among the trees were standing, looking down upon them, idly turning over silver coins within his pocket.

"My God!" she exclaimed. "It is!"

"Is what? Don't speak in riddles," Peter said.

"Slim," she answered.

"Slim?" he questioned. "Slim?" he asked again. "The one who was at the dance with you?"

Selva regarded him in amazement, realizing how far apart, after all, their thoughts had been. Until then she had felt that each experience of the afternoon had been shared between them — the view of the town and mountains, the graveyard, the walk across the bridge. She had assumed — without reason, as now she recognized — that every thought of hers had been his as well. And for half an hour, since from the hilltop she had seen the break-up of the poker game, Slim's steps behind them had been but the dark echo of her own.

"Yes, Slim," she told Peter. "He's riding. He came across by the ford above the bridge. A moment ago I heard the tinkle of his spurs. No one else would be riding by here . . . and in the rain."

"Not married to him, are you?"

"Of course I'm not married to him."

"Well, then . . ." Peter lifted his shoulders in a gesture of dismissal.

"You don't know Slim," Selva replied, looking about the small clearing, seeing herself hemmed in by water, by willow bush and forest.

Decision was taken from her by a horse's snort and trotting hooves upon the trail above. A rock rolled, branches cracked and broke, the shifting earth sighed as the horse slid on his haunches down the path from the fir tree. Slim swung from the saddle, dropped split lines to the ground. He wore a green mackinaw and heavy cowhide chaps. The black slicker rolled behind the saddle cantle bulged with a feed of oats tied in the gunnysack within it.

He stood a moment by his horse's drooped head. Rain dripped from the brim of his black Stetson hat. The horse stretched his neck, shook himself under the saddle. He was wet to the belly from fording the river.

Peter, hands in his jacket pockets, stood back against the school-marm tree. He had slipped the haversack from his shoulder. It lay on the ground at his feet. Selva looked from Slim to him and back to Slim again.

Slim said, "I'm pulling out for the ranch."

"Tonight?" she asked.

"The foreman sent word up. They've got to get some horses in and he wants me there in the morning." Slim spoke as he walked, deliberately, without hurry, one word at a time.

"Why didn't you tell me?"

"I went by to tell you," he said through tightened lips. "You weren't there. No one was at home. So, after I saddled up" — he patted his big bay, Tony, on the neck — "I figured I'd come along and say good-bye. I knew I'd find you here."

"You and him, see?" Slim drawled, staring past Selva to Peter by the tree.

He looked again at Selva. "Sort of showing him around, aren't you?" he said, hitching his chaps. "Suppose you took him to the cemetery too?"

"That's where she goes to sit and look at the mountains," he said to Peter, "and to make 'plans.' She's asked me to go there too, but I never went."

He stuck out his chin and spat and the ball of spittle fell and rested in a rose bush by the pool. "Who wants to look at mountains?" Slim asked the world at large.

Addressing Peter again, he added, "And then she brought you here. Because . . . well, maybe she knew I'd come by and find you."

Selva tried to interrupt him. He raised his hand. "I mightn't have come here either, but I rode down the road a little ways and I saw your tracks where you crossed it and where you climbed up from it to the railroad bridge. I know those new shoes you're wearing, that you bought on your trip to Edmonton."

Selva stepped forward, her face white and drawn, her hair plastered down by the rain, to which she gave no notice. She lifted her two fists as if to strike Slim on the chest. "It's a lie!" she said to him in a voice no louder than a whisper, "I didn't know you would follow us." Yet she glanced quickly at Peter, half in fear that he would believe what Slim had said. He stood impassive, without movement, against the school-marm tree, a slight figure in grey, rosy cheeked, wide-eyed as a schoolboy.

Still, in part, Slim had spoken truth. Fleeing from him, she had also gone towards him — at least towards that portion of him which was hers. More than the Wamboldts' front room, more than the point of land by the cemetery, this was hers — this beaver meadow, this vale, this place of grass among the trees where water streaming from the mountain side pooled behind the dam and emptied to the river. Here with Slim she had seen the sun go down, seen the stars come out and heard the distant owl hoot to his fellow. Here they had learned all that they would ever learn of one another.

Now she bit her lower lip and waited while the word she had spoken seemed to hang above her, persist in the clearing, as though it had a strength apart from hers.

The shower was passing and the westering sun, shining below the clouds, touched with gold the beads of rain on the poplar leaves behind Slim's hat. It shone upon the silver rosettes of his horse's bridle and his chaps and sheened his horse's haunch. It laid a quick yellow mask upon his face.

He moved out from his horse whose head was down as he cropped the grass. "Take it back," he said to Selva. "Take back what it was you called me." He rubbed the back of his hand across his mouth.

In the next instant, with palm and then knuckles of his open hand, he had struck her twice across the face.

"Here, I say, you can't do that!" Peter stepped out from under the tree. Selva, hands to her face, was astonished to hear his voice and vaguely resented it. She had virtually forgotten that he was there. The place, the problem now belonged to her and Slim alone.

"Who said I can't?" Slim, said, taking another step towards her.

Peter put himself between them, moving his head in an unuttered "No!" Selva, behind him, drew back. Slim, taller and heavier, reached out to push him aside. Peter knocked his arm up, shifted his weight and his right fist hit with a thud just under Slim's heart.

Slim gasped, dropped to one knee as though he had found a sudden and perplexing sorrow among the grasses. His hat rolled on the ground. Elbow on his knee, he shook his head, while instinctively his right hand reached for his hat. He let his hat lie where it was, tilted on its brim. He shook his head again vigorously. Lifting it, baring his teeth, he said to Peter, who stood with his back to the pool. "You asked for it and now you're going to get it."

Peter's black tie fluttered in a puff of wind and as Slim got to his feet he put up his hands. Slim pushed at him, head down, arms flailing. Peter tried to duck, to dodge. Slim's blow landed on his mouth.

Peter did not go down. Instead, he staggered, looked drunkenly around the clearing. He saw Selva. His mouth seemed twisted, a patch of red smeared on his face by Slim's fist. It opened as though he laughed. In the next instant, aged and weary, it was as though he tried to call out, to ask a question.

"No, no!" Selva cried in spontaneous answer, running to interpose herself between him and Slim. "I didn't know he was coming. I swear, I didn't know!" Slim's elbow, hard as a knot of fir wood, caught her squarely on her throat, sending her reeling against the school-marm tree. She fell, blind with pain, and the world retreated, whirled around her in redness and in fury.

It returned, flickering grey and uncertain on her consciousness. She felt her throat. She coughed. Her fingers touched pine needles on the ground. Her eyes opened and she saw pine boughs against a washed blue sky. A golden crowned sparrow made its plaintive call of "Here dearie! Here dearie!" and from Yellowhead she heard the chuffing of a locomotive. Dimly she knew it was the eastbound passenger changing locomotives. Closer to her, water riffled through the broken beaver dam like low voices muttering an ominous foreign language whose meaning was just beyond her grasp.

She raised herself on an elbow, saw the clearing, shadowed now and quiet, fenced with sombre trees which seemed to lean to listen. Slim and his horse, Tony, had gone. She looked for Peter. She could not see him.

She whispered his name and rising, chilled with fear, called it louder. As the echoes fell, she heard a further sound. She heard drumming hooves above, receding on the trail. She turned but could not see the man whose horse, beyond the marshalled forest, along the river, close against the mountain galloped through spring twilight into night.

five

As Selva rose slowly to her feet, hand upon the trunk of the school-marm tree, the trees edging the clearing seemed to draw back, to dwindle, until the beaver meadow stretched before her vast as a green prairie and the forest shrank to a hedge which bound its distant limits. Abruptly the scene changed, contracted in her vision. The pine trees approached, their tips downbent, their branches crowding against her. She pulled her elbows into her side, feeling a cold wind upon them.

She heard no sound but the gurgling water at the meadow's foot. To her right, where the pool narrowed and merged with the stream from the mountain which fed it and where goose grass speared the shallow waters, a bush of willow, high as her shoulder, trembled, shook and was still. It came to life once more. Its branches waved like arms in signal to her. They called her on, they bade her stay. Sometimes in the high mountains, in winter's loneliness, a trapper would leave his cabin and go out to shake hands with the willows. His eyes would burn, his voice would rise and he might be found one day on hands and knees by the railroad track, howling like a timber wolf.

Selva observed the bush, holding her breath, but making no move towards it. Under the leaves she discerned the forks of its branches and they were like hands, fingers out-stretched, tense in agony. From among them she heard a grunt, a groan, a blubbering — a cry more animal than human — which from its station was above the water but came as if forced up from beneath it.

In the next instant, Peter stood between her and the bush. He had stepped from behind it. He had taken form from within it. She looked to see leaves and grass and warm moist earth fall from his shoulders. His grey clad shoulders were unsullied but his trousers were drenched with water to their knees. His chin was pushed against his chest. He held his silk handkerchief to his mouth. Blood had stained his shirt and rusted his black tie.

He came towards her, stumbling and unsteady. He put his left hand to her head and from her head to his chin. He tried to speak but the words were drowned in his mouth. He made the same motion again from her head to his chin.

Not knowing why, Selva thought he wished her to put her head by his chin, but when she attempted to do so, he shoved her away, shook his head.

"Poor Peter!" she said, laying an arm around his shoulder, lowering her head to his. "What has happened? Tell me, what happened?"

He gazed wildly at her, at the clearing, pointed to her head and to his mouth from which blood bubbled and frothed turning the handkerchief from white to red. He breathed with effort, like a man who climbed a hill.

Selva thought of Slim, by now across the river and on the road behind the town, shoulders shaking as in laughter to his horse's trot. What had he done to Peter, to her, to both of them, before he rode away into the hills? This before her . . . She had come down to the beaver meadow with a man. Now she was confronted with the helpless stare and the muteness of an idiot. She had seen him hit Peter on the mouth, but a blow on the mouth did not account for a flow of blood which seemed to well up from the throat and for the daze and madness she saw within those eyes. For a moment, she felt she was to be sick to her stomach. Then she gathered herself together, moved to take Peter's hand from his mouth that she might see his hurt. With his free hand he repulsed her roughly.

She said to him, "We'll go find the doctor. Do you think you can make it across the trestle?"

He nodded — yet he did not nod so much as he moved his head up and down with the hand, three fingers of which, holding the handkerchief, were sunk in his mouth to their second knuckles. Blood oozed out between the fingers, ran down the back of his hand and into the sleeve of his jacket.

Passing under the school-marm tree, Selva picked up the haversack, hung it from her shoulder. Peter made no endeavour to relieve her of its burden. He followed, head down, wheezing through his nostrils.

They climbed the path to the fir tree and the trail, torn and dug by the hooves of Slim's horse, Tony. Slim was now too far away, his figure whittled by distance, a shadow among the shadows, to be a satisfactory object of her anger. Her resentment demanded what was at hand, herself or Peter. Why had she brought him to the pool at all? She had known that there of all the places in the valley Slim would most likely come to find her. And why had Peter not been able to stand up, to give as much as he had taken? She would have borne it more easily if he had received an ordinary beating, a swollen eye, a bleeding nose. As it was, he bore the mark, but she was its intended and ultimate victim, and his failure against Slim was her own. If he would emerge from his incapacity long enough to tell her what had occurred after she had been knocked against the school-marm tree, she would be less conscious of being bereft, of having brought a man down to the pool and of leading away in his stead a creature stuttering and incompetent. She looked back along the trail and realized that whatever the beaver meadow had had at one time to offer her, it was hers no more. She realized too in a dim, far recess of her mind that the pool and beaver meadow nevertheless were a part of her as they had not been before. They were firm now, hinged deep within her conscience.

Seeing Peter behind her, compassion flooded her like warmth. She remembered what she had said in the kitchen — it seemed so long ago — when he had asked her to call him by his first name. "Peter," she had said, "it's a nice name. It's like a boy's name." And that was what he had become — a boy, fingers in his mouth, dependent upon her. She felt herself infinitely older, stronger, wiser. At the foot of the railroad embankment he confirmed her dominance. He stretched forth his hand, touched her arm and sat down upon a boulder. He hung his head, took the handkerchief from his mouth and a blob of blood, round as a butter dish, spurted onto the gravel. Selva turned away, her stomach drawn up under her chest. when she looked back, the handkechief was again in Peter's mouth. His head wobbled and she stood above him, steadying it in her hands, studying the sharp rise before her and wondering if he would be able to reach the top where the tracks led level across the river.

She helped him to his feet. Wearily he subsided when a locomotive whistled at the mile board. It was a freight, westbound up the valley. As it went by, Selva smelt cattle, heard the dirge of their sad lowing, saw cattle cars and box cars and coal cars coupled one to another as if they were gravely shaking hands. The passage of the train was slow, rumbled conversation. Like an afterthought the caboose bounced by with a black hat, as a period, in its cupola.

She put her hand under Peter's elbow, assisted him to stand, and they climbed the shifting gravel of the embankment. Crossing the trestle, her arm around his waist, Selva said, "Poor Peter . . . It's all my fault. I'm so sorry and I don't even know what it is that happened to you." He paused, gagged, indicated his mouth. Yes — it was his mouth. What she could not understand was that it was, apparently, inside his mouth, or deeper still, and nothing that she could see.

At the end of the bridge, rather than dropping down to the wagon road, she guided Peter to the right, to the trail though the pine woods which she and Slim were accustomed to use as a shortcut. The need of reaching the doctor hurried her on, but Peter caused her steps to lag in the lowering gloom of the pines.

They came out from the pines onto the street. Half a block away the first house showed and beyond it other houses, scowling behind their porches, night lapping at their thresholds, set back among tall fir trees, among dwarf pines and poplars. The doctor's house was two blocks down the street, three blocks to the left.

A motor car moved slowly up the street. It was a black car

of the size and shape of a covered delivery truck. It had side windows in which black velvet curtains hung and its polished hood and nickel trimmings reflected the waning light of a clouded sky. The car drew up before the last house on the street but one, a brown cedar bungalow with young pines grouped by its door.

As she approached, Selva saw Mr. Winnie step down from the car and walk around its front while his mother, an elderly woman in a grey cloak, descended on the side nearer to the house and picking up her long skirt, as though the sidewalk were a puddle that she crossed, went through the gate and indoors. Mr. Winnie had climbed onto the car's running board and was reaching in behind the seat.

He was a man, Selva had been told, who had come to Yellowhead six or seven years before. At the time he owned a Ford truck and for a while delivered wood and coal and small consignments of freight from the railroad. Then in the summer, when the hospital was being built, he had gone away to Winnipeg to "take a course." He returned after six months with his mother. Her money had enabled him to buy their present home and to rent a one storey stone building facing the tracks a few doors below the pool hall. His office was in the front of the building. Behind the office was a large dim room into which no one but himself and his part-time assistant — the McGonigal boy whom he had hired to drive the Ford truck — had been known to enter. Over the entrance to his office he had erected a sign in the form of a half circle. It read, pink on white, "Valley of the Flowers." Underneath, in smaller letters, was his name, "A. J. Winnie, Mortician."

He had already purchased a new car which served, according to the occasion, either as an ambulance to bring people to the hospital or, more rarely and profitably, as a hearse to take them away. Mr. Winnie, a man with a feeling for the rightness of things, had been heard declaring to strangers that he "followed the medical profession."

Now, as Selva and Peter were about to pass, he backed out of his two purpose vehicle, carrying the picnic hamper which he and his mother had had with them on their usual Sunday afternoon drive. He stumbled against Peter and turned, surprised. Peter's face was pale in the half light. His sleeve was blood to the elbow and the handkerchief against his mouth was clotted with blood. Mr. Winnie's avid and professional eye immediately accepted the situation.

He held the car door open. "Get in!" he commanded. Peter looked at Selva. She had been ready to hail a car had she seen one going by, but she was unprepared for Mr. Winnie's abrupt proposal.

"Get in!" he said again to Peter. "Get in and I'll take you to the doctor. That's where you're going, isn't it?" He addressed the last words to Selva.

"Yes," she said, "the doctor. He's hurt."

"Looks like a haemorrhage, internal, to me," Mr. Winnie said. He stood by the door. Peter set his hand upon it and with a final glance at Selva, as if asking her permission, climbed weakly in. Mr. Winnie slammed shut the car door, pushed the picnic hamper into Selva's hand, walked around the front of the car, took his seat beside Peter, started the engine, switched on the headlights, shifted the gears, wheeled up on the far sidewalk to turn the car about and drove away with a wink of his red taillight towards the doctor's house. Selva watched the black car swaying in its progress down the street between the pines, diminishing before her eyes, a piece of darkness called home to the night which gave it birth.

Mr. Winnie had not invited her to go with them. Perhaps that was because the night before at the pool hall he had asked her to dance with him and, as formerly when he had presented himself, she had begged to be excused. She was tired. Her feet were sore. The dance was already taken. She could not sufffer her hand in his, nor his arm around her. Yet Mr. Winnie, she supposed, was sufficiently personable in his way, if one could forget his calling — a round, cheerful little man in a bright tie and brown suit, a man given to looking up at the sky. He had been looking up at the sky one early morning in the previous fall when she had seen him. At the time she was still with the station restaurant and had been crossing the vacant lot behind his office to go to work. It was the morning after Lucinda, the small daughter of the section foreman from up the line, had died in the hospital from a ruptured appendix. Mr. Winnie stood in the doorway at the back of his office, head tilted to the blue beyond the western mountains. His lips were pursed. He whistled, shirt sleeves rolled above his elbows. He had been scrubbing his forearms and hands and had come outside for a breath of air, for a touch of the sun, while he dried them on a towel. Steam rose from them in the frosty air. Selva quickened her pace, but Mr. Winnie, rubbing his pink forearms with the rough towel, was not to be easily dismissed. He nodded. He bowed. He remarked upon the fine morning.

Now she stood before his house, his picnic hamper in her hands. She took it with the tips of her fingers and set it by the trees inside his gate and walked down the street, fresh smelling after the rain, to the green frame of the Wamboldts' house. Peter by this time would be with the doctor.

It was the indecisive hour between twilight and dark. In some windows that she passed, lights shone, while in other houses people waited upon the porches, drinking to the full the dregs of the sabbath day. Someone called her name. Selva waved her hand, walked on. She did not wish to stop and talk. No light showed in the Wamboldt house, although as she touched the gate, it seemed that from the front window she saw a flicker of flame, as though someone in the darkened room were lighting a cigarette. She thought of it no more and entered the back door to the kitchen, flipped the switch to the right of the door, pulled down the window shades, sorted from the haversack its unused contents, and considered again Peter as he had come from behind the willow bush in the beaver meadow like an apparition sprung from the ground. Nor could she rid her conscience of the fact that it was an apparition of her own making. She had brought him there. Reviewing the dance, their walk up the hill to the cemetery and along the hill top and over the bridge she was bewildered that an outing, innocent in inception, should have so inexplicable an end. Peter was hurt, but she did not know the extent of his hurt, nor what had caused it. Even more vital than that, was the suspicion that he might believe that somehow she had contrived it and that, except for its details, it was, as Slim had hinted, all according to a plan. Peter's face came so close to her that she wished to brush it aside and she saw once more the black car in its journey down the street and the red taillight blinking at her in knowledge and in mockery. She would put away the cups, the tea-billy and the haversack and go at once to the doctor's house.

As she went to the dark stairway leading down to the basement, she drew back, stifled a cry in her throat. Something palpable, undefined as the shape of her thoughts, brushed against the calf of her leg. She leaned down, scratched the back of the Wamboldts' brindled tomcat. Fright was still within her. When she and Peter had left the house, the cat had been outdoors. Someone had let him in. She did not think that the Wamboldts had yet returned from their drive down the valley to Entrance. In that case she would have heard them moving, talking. She would have heard the rustle of a newspaper or Mr. Wamboldt's chronic cough from behind it. She would have seen a light. The Wamboldts did not retire early. Until midnight or later they sat in the front room, Mrs. Wamboldt engrossed in a Christian Science tract from Boston, he reading the day-old newspapers which had come in from Edmonton and Vancouver. They were quiet people. Elsie Wamboldt had a grown son by another marriage who was in the lumber business in Australia. She herself was in her late forties, tall, black haired, with the quick, direct eyes of a bird. She was broad shouldered for a woman and complained because she had lately grown stout. She spoke frequently of Toronto and of Toronto people and of the horses there that she used to ride and of the country club society in which she rode. It was evident that she was habituated to many amenities lacking in Yellowhead. Nor nowadays did she often ride. She had a distaste for the short-barrelled mountain horse with his jolting, uneven trot and it pained her, she claimed to hear a horse's shoe strike against a stone.

Mr. Wamboldt may have been a year or two younger than his wife. He was one of the most prominent men in town. In addition to managing his apartment house, moving picture theatre and garage, he had recently been elected president of the local Board of Trade. Many times he had gone into Edmonton and twice had travelled all the way to Ottawa to urge the building of roads and other improvements in and around the town. Selva had heard reports that he was quite a "gay dog" on these journeys away from home. She thought it incredible, because around the house he was so quiet, well behaved, his head behind a newspaper or bowed over a bowl of soup, listening while his wife advised him about "putting up a proper front" or "making an impression." When she had finished speaking he would lift his head, cheeks puffed and flushed, eyes blinking behind his square-framed glasses, as though he had just wakened from sleeping on his face.

Though the house had three bedrooms, the Wamboldts slept in the same bed on which Selva weekly changed the sheets. In the four months she had been with them she had seen no sign that they did more than lie one beside the other. And one evening after dinner, going from the kitchen to the living room with wood for the fireplace, she had stopped behind the plush curtains hung from the archway in the dining room. The silence beyond them forbade her to step boldly out. She heard the crackle of the open fire and at her toes saw its glow upon the polished floor. She was about to cough to announce her coming. Instead, she moved the curtain slightly aside, peered into the living room. The Wamboldts were sitting in a big chair pulled up before the fire. He was on Mrs. Wamboldt's lap, his head against hers, while in the yellow firelight she slowly, ever so slowly, patted his cheek. His feet were off the floor. Selva drew back from the curtain, eased herself quietly into the kitchen. She was shocked, stirred, filled with uncomprehended pity by what she had seen.

She had tried to explain it to Slim when they went walking two days later. "But don't you understand," she said to Slim, "his feet were off the floor. They were just hanging there. And he always keeps his shoes so well polished. They looked so useless over that expensive carpet."

"What's the carpet got to do with it? And of course they'd be off the floor," Slim said. "If he was sitting on her knee, what do you expect?"

"Yours wouldn't be off the floor, if you were sitting on my knee," Selva retorted.

"I wouldn't be sitting on your knee. You can sit on mine. That's good enough for me."

Now at the top of the basement stairs, thinking of Slim, of Peter, trying to account for the presence of the cat inside the house, Selva waited, and stillness was around her like a breath withheld. Quickly she switched on the lights in the basement, ran down the creaking wooden stairs, hung the haversack and the canvas bag with the tea-billy from their proper nails, and shadows dogging her heels, fled as quickly back to the kitchen. There she stood indecisive, knowing that she should go into the front of the house to learn whether or not she were alone in it or if the Wamboldts had returned or — and she remembered with a pounding of her pulse the match flicker she thought she had seen before entering the house — perhaps, before she had time to turn on the lights, to feel a hand upon her arm, a hand across her mouth and against her ear a husky voice she had never heard before. Or through the half dark of the front room from the sofa by the grandfather clock, a face gaunt and white and sulphurous would stare out at her. Its character altered. She saw Peter sitting there, as he might have sat that afternoon, immaculate, curly hair upon his brow, gazing into her with accusing eyes. As her fancy roved, flesh gathered in goose pimples on her breasts. Suddenly she thought again of Slim — but Slim would not be there behind the curtain. Slim might have waited outside behind a tree. He would not have come into the front room. And anyway, she felt herself capable of meeting Slim. She would welcome the chance to upbraid him. It was the unknown that she feared — the threat, inherited from childhood, of a night haunted house.

Caruso, the tomcat, sat on his haunches, held up to her a green eye like a proffered jewel. He had only one eye, having lost the other in a night of tumult underneath the moon. His frayed ears were cocked. His pouched, grey face bore old scars gained in stubborn service to his ecstasies. He purred, swished his tail. Mrs. Wamboldt was proud of Caruso, boasted of his knight errantry to her husband and to others, twittered to the cat in baby talk.

Standing in the kitchen before the swing door into the dining room, failing in courage to step through to what lay beyond it, Selva squatted on her heels, petted the cat, picked him up in her arms. As she stood, she heard the floor creak in the dining-room. The white swing door was pushed towards her. Then it settled back into place. She watched, muscles tense, body wooden. She squeezed the cat until he ceased to purr and watched and listened with her. In the railroad yard a switch engine puffed and laboured, shunting cars. Nearer to the house, but half a block away, heels crunched on the gravel of the sidewalk. Selva was tempted to turn, to run, to flee from the house, to scream, to call, but the smooth and unmoving door held her eyes in a bond she could not sunder.

The door moved on its hinges, swinging without sound into the kitchen. She stepped back farther from it. The tip of a stubby finger stained with tobacco showed on its panelling and around its lower edge the sharp, polished toe of a shoe and a dark trouser cuff. The door came wide against the wall and Mr. Wamboldt was before her. He released the door and it swung to behind him.

"Mr. Wamboldt!" Selva exclaimed.

He did not reply. His thin, fairish hair was mussed. His breath came heavily. Sweat glistened on his nose. His chest heaved and his plump body seemed padded as though beneath his clothes he wore an overcoat. His eyes, behind their glasses, small and inflamed as a bear cub's, searched the room to rest at last in slow insolence on Selva's blouse revealed beneath the open jacket. Mr. Wamboldt threw back his head, put his hand to his mouth. He hiccoughed, shaking as if from a blow on the shoulder.

"My God, Mr. Wamboldt!" Selva said.

He wagged his head, twitched his lips. His hand went to his vest pocket. He pulled out his watch and held it dangling from its thin gold chain. He studied it thoughtfully, wagging his head again, then replaced it in his vest.

"But Mrs. Wamboldt . . ." Selva stared despairingly at the door into the dining-room. He shook his head in negation. She realized that Mrs. Wamboldt was not in the house. Probably she was staying the night at Entrance as she had done before for an early morning ride. Her friends there, the Fishers, owned a horse that she was fond of. They would then drive her up to Yellowhead in time to be home for lunch. Mr. Wamboldt, Selva concluded, had been sitting alone in the front room, waiting. His was the match which had flared as she came in the gate.

Now a glaze had come over his eyes. They emerged from it as bright as before and fastened upon the cat in Selva's arms. Mr. Wamboldt lunged forward but Caruso sprang free, lit hugging the floor and made a rapid circuit of the kitchen. The three doors were closed against him and he took shelter behind the stove.

"Damn cat!" Mr. Wamboldt muttered. "Elsie's cat, wife's cat, a tramp, not my cat." He grabbed the poker from the coal scuttle, thought better of it, threw the poker clattering on the stove top.

Selva was dismayed. This was the Mr. Wamboldt of whom she had heard but in whom she had never believed. She was amazed at the transformation liquor had wrought because until now never had he shown the least interest in her. He had become a different man, aggressive, forward moving with menace in his bearing. She would not have been more taken aback had a mouse turned upon her with a growl.

"Let me make some coffee for you," she said.

He swung about, turned a moment to glower at the stove behind which the cat lay hidden. He smoothed his hair, tightened the knot of his tie. He half spread his arms and came shambling towards her. As he drew near she felt oppressed as if the room were crowded. "Ever since the first day you came to the house," he mumbled. Little blue veins showed on his cheeks, his lower lip sagged, tongue sluggish against it.

Backed up to the kitchen table, Selva wished that she could become small, draw in her arms and legs, become a ball, grow quills like the porcupine and throw herself at his face. She scorned him as she had scorned no one in her life before. He thought because she worked in the kitchen . . .

She moved to her right, past the door to the basement, eluding him, until she stood before the door to her own room. She put her hand behind her, turned the knob. Opening the door, still facing Mr. Wamboldt, she retreated a step within her room. He followed. Reaching forward he set his hand full upon her breast where it showed beneath the blouse.

Selva shut her eyes, gritted her teeth, drew back her head. With all her strength she brought up her right hand, slapped him so hard across the cheek that bristles stung her palm and his head knocked against the jamb of the door. She slammed the door and in the dark stood trembling, suddenly weak, against it.

For half a minute she heard nothing but Mr. Wamboldt's enraged breathing and waited to feel his hand upon the knob, his weight against the door.

Then she heard him grunt and murmur. His soles shuffled on the linoleum. She heard him take the poker from the stove and strike the wall behind it. Caruso apparently ran from his hiding place because he growled deeply and there was a scuffle on the floor, succeeded by a yowl like a linen sheet being torn. Mr. Wamboldt said, "Devil! Scratch me, will you?" Because Mr. Wamboldt's voice came from low down as if he were on his hands and knees trying to reach him, Selva concluded that Caruso had again succeeded in retreating under the stove. Mr. Wamboldt raised his voice, shouted and cursed, but the cat, with his frayed ears, his lonely eye, badges of success and daring, remained untouched where he had withdrawn.

Soon dishes rattled when Mr. Wamboldt rose and staggered against the cupboard. He went through the door into the dining room, walking heavily on his heels and up the stairs to his bedroom.

Selva did not turn on the light in her room. Because the door lock had no key, she pulled her squat steamer trunk from under the cot on which she slept. She kept it there to cushion the sag of the flat wire springs. She shoved the trunk against the door. Without undressing, she flung herself, stomach down, upon the cot and, head cradled in her elbow, sobbed beyond the verge of tears until spasms, like angry hands, grasped and shook her body.

six

In the wan light of early morning, hanging on the bedroom wall by the dresser was the yellow print dress. This was Monday morning and it was the dress Selva wore for doing the week's washing. The dress had belonged to Gretchen, the German girl who had preceded her at the Wamboldts' and who had gone away, married to a track-walker over the divide in British Columbia. Selva, on her arrival, had found it suspended like an exhausted wraith from its hook in the bedroom. Though it was short and tight in the sleeves, she had worn it to save her own clothes. Now it impended above her, a faded doom from which she could not escape — a doom of Monday mornings, of lonely work in another's house, of tending things which were not her own, of answering bells and bowing to commands. True, Peter Wrogg and spoken to her of another sort of life, but Peter had fallen before Slim in the beaver meadow. Peter was what might have been. Slim was the implacable, that which was. Slim, and now Mr. Winnie, who had driven Peter away in his black car and would talk about it. And there was Mr. Wamboldt too. He would bear a grudge against her because she had had to slap his ugly face.

Selva's eyes shifted from the dress. She saw the blue bells on the dresser. They were already wilted, drooping from their stalks. The dresser was formed of two apple boxes, one up-ended, the other laid across its top. The divisions of the apple boxes made four compartments in which she kept her handkerchiefs, her waists, her stockings, her slips and the other few intimacies of her being. She had tacked on a blue cotton drape to give them cover. Over the dresser was a small mirror hung on the wall. To its right, her blue party dress, her dark blue suit, her mother's Persian lamb jacket, a brown woollen dress and the black uniform and white apron for serving dinner were on hangers hung from hooks. At the foot of the bed, to the left of the mirror, was the window showing, through cotton curtains, part of a mountain side with the sun bright upon it, the red shingle roof of the house next door and a young birch tree across the road, its leaves gleaming like twirling two-bit pieces. Above the bed on the grey plaster wall was a calendar from Calder's feed store. It displayed a picture of a canal in Venice. Soon, Mrs. Wamboldt had told her, they would buy a new dresser for the room, put in a closet for her clothes, replace the thin straw mattress with a better one. Soon, when times were better, when Mr. Wamboldt did not have so many demands upon him. Still, at that, there were worse people than the Wamboldts to work for. The Wamboldts paid her thirty dollars a month instead of twenty-five. She had Sunday afternoons free and every evening after dinner, unless company came in to play bridge when she might be expected to serve coffee and cake at eleven. The Wamboldts were not stingy with what she ate nor with the food she took from the pantry for picnics, nor, like some people she had heard of, did they insist on calling her by the name of the girl who had been in the house before her as though a hired girl were not an individual at all, but merely a package of energy whose name and content, whatever the cover, were always the same.

Selva looked again at the faded yellow dress. Yes, she would get up, pull it on. She would pin up her hair, bind a handkerchief around it. She would go out into the kitchen, light the fire, fill the kettle and clothes boiler and set them on the stove. She would go to the basement, wash her face and hands, come up and damp the stove, return to the basement and put the clothes to soak. She would go through the front of the house, dust and tidy it, take out the ashtrays and empty whiskey glass left by Mr. Wamboldt the night before. She would prepare his breakfast of orange juice, soft-boiled eggs, toast and coffee and set it on the table in the dining room . . . leave it there for him and return to her washing in the basement before he appeared.

But Mr. Wamboldt did not come in for his breakfast. From the basement window, over the laundry tub, she saw him, hat pulled low, walking down the street studying his shoe toes. Likely he would go to the station restaurant and from there to his office above the garage.

By ten o'clock, Selva had her washing on the line, the sheets, the pillow slips, the table cloths and serviettes, the silk socks and the shirts torn where Mr. Wamboldt who had piles had scratched himself. All of it had been done by hand. Mrs. Wamboldt had not bought a washing machine because good linen lasted longer if it were washed by hand. Selva stood back, wiping sweat from the tip of her nose with the heel of her thumb. To wash clothes and see them hung on the line and drying in a gentle breeze satisfied her, gave her a sense of accomplishment not to be gained by hours of cleaning and dusting and polishing floors when at the end all seemed much as it had been before.

Shortly after eleven o'clock, when she had made the bed upstairs, returned the breakfast dishes to their shelves after washing them and put in order her own room, she ran from the back door, down the lane and out to the street. Down the street, lined with poplars, were three box cars painted a dull red sitting on a siding just north of the station. As she ran down the street, out of the corner of her eye she caught the white steam of a locomotive and, remembering it whistling in a few minutes before from the mile board, guessed it to be the way freight from the west. Even as she watched, the locomotive — because someone had forgotten and left the switch open — swerved from the main line and plowed into the box cars. They were loaded with lumber and in an instant their dull red outlines were converted into white kindling.

So vivid was the image of disaster that afterwards Selva could not recall any sound that accompanied it. In the succeeding hush, as though the whole town held its breath, she gasped, opened her mouth, put a hand to her throat and considered for a moment following the other people whom she now saw hurrying to the siding. She thought better of it and after a few more steps down the street, turned up another lane to the kitchen door behind the hotel. She put her head inside the screen door, its wire mesh clogged with grease, and asked Charlie, the Chinese cook, to call Rosie, the maid, from the dining room. Rosie was the girl who sang with her in the church choir.

"Lossie busy," Charlie said, throwing up his head as he sharpened the butcher knife on the steel held erect on his round, white aproned belly.

"Never mind. You tell her that I have to see her."

"You go tell," Charlie said. "You lots' time."

Selva tiptoed into the dining room where Rosie was setting the tables for the noonday meal — "lunch" for those from out of town; "dinner" for the ranch hands and railroaders who ate there regularly. Rosie was short, upward looking with a wide freckled nose.

"He didn't come in to breakfast," she replied to Selva's question about Peter Wrogg, rubbing her hands on her hips. "I would have noticed him. He left me a four-bit tip yesterday."

"Go and find out if he's all right then. I can't go in to the front looking like this." Selva glanced down at her yellow dress splotched with soapy water.

Rosie was puzzled. "Why shouldn't he be all right and what do you want to know for anyway?" she asked.

"Never mind. I have to know, that's all. Go on. I'll wait."

While Rosie was absent on her errand, running quickly away, head back as though she were a mannequin pulled on rollers, Selva looked around at the white clothed tables, each neatly set with its knives, forks and spoons, its paper serviettes, its salt and pepper shakers, its bowl of sugar and bottles of H.P. Sauce and tomato catsup, each chair empty, receptive to an anonymous occupant. She wondered if Rosie had a better job than she had. Tips and regular hours and a chance of meeting people . . . these were advantages not to be lightly disregarded. And Rosie, when she worked, was not alone. She had people to talk to.

Rosie came back, shaking her head. "Sam says he came down this morning and checked out on Number One." Sam was the day clerk and Number One was the passenger train which had already left for Vancouver and the Coast.

"You're sure?"

"Sure, I'm sure. Sam wouldn't lie about it." Rosie looked down at Selva's hands still pink and soft from the washing. They were clasped tightly, held across her dress front. Selva let them fall apart.

"Say," Rosie said, "you seem all hot and bothered."

"It's nothing," Selva said. "Nothing at all. I just wanted to find out, that's all."

"He's good looking. I bet he's got money, that Mr. Whatever-you-call-him." Rosie sang out in her high pitched voice as Selva passed through the swing door into the kitchen.

In the kitchen, the Chinese cook was in the act of latching the screen door. "People," he muttered to Selva, frowning, "all time, people. This morning early one man come. He old, he no grass on his savvy patch. He hungry. I give him eat. I busy, all time busy. Then, bye n'bye, you come. You want Lossie. I give you Lossie. Now this woman come . . ."

"What woman?" Selva asked.

"You savvy what woman. She come every day. She Indian woman from outside. She come with little boy. Little boy I give biscuit. Woman no want eat. She want work. I no have work. How she work? She got eyes. No can see."

The "Indian woman from outside" was Marie Pierre from Calling river in the foothills. She had been in the town now for three weeks looking for work and had become a familiar figure in Yellowhead. Stepping out into the lane, Selva saw her being led by her hand by her four year old boy towards the street. "Marie Pierre" — it was a beautiful name. The woman herself, Selva thought, was beautiful. No one would know from her deep and luminous brown eyes that she was blind. Her face was brown, oval, shaped like a poplar leaf, and seemed as fragile. Selva guessed her age to be about twenty-five. The story was that the man she lived with, a white man in Calling river — a town of a few cabins and a trading post — was not her husband though the father of her child. She had left him because he beat her unmercifully whenever he got drunk, which was often. In Yellowhead she stayed with cousins in a shack on the north edge of the town. But she could not stay there long because these people, living on the gleanings of one man's trapping, could not afford to support her. Failing soon to find work, she would be forced to return to Calling river. What work could a blind woman do in a place such as Yellowhead? Selva did not know.

Turning the corner into the street, she watched Marie being led down it by her son who strained forward like a bird dog on a leash. He wore a little buckskin shirt. His mother's dress was of a purplish cotton which hung with grace from her shoulders, touched lightly her hips and fell away to the little moose-hide moccasins which dressed her feet. By a store window, the boy paused, pointed and then gazed hopefully upward to his mother. She did not respond. Was it possible, Selva wondered, that he failed to comprehend that his mother was blind, that she lived in one world, he in another?

With all her heart, Selva wished them well. The Cree-Iroquois, of which they were a part, were a proud and independent people living much as their forbears had done, hunting, trapping and fishing. The Iroquois, carrying with them French names from Quebec, had come into the country beind the jingle of harness bells with the early fur traders. Some of them had remained to mingle their blood with that of the native Crees.

Selva turned about and came face to face with a stranger. She thought he was a traveller. He carried a briefcase. He was carefully dressed in a dark, double breasted suit. He wore a grey shirt, a grey tie and grey hat with its narrow braided brim turned up. He was sallow faced and had a pointed nose and a thin black moustache.

She had confronted him so suddenly that she went to her right to pass him and he went to his left. They seesawed from side to side. In her hurry she was ready to cry out, to push him aside when, finally, the mute, hypnotic conflict was broken. She looked back over her shoulder and flushed to see her late adversary staring after her. He turned, went down the street with stealthy steps, his sleek appearance, little moustache and pointed nose reminding her of a mink along a river bank.

Returning to the house, she hastily pulled off her yellow dress, changed into the one of brown wool. She took off her felt slippers, put on high heeled black shoes. She stood up, combed her hair, daubed her lips with rouge against the mirror. She stepped into the kitchen and out of it, half running, to the lane and turned left towards the doctor's house. Her shadow, dwarfed in the noonday sun, scuttled before her, dodging over a stone, losing itself in a hollow, forever evading the oncoming footstep as if it had a life of its own and might at any moment forsake her for its affinity under the ground.

She hurried on, past open back doors from which babies cried, past overturned garbage pails and washing hung on lines until, after two blocks, she crossed the street to the doctor's office in the corner of his red brick house. A dark coupe — she recognized it as belonging to Jim Galbraith, the station agent and first-aid man — was parked in front of the pebbled walk which was bordered by yellow Icelandic poppies. Selva, remembering the locomotive which a few minutes earlier had plowed into the box cars and knowing that the doctor would have been called there if any one had been hurt, wondered if she would find him in his office. As she went around the front of the car and was about to pass to go up the pebbled walk to the office steps, a voice arrested her.

"Say!" said the man sitting in the seat on the right side of the car, "You're in a hurry now, a real hurry, aren't you?" It was a wistful, sing-song voice, one that had been long used to speaking to horses or even to singing to cattle at night out on the range.

Selva, glancing over her shoudler, was about to toss her head and continue on her errand, but the pallor of the man's face, the gleam of his eyes rimmed by coal dust, held her in her tracks, compelled her to turn wordlessly towards him.

"And such a purty girl too. I guess the purtiest I've seen since I've been in town. Of course, I'm not here long. Just passing through, so to speak, looking at the scenery."

"Say — who are you?" Selva came closer until she smelt the whiskey on his breath.

"Yes," he said, "one of the boys gave me a drink. Figured I needed it. I guess you can smell it off of me."

"But . . ." Selva began.

"Oh, yes. You want to know who I am. Who am I? Funny,

I never thought much about that. But I guess you've seen me before, riding behind the locomotive tender, sitting in the door of a box car, going west, down to the Coast. They say there's work down there and the nights are warmer. I'm just a man with coal dust in his eyes."

Now she saw who he was. Like the man riding the rods who had been found in the log jam in the Athabaska, his eyes open to the sky, he was one of the homeless ones against whose foot soles the earth was forever hot. Their home was around the bend in the tracks, on the other side of the river, over the hill, always where they had never been and their promise waited for them in a tomorrow which could only be another yesterday. But, if so, why was he sitting outside the doctor's office in the station agent's motor car? He answered the question for her.

"That's what I was doing," he said to her, "sitting, resting in the open door of this box car loaded with lumber. I guess it's not more than fifteen minutes or so ago I'd stopped off here, you see, to break my journey just like the tourists do in the summer and I was thinking of pulling out on the next freight west. Then this locomotive plowed into the line of cars and there I was lying across the tracks with someone holding up my head."

"You mean . . ." Selva uttered, with a tightening in her throat.

"Yes, there was an accident. I heard one of the boys say before they gave me the whiskey that I had lost both my legs above the knee."

He smiled at her and she saw that there was coal dust even on his teeth. "But I don't believe that for a minute because I can still feel my toes when I move them. But they've put a rug over my legs and I can't see them." Also, she supposed the first-aid man had applied tourniquets.

Selva, from outside the car, was able to see only his head and shoulders. Involuntarily, she looked down. From under the tightly closed door of the car, bright red blood was dripping onto the running board. The sight of it made her feel faint. She put her hand against the car for support.

"So they brought me up here to the doctor on the way to the hospital, but I guess the doctor's out, maybe making a call somewhere else in town." The voice beside her was unperturbed and, apparently, effortless.

He took a deep breath. "Funny, isn't it?" he asked, as if talking to himself. "When a man's got two legs, sometimes they won't do anything for him at all. Then when they say he's got no legs, there's not enough they can do to help him."

Selva, her own legs unsteady, her eyes still fixed on the crimson trickle from beneath the car door, now soaking in three separate channels through the dust on the running board, was slowly drawing away, the purpose of her visit to the doctor's office forgotten.

The man in the car reached out. His hand had the strength of iron as he pulled her to him. His other hand caught her behind the head. "Kiss me, purty girl," he said, "because I'm going away. I just heard a locomotive whistle and when I hear a locomotive whistle I know I'm on my way."

She yielded, protesting, tasted the whiskey on his breath, felt his lips dry and hot against her own.

Swinging about, she saw Jim Galbraith, the station agent, coming down the steps of the office. Apparently the doctor was out, possibly at the hospital where Jim would now take the injured man. Rubbing the back of her hand across her mouth, she turned and ran up the lane towards the Wamboldt house.

Nor did she return to see the doctor until mid-afternoon. Another car, his low grey one with the medical association insignia upon the front of its radiator, was this time parked before the doctor's door. As Selva's hand reached for the bell, the door opened and Dr. Ormsby himself stood before her, hat on his head, carrying his little black bag on his way to make a call.

"Well," he said, "Selva! And what can I do for you? Something amiss at the Wamboldts'?"

She shook her head. No, nothing was wrong at the Wamboldts' in his sense of the term, but now that she stood before the doctor she did not quite know what to say. They had met before. She had served him coffee in the early morning when he had come into the station restaurant weak an wearied after an all night case and, in later months, had shown him into the house when Mrs. Wamboldt was confined to bed with one of her dizzy spells. More than once he had had supper there. He was a spry little man with a neat grey moustache, its fringes ever so slightly stained with tobacco juice. His cheeks were pink, glistening, and his expression one of steady amazement as though a moment before a handful of snow had been dashed against his face where his eyes twinkled like bits of chipped blue ice. The doctor's wife, Selva knew, had not been out of the house for years. She was a chronic invalid, her world an upstairs bedroom, its shades forever drawn against the sun.

Standing beside him, observing that he did not stand back to show her into his office, she heard the creaking of the doctor's immaculate starched front of shirt. This little man, sparkling and brittle as an icicle — were she to touch him roughly, he would shatter, fall in gleaming pieces at her feet — this little man with sorrow in his house who faithfully attended the sorrows of others, going about the streets on his daily rounds, carrying his black bag, repeating quick, happy words of cheer was, in his way, a champion — the town's champion pitted against the Grim Antagonist. For forty years, here and in other mountain towns, he had fought with death. He had won and he had lost. Always, of course, in the end he must lose. He was familiar with the cry of protest as life came from darkness into light and with the struggle and at last the peace as darkness claimed its own again and Death had won another game across a lamp lit bed.

"I haven't much time," he said to Selva. "A baby is waiting . . ."

"I wanted to ask you," she began. "I mean that man who lost his legs this morning."

Dr. Ormsby shook his head. "Shock. Loss of blood, I'm afraid . . ."

"But he talked to me! He was out here in Jim Galbraith's car."

"He felt no pain. Shock kills pain at first. Even now he doesn't know he's lost his legs."

And he had kissed her! Remembering his fevered eyes, his parched lips, a chill tremor ran down her spine.

The doctor touched her arm and she went with him down the steps to his battered and dusty roadster.

"And there's something else," she said to him hesitantly, standing on the steet. "A young Englishman last night . . ."

"Of course," the doctor said, still holding his bag, one foot

84

on the running board of the car. "Winnie mentioned you to me. Peter Wrogg, is that the name?"

Selva nodded.

"Nothing serious," Dr. Ormsby said. "Unusual, but hardly serious, barring complications naturally. The tip of his tongue was partly severed. I stitched it up. The lingual artery was cut which accounted for the excessive bleeding and, of course, he had great difficulty in articulation."

"He's gone on to Vancouver," Selva said.

The doctor seemed surprised. "He was to have come by the office this afternoon," he said. "He needs attention."

He regarded her with his quizzical, dancing eyes. "What was it that happened?" he asked. "He must have received a tremendous blow on the chin."

A rising tightness in Selva's throat prevented her from answering. She turned on her heel, fled across the street, up the lane, leaving the doctor with his mouth open as though he would suck in from the air the response she had denied him. She felt a strange, unreasoning rage that Peter should have permitted such a disability to be visited upon himself.

When, breathless, she reached the house, she found Mrs. Wamboldt waiting for her in the kitchen.

"Where have you been all this time?" Mrs. Wamboldt asked severely.

"I was over seeing Rosie, Mrs. Wamboldt." To have said that she had been to see the doctor would have involved too many explanations.

"Rosie? The girl at the hotel? Whatever did you want to see Rosie for at this time of the day?"

"She wanted to borrow my brown hat, the one with the flowers on it." It was a lie, the defensive weapon of the dependent.

Mrs. Wamboldt, standing by the cupboard, lifted her chin, tapped a neatly slippered toe on the floor. She asked, "Why doesn't Rose come over here to get the hat then? And anyway, you may see her on your time off and not when you should be working. You have lots to do today."

Selva lowered her eyes. "Yes, Mrs. Wamboldt," she said.

"Besides, you're too untidy to be gadding the streets."

"I changed my dress," Selva replied.

"Yes, and it's wrinkled and its hem is showing and your

hair is bouncing around your ears." Selva flipped her head back, put her hand against her hair.

Mrs. Wamboldt was observing her from the corner of her eye, a studied and habitual attitude, chin high in profile to erase the creases from her throat. It was the stance of a robin on the lawn, attentive to the worm.

Just back from her trip down the valley, she wore her tailored black and white checkered suit with the purple blouse. She had removed her round black hat with the white trimming and set it on the table by her purse. Despite her broad shoulders and her full hips, Selva could see that in her time she had been a handsome woman. Youth still showed in an erect carriage, the quick movements, the freshness of her skin, the shadow not the substance like an image in an attic's dusty mirror.

"And there is something else, Selva," Mrs. Wamboldt said. Selva perceived threat in the words. She braced herself, confronting the older woman across the years, across the barrier between those who pay the money and those who earn it, compassionate and not defiant, drawing strength for herself from the occasion. After all, remembering Mr. Wamboldt and the night before, she had more to say to Mrs. Wamboldt, if she chose to say it, than Mrs. Wamboldt could easily find to say to her. Mrs. Wamboldt was no longer the invulnerable giver of money. Unknown to herself, her defences had been pierced.

Mrs. Wamboldt glanced around the kitchen. Outside the window the clothes were flapping in the wind. She stepped over to the window, ran a fastidious finger along the sill, looked at it for signs of dust. Selva knew she would find no dust. Mrs. Wamboldt turned and sat down on the chair by the table. She crossed her knees, showing a well rounded calf. Selva remained standing by the stove, the kettle in a slow purr behind her.

"As I was saying," Mrs. Wamboldt began, clearing her throat. "As I was saying, Selva, there is something else."

Selva waited.

"What time did you get home last night and where were you?" Mrs. Wamboldt inquired.

"I went for a walk. I got home early, maybe a little after ten."

86

"That's what I have to speak to you about, Selva. It is not pleasant for me, I assure you."

"About what, Mrs. Wamboldt?" Selva reached up, tucked into place a wisp of hair which had fallen over her forehead.

"Selva, you know to what I refer."

Selva shook her head in denial.

"The whole town is talking about it," Mrs. Wamboldt said. "Mr. Winnie met you and this Englishman coming out of the woods last night . . ." Selva felt the blood rising behind her ears and colour flare like flame in her cheeks. She tried to speak, but Mrs. Wamboldt silenced her with a lift of her head. She continued with what she had to say, a crackle in her voice that was like dry twigs burning.

"He was covered with blood," she said. "They had to take him to the doctor. He couldn't or he wouldn't say a word, but he had been in a horrible fight of some sort or other. That was plain to be seen. And he comes of a good family too. I'm sure of that because I remarked on him at the dance." Mrs. Wamboldt paused, breathing deeply.

"I saw Mr. Wamboldt just now in his office," she said after a moment. "It was he who told me about it. He is very upset. He says it reflects upon me, upon him, upon both of us. In his position, he can't afford to have people talking . . ."

"In his position . . ." The phrase rang through Selva's head. She made no reply. She was so full of speech that speech choked her. Mr. Wamboldt . . . and his "position." It was unjust. It was unjust that she should be able to go out for months with Slim and that she should now be called to task because once she had gone out with Peter Wrogg. It was true that what had happened should not have happened, but it was Slim and not herself who should shoulder blame. Slim shouldered nothing because he could always ride away into the hills. And Mr. Wamboldt . . . how could he dare to say a word when the night before he had come into the kitchen and put his hand upon her? Selva bit her lip in vexation.

Mrs. Wamboldt's voice came to her as through a haze, "And so we decided after talking it over that it would be better — better for you as well as for us — that is to say, it was bad enough, it caused enough gossip, as Mr. Wamboldt says, when there was only this one man, this ranch hand, whatever his name is . . ."

"Slim Conway," Selva murmured numbly.

"Yes, of course, Conway. Slim! What a horrible name! As I was saying, it was bad enough with you going out with him — and he drinks a lot, too — and comes in at all hours and being seen with him at dances . . ." Mrs. Wamboldt ceased to speak. She patted her chest and began once more.

"Mr. Wamboldt and I decided," she said, "that it would be better for you as well as for us, if you found some other work to do . . . That is, after I have someone to take your place. In two weeks or so. Perhaps you could go back to the restaurant. You would have greater freedom there. Be sure that we will do what we can to help you."

It was Mrs. Wamboldt's voice, but it was Mr. Wamboldt speaking — Mr. Wamboldt, whose face Selva had slapped the night before as he tried to follow her into her room.

The interview was at an end. Mrs. Wamboldt gathered up her gloves, her purse, her hat. Head held high, she swept from the kitchen like a gust of wind from a forest clearing.

seven

Selva watched the swing door slowly settle on its hinges after Mrs. Wamboldt's passage.

The kitchen was quiet. The clock ticked complacent in its journey down the hours. A piece of coal crumpled in the stove. A wisp of steam came from the kettle's spout.

The stove was an old antagonist. She knew its every humour. Winter mornings she had battled with its drafts that its fire might draw against the cold chimney. She had fed it wood and coal and taken from its wide oven roasts and cakes and pies. She had polished its top and burnished its nickel. She and the stove had fought with one another and they had worked together. Her life in the kitchen had been a sort of marriage to the stove. Now she was close to it no longer. She was a face at the window looking in from the outside.

Two weeks, Mrs. Wamboldt had said. They would be two weeks of strain, of silence when she took food into the dining room, and silence would be with her as she worked around the house. Then there would be another job — she had no fear of being unable to find another job, a job behind a lunch counter or in a stranger's kitchen. Before she had gone walking with Peter and listened to him talk of Montreal, she would have accepted the prospect as one natural to her. Now she rebelled against its necessity — a notice, her name upon it, in the post office, as though she were a thing for sale.

Nor would she, had she so wished, return to the homestead in the foothills. Her mother, before her death, knew that she would leave the homestead and go away to make her living. She had given Selva an address in Winnipeg. "Remember," she had said, "if you are ever in trouble . . ." It was more than a year ago and her mother had been sitting by the window which framed the distant mountains. She had written the address on a piece of mauve writing paper and handed it to Selva. Later, Selva had burned it in the stove knowing that she would never use it. It was a man's name and he lived in Winnipeg.

The day her mother penned the address was the day after she and Selva had returned from their last trip together into Edmonton. On the train, her mother, wearing the Persian lamb fur coat with a mink muff and a mink hat like a cadet's cap, had told Selva a story and continued it as they drove home from the railroad in the sleigh under the stars. She sat next to the window in the day-coach with the snowy prairie disappearing behind her face. She had a soft, a very gentle voice, and spoke as though she were tired and as though each word that she uttered would be the final one. Selva had to listen carefully to hear what her mother was saying.

Her mother was telling of some twenty odd years before and of a Hudson's Bay Company fur-trading post in northern Manitoba and of a girl of sixteen who lived there with her parents who were strict Presbyterians and who said grace at meals and read the Bible aloud at night and got down on their knees and prayed to God before they went to sleep. The fur-trading post was miles beyond the nearest railroad line and mail and news of the world came to it infrequently, brought by canoe in the summer and by dog team in the winter.

During this winter that she spoke of, Selva's mother said, the dog team driver fell in love with the girl who lived alone there with her parents. He was young, handsome, full of laughter, his comings and goings attended by the jingle of harness bells. Sometimes they went walking together on snowshoes into the forest. Then, because he smoked and once had had the smell of liquor on his breath, the girl's father forbade her to be seen with him again.

But already it was too late and when the day came for the arrival of the mail, the girl went up the trail to listen for the approaching harness bells. The mail was late and did not come and the next day she went up the trail again. Selva's mother turned to her and said, "She listened until the silence became a roar in her ears. She learned then what winter silence was. It was the sound of time passing by."

Selva saw a tear form in the corner of her mother's eye, roll slowly down her cheek holding for a glittering moment the reflection of snow beyond the coach window. The snow, the cold, the loneliness of the vast frozen earth were there for a moment in a tear upon a woman's cheek. Later, her mother said, the mail came by, but the driver was a new man, an older man with grey hair. In the spring the girl's father saw that she was growing big. He made a bundle of her clothes, set them on the doorstep and turned her out of doors. The girl's mother cried and hid eighty dollars in a small Bible which she slipped into the bundle of clothes.

The river was now flowing free of ice and the girl went upstream in a canoe with two trappers who were going out to the railroad. She took the train west to Winnipeg thinking that there she might find her lover. In the telephone book there were several names the same as his. After she had called four of them, she was told that he had gone away to the United States, to St. Paul and then to Chicago. She wrote to him at the address she had been given but she received no reply to her letter.

She had her baby in the public ward of the hospital. Afterwards she supported herself and her child by doing housework during the day and taking in sewing in the evenings. All this while, she had had no word from the man who had been her lover and then, after three years, another man came by. They were married. He owned a ranch in Alberta and they went out there to live, taking the little girl with them. Other children came, a boy, another girl, and she was brought up with them as their sister.

"Only it wasn't a ranch," Selva's mother said. "It was only a homestead. Chickens, two cows and a herd of horses that were good for nothing, and men constantly coming and going."

"And the little girl?" Selva asked, playing the game as she knew her mother wished it to be played.

"He was good to the little girl. That much must be said for him. He was good to her from the beginning."

"What was her name?"

Her mother looked away, out of the coach window. After a pause, she said, "It was a name her mother found in a book while she was in the hospital waiting for her in Winnipeg. It's a Spanish word that means 'forest.' She called her that because that was where . . ."

"That's why you called me Selva," Selva said to her mother. "I've often wondered because it's a funny name, it seems to me."

Later, driving towards home behind the bay team which they had stabled in the little town while they were away in Edmonton, her mother explained that she had seen in the newspaper the name of the man who had known her so long ago. He was now a mining engineer and she had written to him in Winnipeg. His name was Robert Fibert.

"Is he married?" Selva asked.

"No. He never married." Her mother's voice had a ring of pride. "And he wants to see you," she said to Selva, "and to send you away to school."

Selva said, "No!" She had no wish as yet to leave home, nor to accept a favour from a man whom she had never seen, an intruder from beyond the horizon. Indeed, she would have preferred to have heard nothing at all about him. Now she had become an outsider in the house where she lived. Her brother and sister were brother and sister no more and the man with the deep voice and the black beard who stood with his feet apart as though he had roots in the ground was her father no more. She felt that she had been deprived of what was hers and given nothing to take its place.

And two months later when her mother died — from a chill and then pneumonia — and was buried among the birch trees on the hillside, Selva felt a sudden change in her status. Jed Williams, whom she called "father," developed the habit of staring at her long and speculatively for a minute, for two minutes at a time, not as he would at his oldest daughter, but as he would regard a woman stranger in the household. When she went away, Selva shed tears. She would miss her brother who was now fifteen and her little sister whom she had taught to make bracelets of grass and wildflowers. She went to Edmonton. There an employment agency sent her to the station restaurant in Yellowhead. After six months, she had come to work for the Wamboldts. Everyone spoke well of the Wamboldts. Because they had no children, the work would be light. Besides, they travelled and when they were away from the house she would have time to do as she pleased . . .

Now, after four months, she was leaving — leaving the security of their house and the shelter of her small bedroom with its blue hangings. From before the stove, she stepped over, opened the door and looked into the bedroom, walking on tiptoe as though to surprise someone already there in her stead.

Mrs. Wamboldt's voice came down the stairs. It was time, she said, to prepare lunch. Mr. Wamboldt would soon be home. The orderly routine of the house, Mrs. Wamboldt's voice implied, would be uninterrupted — the making of meals, the dusting of tables, the sweeping of carpets, the polishing of floors, all of this would continue as before as though nothing were changed. Selva had been reminded that she would undertake her duties and carry them through at least until the other girl came to take her place . . .

That evening, dust rising like angry puffs of smoke from her sharp heels as they hit the gravel of the road, she walked down to the station to see the eastbound passenger go through. Her hair, freshly washed, was upswept, a smouldering crown upon her head. She wore her white blouse, her blue suit, a necklace of glass beads around her throat and a pair of open work black silk stockings. These she had bought on an impulse weeks before. Until this evening she had not worn them because, on second thought, she had considered them "too daring." Now, however, they touched her with a subtle warmth, made her feel taller than she was without them. Furtively and quickly, passing the drugstore, between thumb and forefinger she pinched a glow into her cheeks.

She walked with others of the town on their daily pilgrimage to see the world go by, down stone steps to the station platform and along the platform by which the locomotive panted from its climb through the mountains. She turned from the locomotive and baggage cars towards the other end of the train and had walked as far as the observation car, mingling with the well dressed, well fed travellers who emerged from it, when a voice spoke from behind her.

"Going away?" she was asked.

Selva swung about and was confronted by Mrs. Weaver, a woman with whom she had a nodding acquaintance and who now, like a mouse from its hole, peeped out at her from the tight cowl of her hair.

Selva smiled weakly. "Not today," she replied. "I just came down for a walk, to see the people."

Mrs. Weaver glanced down the platform as though in search of a face. Then, looking at Selva, she inquired secretively, "Where's the boyfriend?"

"Slim's gone back to the ranch, Mrs. Weaver."

"Don't call me Mrs. Weaver. Edna's the name. See, they go well together. Selva . . . Edna. Anyway, I didn't mean Slim. I meant the one with the curly hair you met at the dance . . . and went walking with afterwards."

"I went right home from the dance."

"I know. I mean the next day you went walking with him. Yesterday. Sunday."

Selva blushed. It seemed already two weeks ago that she had been out with Peter.

"I guess he's gone on to Vancouver," she told Mrs. Weaver.

Mrs. Weaver smiled slyly. She had a pale, smooth and narrow face. Like Selva, she wore no hat and her dun colored hair was parted in the middle and pulled down over her ears. She was not so tall as Selva, and so slight that the wind might blow her away and now, as in her grey woollen dress she leaned back into it, she seemed not to stand at all but to sway, to be suspended like a figure stretched on a clothesline, the hem of whose skirts at any moment might be lifted up to shoulder level. She was a widow and an older woman than Selva. They had met while shopping and had seen one another at dances. Had she had more money Mrs. Weaver would have been known as "fast." As it was, she owned a rooming house in the northern and lower end of town and Selva had heard Mrs. Wamboldt speak of her as "that loose Weaver woman." It was common knowledge that when the government liquor store had closed its doors, a bottle could

94

always be had at Mrs. Weaver's by the proper individuals. Her husband had vanished under peculiar circumstances. In the summers he had packed for survey parties with his own string of horses, and in the winters he had run a trapline. Two springs before, he had failed to come in with his furs. The search party had found his cabins in perfect order, stocked with food and wood. It was thought he might have fallen through an air hole in the river ice and drowned. Other opinion was that he was still alive. It was said that he had gone north, or down to the Coast and changed his name, that he had "walked out" for his own good reasons.

Gossip had it that Mrs. Weaver could not keep skin and bone together, much less pay for the upkeep of her house by the three rooms she rented. About this, Selva, who kept to herself except for her outings with Slim and an occasional evening at the moving picture theatre, did not know. Instinctively, however, though she shared no prejudice against the other woman, she was aware that a sharp hard line separated their two worlds. It was not a question of up or down. It was simply one of crossing over.

"And I always thought," Mrs. Weaver was saying to her, in pointed reference to Peter Wrogg, "that you were such a quiet girl. Stand-offish, I almost said."

"I am a quiet girl. I'm kept pretty busy. I don't go around very much."

"That's what *you* say." Mrs. Weaver hesitated, then added, "Why don't you come down to the Lotus with me and have a glass of beer?" The "Lotus" was the new beer parlour on the southern edge of town.

"I couldn't," Selva said. "I'm going to meet Rosie from the hotel later." It was not the truth. She had no such commitment.

"You can't meet Rosie," Mrs. Weaver replied, "unless you come to the Lotus. She's going to be there. She told me she was. Come along, just for a few minutes. It won't do you any harm." She put her hand on Selva's arm.

Selva drew away, jealous of her person. "I can't very well," she said. "Mrs. Wamboldt would hear of it . . ."

She ceased to speak, her mouth still open. What did it concern her now what Mrs. Wamboldt thought? She still worked for the Wamboldts, but would be with them little longer. She looked past Mrs. Weaver to the town itself, its street of stores with their dark windows like eyes lidded for the night, and it seemed that it too was passing by her and away from her and that she was here on the platform merely resting on a journey.

"Come along," Mrs. Weaver insisted. "Never mind the Wamboldts."

A brakeman came by swinging an unlit lantern. His eyes met Selva's, then dropped to her legs and she was aware again of the black silk stockings she wore and of the warmth in which their fragile covering enclosed her legs.

"Well, maybe for a minute," she said in response to Mrs. Weaver. After all, tonight she would enjoy company, though she desired to speak to no one of her impending departure from the Wamboldt house, nor much less of what had brought it about. Slim was at the ranch and for that matter, had he come riding down the street, she would have turned her back upon him. Nevertheless, she was surprised that Mrs. Weaver had invited her. They had not been out together before. The fact that Mr. Winnie had met her with Peter when they stepped out of the pine trees on Sunday night and afterwards had talked about it appeared to have established grounds for the approach — at least in Mrs. Weaver's eyes. As they walked up the street and away from the station, Selva paused momentarily, inclined to turn back, astonished to find herself going to the beer parlour with Mrs. Weaver. She, Selva Williams, had not altered. She was what she had always been and yet, since she had been out with Peter, even Mr. Wamboldt had acted towards her as he had never acted before. It was as though Peter had touched her and revealed what until then lay hidden. She wished that he were beside her and that they were climbing up the hill again.

Mrs. Weaver clutched her elbow with fingers sharp as pincers. "Look!" she said, "What do you say that's worth?"

Because Yellowhead was a divisional point on the railroad, the eastbound passenger stopped there for half an hour to change engines and crews, taking on ice for the dining cars, and to have its wheels inspected. During this interval people spilled from its cars to pace the station platform or to stroll singly or in pairs from the pullmans, in groups from the coaches, on to the main street of the town, lifting their heads to the mountains flushed by the westering sun, or gathering before the drugstore window where miniature and imitation totem poles and other cheap knicknacks mainly of Japanese manufacture were for sale.

Among the strollers was the woman who had aroused Mrs. Weaver's question. Her husband, a tall man in a brown tweed suit, was at her side. They walked up the street past the pool-hall, the woman's flaxen hair coiled in a tight braid on the top of her head, her mink coat reaching to below her knees. Her legs were young.

Mrs. Weaver replied to her own question. She said, "I'll bet that coat cost two thousand dollars if it cost a nickel." As she spoke the man and woman stopped before Calder's feed store. He spread his legs, put his hands in his trouser pockets, looked down the street, up to the mountains. His lip curled in a remark to his wife as though what he looked at were for sale and as though he could buy it but disdained the bother. His wife turned her face. It was a face that had been tended, that might have been put away for a while and folded and now that it was taken out and worn the intricate lines of its folding still showed upon it. It was white, so white that the dust of powder upon it appeared blue, and the two small eyes were like holes burned through it.

The woman's legs were young. The fur coat was well cut and lustrous, the best that money could buy. She had, apparently everything that she needed. Yet her face was aged, was like a death's head, with mere satiety or with fatal sickness. Selva stepped over to one side to let the woman and her husband by.

"It's a nice coat," she said to Mrs. Weaver.

"Nice . . . nice," repeated Mrs. Weaver, who did not notice faces, but whose husband had been a trapper. "Why one man trapped all winter so that she could wear it."

Mrs. Weaver sighed. "Anyway," she said, "it's not a coat for the likes of you and me." Selva, resenting this casual linking of their separate destinies, and remembering Peter Wrogg's talk of Montreal, wished to be able to contradict her, but she supposed that Mrs. Weaver spoke what was fact. They were alike in that the woman in the mink coat, all women in mink coats with husbands by them, were adversaries. They were the possessors. Mrs. Weaver and herself possessed nothing but the strength or promise of their bodies, the artifices of their cunning, rooms to rent and hands to work with. Men like Mrs. Weaver's husband, who caught the furs, could not afford to buy them back.

Selva experienced a new understanding of the woman beside her, a gentleness toward her. She was neat. Each tightly pulled hair was in place. Her dress was clean and simple. She did not at all appear to be the woman she was said to be and Selva was prepared to discount the stories told about her. No harm could come, she thought, from going out with Mrs. Weaver. Mrs. Weaver was as good as the rest of them. Peter, she believed, would have liked Mrs. Weaver had he met her.

It was odd that she was now attempting to see things as they would be to Peter. "What would Peter think . . . what would Peter say . . ." the query came and went. Not once had she consulted herself in similar fashion concerning Slim.

Mrs. Weaver, as they walked towards the beer parlour, asked about the Wamboldts. Yes, Selva agreed, making conversation, they were good people to work for.

"I've never been in their house," Mrs. Weaver said wistfully, "but I understand it's very nice inside."

"It's a big house to keep clean," Selva said.

A locomotive engineer, "Drag" Perkins, carrying his lunch-pail, crossed in front of them on his way home from the roundhouse. He touched his peaked cap to Mrs. Weaver. A heavy man in blue striped overalls, he trudged wearily on, his feet lagging as though the drag of the long passenger train were still behind him. He had done his job. He had brought the woman in the mink coat and her husband as far as Yellowhead. Others like him would take them on across the country, through the foothills, out onto the prairies where hotelkeepers and storekeepers would bow their heads and give them what they desired because they had money and leisure in which to spend it.

Coming towards her along the street Selva saw Nancy Carstairs with a frill of lace about her snow white throat. She had last seen Nancy dancing with Peter above the pool hall. With her now was Hank Barton, the son of the bank manager. Nancy stared at Mrs. Weaver, stared her coldly up and down. She glanced at Selva, sniffed, twitched her narrow buttocks and passed on.

Mrs. Weaver said, "What that one needs is a man instead of the young boys that she's always running around with."

Selva said, "I guess she takes what she can get."

They approached the beer parlour with its sign, "Licensed Premises." A horse was tied to one of the pine trees outside its door. Selva was reminded of Slim and, for a moment, she wondered if he might be inside. But it was not Slim's horse. He was a tall black with a Roman nose showing the white of his tempestuous eye. Instead of a curbed bit, his head wore a rawhide hackamore. The saddle, a rope strapped to its pommel, was well oiled and black from long use. A two and a half pound trail axe hung from a scabbard below the saddle skirt. As Selva passed close to him, he lowered and shook his head, pawed the ground.

eight

Selva and Mrs. Weaver went into the beer parlour by the women's entrance at the side. They took their seats in a high walled booth near the door. Although it was broad daylight ouside, in the beer parlour the sun entered only through long, narrow windows near the ceiling and under the electric lights a haze of tobacco smoke hung. Men's voices and the clatter of glasses filled the room which, with its stalls and rafters and high ceiling, Selva thought was like a stable. She faced towards the counter at the far end where the beer was handed out to two white coated waiters.

"I've never drunk much beer," she said to Mrs. Weaver.

"It won't hurt you. It's like water. Personally, I always order ale. It's quicker."

"Quicker?"

"Makes you feel relaxed quicker."

When the waiter came by Mrs. Weaver ordered two bottles of Calgary Ale and paid for them when they were brought.

From the partition behind Selva, a man's voice rose. "I tell you," he shouted, "the world's a piss pot. And I've been all around it looking for the handle."

Selva, astounded, set down her glass. "It's nothing," Mrs. Weaver assured her. "That's old Tom Throstlebottom. He's always bragging since he made that trip to California."

Rosie, the dining-room maid at the hotel, walked over from another booth and put her upturned face like a cherished exhibit beside Mrs. Weaver's shoulder. "My!" she said to Selva, "I'm surprised to find *you* here. What will Mrs. Wamboldt say when she finds out about it?"

"Never mind Mrs. Wamboldt," Mrs. Weaver said. "There's no harm in coming to a beer parlour. It's legal. The government says so."

"Did you find out?" Rosie asked Selva.

"Find out what?"

"Find out what you were asking me about this morning, silly!"

Mrs. Weaver leaned forward to listen.

"I found out what I needed to know," Selva replied to Rosie.

She looked around the beer parlour and decided that Peter probably would not have liked it. It was not his sort of place. No, he would not have brought her here. She thought she would have one more bottle of ale then she would go home.

But after the third bottle, she was still sitting at the table with Mrs. Weaver and Rosie. She left them to go to the toilet. Returning, she was conscious of men's eyes upon her. Some of the fifty odd men in the beer parlour she knew by name and almost all of them by sight. Many of them had been at the dance above the pool-hall. Their eyes searched, they probed, they asked, they demanded. Yet most of the men, she supposed, knew all that they searched for and had received already what they demanded. The eyes were wise and they were knowing. Blouse and skirt were no shield against their inquiry. Walking towards them to her table fronting the length of the room, she waded as if naked into their scrutiny. They must know, they would see it in her, that soon she would not be working in the Wamboldt house. And they would know too the reason for her leaving. Losing her job, she felt half unclothed.

When she had seated herself, a man came over to the table and joined them. Because he wore moccasins, he came silently — silently and quickly as he might flit from tree to tree along a river bank. He set a chair gently at the table end, turned it about, nodded without speaking to Mrs. Weaver — every man in town seemed to know Mrs. Weaver — sat down and leaned forward, his elbows on the back of the chair.

Turning to Selva, he said, "I'm Clay Mulloy." He drew in his breath, spoke again. "I saw Slim Conway today," he said.

Selva did not immediately answer. She surmised that Clay Mulloy, the newcomer to the table, was one of "the boys," one of those who worked or played poker with Slim. She remembered having seen him once or twice upon the street. She had then remarked on his small, high-arched moccasined feet, and looking at him now after he had spoken, she sensed the quietness about him as though, even in the noise of the beer parlour, he were listening for a sound, for a call, for a summons from afar that only he could hear. The smell of wood smoke was in his worn buck-skin shirt and the sheen of the campfire seemed to play upon the tanned tight skin of the cheekbones where the shape of the eager skull showed through. Yet his eyes were heavy lidded, as with sleep. Remembering the rawhide hacksmore, Selva assumed that it would be his horse tied to the pine tree standing beyond the door.

After waiting for her reply and receiving none, Clay Mulloy added, concerning Slim, speaking through lips which did not open so much as to reveal his teeth and in a voice that was no more than a hoarse whisper, "I passed him on the trail. He was bringing some horses into the ranch." He spoke as though he and she were bound together in a conspiracy of silence.

Selva said, "Oh!" She glanced over at Mrs. Weaver and Rosie. A young railroader had moved in beside Rosie and the three heads were together in a huddle of intimate talk.

The voice of the man beside her continued, subdued, so close to her that, had she shut her eyes as its soft cadences invited her to do, it might have seemed but an echo of her own unuttered musings. "He's a good man with horses," it said.

"Is he?" asked Selva.

"One of the best. He understands them. I've seen him up all night with a horse with the colic and he never puts a hobble on them."

After a moment, "Funny thing about Slim. He was born in Philadelphia." As he spoke, he pinched his lower lip pensively between thumb and forefinger.

103

"Philadelphia?"

"Yes. That's in the States. His old man moved up here on to the prairies and started farming when Slim was just a kid."

Selva was not seeking information about Slim. It amazed her now in thinking of it that she should know, and had been satisfied with knowing, so little of him. She had not known where he had been born, nor that his father had been a farmer. She knew no more of his antecedents — less, indeed, than she did of those of the horse he rode. He was "Slim," without even a full Christian name, accepted like his horse as part of her environment. What had they talked of, what did they do, when they were together? A few questions and fewer answers — a matter of small trouble at the ranch, a disagreement in the Wamboldt house, her blouse and why it was not a different colour, and what it cost and what she had done on her trip into Edmonton. Names of those they knew, idle words, a dirty story by Slim, the shadows of the forest around them, the quick urgency of the embrace and with it, grass fingering her hair and above her, the vision of pine branches against the sky and afterwards, when she had risen and dusted twigs from her skirt and Slim had rolled his cigarette, the slow walk home with only a scarce word spoken.

"He may be working with me up in the High Valley," said the man beside her.

"Who?"

"Slim . . . I've got my horses back in Wilkins' corral. I'll be packing in supplies to the new chalet. I'll be packing in lumber and mattresses. They're hardest of all to pack."

"What new chalet?" Selva asked.

"It's for tourists. Sort of a hotel, only it's two days by trail back in the mountains."

He got up from his chair. "Anyway," he said, "I thought I'd like to tell Slim I'd seen you."

"Yes, tell him . . ." Selva said looking up. Then she hesitated. What was there, after all, to tell Slim?

"Tell him," she said in decision, her voice cracking, rising from her throat more loudly than she had intended, "tell him that I'm not working for the Wamboldts much longer."

"Oh, that's too bad," Mrs. Weaver said. Selva looked over at her, realizing once more that she was at a table and that her remarks might be overheard by one to whom they were not directed.

"It's not too bad at all," she retorted in heat to Mrs. Weaver. "I'm tired of working in someone else's kitchen."

The man standing above her glanced at Mrs. Weaver, looked at Selva again. "Well," he said. "I mean, well . . ." He stared at her as though he would say more, and speculatively, as if to carry away with him every detail of her features. Then, as she slowly flushed, he turned and with his going and taking with him the enfolding presence of his voice, she felt that she had been visited not so much by a man as by a happening. It was strange that he should have come to the table in the first place and then only to speak of Slim and, incidentally, of a mountain chalet. Even in the beer parlour, in her most trivial comings and goings, she was to be reminded of Slim and that, though absent, he was close at hand and she was always to hear Mrs. Weaver or others like her say that it was "too bad" that she was leaving the Wamboldts' as though the only work that she could do was in another's house.

She watched Clay Mulloy's receding figure, buckskin fringes quivering upon his trim shoulders. His hips were narrow, so tightly pressed one against the other that she felt they must give him hurt. She watched him pass among the tables and sit down in the far end of the room and lose himself in the crowd and then, as if a protecting screen had been withdrawn from around her, became aware once more of the hubbub in the room. Boots scraped, glasses rang, words buzzed through the air. A short, fat man with long arms went by the table pushing his paunch before him as though it were cradled in a wheelbarrow. Above him the lights blazed like separate suns.

"But what are you going to do?" Mrs. Weaver asked, putting out her hand, touching Selva's arm. Rosie and the railroader beside her listened.

Selva drew her arm away. "What do you mean, what am I going to do?"

"When you leave the Wamboldts'?"

"I'm not going back to the station restaurant, you can be sure of that." Selva looked away. She did not wish to continue with the subject.

A girl came in alone from the women's entrance. Selva recognized her. They had once worked together behind the station lunch counter. She was a slim blonde. Tonight she wore blue jeans and the man to whose nearby table she walked pointed to the rivet in their crotch.

"What's that?" he asked.

The blonde girl bent over, looked where his finger pointed.

"That's dead centre," she said softly, slipping into the chair beside him.

Across Selva's table, Rosie was talking to Mrs. Weaver and the young railroader. She spoke shrilly, breathless, as though she had just been chased to the top of a hill. She was saying, "It's all right if you're a man to pick your nose with your thumb, but it's not good manners to use your finger. Ma said so one time to Pa at dinner."

Selva liked Rosie, and was sorry for her, going through the world with her pale little face, concave as a plate held up for contributions. And Selva had nothing against the young railroader, nor against Mrs. Weaver, except for her comments, yet she knew that though she was with them, she was not of them. She was apart from them. She was going away. Mrs. Wamboldt had said, "two weeks more." She was going away. She did not know where or how, but she was going away.

She shoved Mrs. Weaver's hand aside when the waiter came again to the table with the bottles. "No," she said, "I'll order this one. It's my turn to buy a drink." She would buy the drink that she should buy and then she would leave and go home.

She tried to count how many bottles of ale they had drunk already. She shook her head and gave up the effort. She leaned back in her corner. Looking up at the ceiling where there was only one light, she saw two. The two merged and became one again. She shut her eyes and opened them quickly because she became dizzy. She saw Mrs. Weaver's hand, palm upward, lying on the table top like a creased and discarded glove. Mrs. Weaver's face was young, smooth, without lines, but her hand was old. Selva's own hands, she knew, were likewise older than her face. Over the table Mrs. Weaver's neck seemed very long, as though it were being stretched by an unseen rope, and Rosie beside her was just a face that she wore upon her grey shoulder.

The railroader reached out a hairy wrist, poured a trickle of whiskey from a flask into Selva's glass of ale. She protested. "A few drops," he said, "they'll do you good. Beside, you're too quiet. You don't talk enough."

"I talk when I've got something to say," Selva replied, pushing the glass aside. She had had enough to drink, she decided.

"Listen then," the railroader said, "listen to what I've got to say, what I've been telling them here. See, there's this creek. It comes down out of the mountains and I pass it every run I make west to Blue River and some day, see, I'm going to ride deadhead and get them to put me off there and I'm going to climb up it and see where it comes from and learn all about it and build myself a cabin. Maybe there's a lake at the head of that creek."

The railroader had his lake at the head of the creek. She had her city at the end of the railroad line. In an instant of intuition she said to him, "Maybe you'll never climb up your creek. Maybe a year from now you'll be telling someone else that you're still going to climb up it, and maybe there's no lake at the head of it anyway."

He sat back. He licked his lip. He said nothing.

Mrs. Weaver said, "You can't have your creek and climb it too." She laughed, but no one else laughed with her. She added, perhaps remembering her lost trapper husband, "Men are always looking for a lake at the head of a creek."

Later, Selva was able to recall only snatches of the conversation at the table and an occasional remark beyond it when, in a lull, a voice would rise clear demanding to be heard. She and Mrs. Weaver talked a while of cooking and she recalled Mrs. Weaver saying, "but I always put the eggs in first . . . always put the eggs in first." Selva had lost the context of the sentence in the general hubbub. More men had come to their table and she was confronted by a half circle of faces which seemed to her to be but one wide, uttering countenance spread along its breadth, and when one person spoke, it was as if all the voices had joined together in a composite statement quite unrelated to what had gone before.

"Anyway, I wouldn't send my boy to college, not until he's learned to work." That must have been Mr. Ogelthorpe, the town lawyer. He was sitting far away across the room, yet his speech through some quirk of acoustics, as if made for her alone, was bounced from the ceiling to Selva's ear. Looking over to him, she saw his lips still moving as he sat behind his red, bristling moustache, spitting out words like a man behind a hedge which spouted sparks.

It was fairly certain, she thought, that Mr. Ogelthorpe would not send his boy to college for the very good reason that he had no boy — at least, so far as she knew he had none who bore his name. The story about Mr. Ogelthorpe, a squat, burly man now in the youth of his age, was that at one time he had had a good practice in Saskatoon on the prairies. He had taken to drink. Just why he had taken to drink no one seemed to know. At any rate, it had cost him, in sequence, his reputation, his practice and his wife. From Saskatoon he had drifted from town to town, finally coming to Yellowhead where he did not so much practice law as suggest in his indolence to prospective clients where, in Edmonton or other parts, competent legal advice might be had. His income came from collecting insurance premiums. witnessing documents and from small speculations in mining stock. Lately he had "settled down" and lived with a "housekeeper" who had moved into his pink stucco cottage on the western edge of town. Selva knew the housekeeper as a florid faced woman, the colour of her grey streaked hair matching that of Mr. Ogelthorpe's moustache, who seemed to be forever beating a rug hung out an open window.

Before meeting Mrs. Jameson, however, Mr. Ogelthorpe's ways had been more devious. He was well remembered for one cold December night. He had passed the first part of the night between the sheets with Mrs. Andy McPherson. Mrs. McPherson's husband at that time was "hog-head" on the time freight, a steady run between Yellowhead and Edson, the next divisional point to the east. Like many engineers, Andy played a few special trills on the locomotive whistle at the mile board to acquaint his wife with his coming. This, as circumstances demanded, might be taken as a hint to have supper ready or simply, to avoid embarrassment, as a warning that her husband would soon be home. In Yellowhead, where many husbands were regularly absent from their wives for twenty-four hours or more, these shrill announcements of arrival piercing the frosty air at times caused, behind masked windows, quick stirrings and excited whispers which presaged an imminent departure as often as they did the preparation of a late supper. Then the wife who had not swept the new fall of snow from her back steps would be quickly out with the broom.

On this particular December night, Andy McPherson had been remiss and had forgotten to give his usual signal or his wife, Sarah, deep in the mysteries of Mr. Ogelthorpe's embrace, had failed to hear it. So it came about that Mr. Ogelthorpe lit on the back porch just as Andy's steps crunched on the front one. The night was cold. The snow was two feet deep. Mr. Ogelthorpe's clothes, all of them, even to the suspensory he wore because of his varicocele, were in the warm bedroom he had left. He could not walk up the street, across the town, naked. Aside from being seen, his feet would freeze. He waited, teeth chattering, on the porch against the wall listening to Andy's enraged denunciation and the long wails of Sarah from within.

After a few minutes, a window in the side of the house opened. An object, two objects, thumped onto the snow. the window closed. Mr. Ogelthorpe put his head around the corner of the porch, his breath rising yellow against the light from the window. He stepped down into the searing chill of knee deep snow. There he found his shoes and socks. The shoes were filled with snow. He emptied them and put them on and waited hopefully beneath the window, like a shorn, shivering and hungry airedale for another bone. His long red woollen underwear and his trousers came next. He had to sit down on the steps, remove his shoes, to pull them on. Snowflakes melting on his bare shoulders, he cursed and mumbled, half perishing with cold, until his shirt, tie, vest, jacket, hat and buffalo hide coat were flung into the snow bank. When, his shirt tail hanging out, his hat askew upon his head, one arm through an overcoat sleeve, he was groping his way through the trees, the window opened once again. As it slammed disdainfully shut with an echo which shook him to his foot soles, Mr. Ogelthorpe discovered at his toes, its belt and strands suggesting a snake strangely writhing on the snow, the outlines of his suspensory. He picked it up, went home a chastened man, it was to be supposed, to his pink cottage.

Nor was the incident one to cause a rift between him and Andy McPherson. Formerly known to one another only by sight and name, sharing a further acquaintance, as it were, by proxy, they had, it now appeared, sufficient in common to establish the basis of friendship. Indeed, as Selva observed from her table, it was Andy who afforded the audience to what she took to be Mr. Ogelthorpe's continuing dissertation upon the evils of sending a boy to college before he had learned to work. As she watched, Mr. Ogelthorpe pushed back his chair and, moustache twitching, holding his finger under Andy McPherson's nose, half rose as he said, "And I'll tell you more. I've been there, see? I know that a university is only an uneasy state of mind surrounded by professors." Having spoken, he glared about the room as if he expected to be challenged. A man sitting alone at the next table, a grey bearded trapper, shifted his shoulders, regarded Mr. Ogelthorpe and, after spitting once on the floor, returned to the morose contemplation of his glass of beer.

The tale about Mr. Ogelthorpe, of course, like others Selva had heard here and there, might not be entirely true, yet she did not doubt that there was substance to it. Behind all these faces sipping beer lurked some history of deception. If they deceived no one else, they deceived themselves. Drink was a deceiver. Here for an hour, for two hours or three, they escaped from what they were and were for a while, in imagination, what they might have been. Stories like that of Mr. Ogelthorpe ran like bright threads through the dull woof of their everyday. Men and women too came to the beer parlour to live their dreams, as the railroader across the table throughout the evening had been climbing his creek to the lake at its head. And she, she herself, had stoutly denied to Mrs. Weaver that on leaving the Wamboldt house, she would ever again work in a station restaurant. And where had she worked, and where could she look for work, but behind a lunch counter or in a kitchen?

Now at the table she was crowded into a corner by the men who sat beside her on the bench. The ale had made her drowsy. Eyelids drooping, she was ready to go home and paying small attention to what was being said, when she felt a hand upon her knee.

She blinked. Hank Barton, the bank manager's son, whom

earlier in the evening she had passed on the street with Nancy Carstairs, was at her side. "Take it away!" she told him.

He smiled foolishly, removed the cigarette from his lips with his other hand. "Take your hand away," she commanded more loudly. He took it away. He turned to the man at his side, apparently continuing a conversation carried on even while his hand sought to rest upon her knee. His upper teeth protruded and he spoke with a slight lisp. "Anyway," said this son of a bank manager, "there's only two sorts of people in the world — presidents and vice-presidents."

"Which one are you?" a gruff voice asked.

Instead of replying, he turned again to Selva. "Mrs. Wamboldt told my mother," he said.

"Told your mother what?"

"You know what she told her . . . and my mother's looking for a maid."

"What's that got to do with me?"

"Well, you've got to work for someone, haven't you — and my mother's pretty broad-minded," he lisped in a whisper.

Hot tears of anger welled up in Selva's eyes. "I don't have to work for your mother or for anyone else unless I want to," she said, her body trembling as she tried to control her voice. All evening long she had protested, and to what avail?

She half rose to go, to leave the booth, to push by Hank Barton and rid herself of his impudence, but sat back again against the wall when she saw that Clay Mulloy had returned and now stood, a deliverer in a buck-skin shirt, at the end of the table. Taking a short, black pipe from his mouth, he beckoned with his head to her. "Someone wants to speak to you," he said.

"Me?" She roused herself in unbelief, pointing a finger to her chest.

Clay Mulloy nodded.

Selva rose, murmuring her goodbyes to Mrs. Weaver and the others in the booth, relieved at the excuse for leaving which had come her way. Hank Barton got up surlily, hung his head and let her by.

Clay Mulloy touched her elbow, urged her towards the women's entrance behind and out of earshot of the booth. There she stood beside him. He was slightly taller than herself, and regarding him, she thought that he had very good, serious eyes, their whites gleaming in the tan of his face. The face itself was battered, the nose slightly bent, the lower lip outthrust and moist.

"He wants to see you," he said to her.

"Who?"

"Bill Wilkins. He's over there in the corner. I've been talking to him." Bill Wilkins was the owner of the outfit for which Clay Mulloy and Slim and many others worked.

"What's he want to see me for?" Selva glanced over the crowded tables to the far corner of the room.

Clay Mulloy tucked the pipe into the corner of his mouth, took it out again, held its stem against his cheek. "It's what I was talking to you about," he said in the voice whose low resonance she found pleasing. "You know, the chalet I'm packing in supplies for." When he spoke it was as though he touched and caressed her with his voice.

"The chalet?" she asked.

"Yes, it's going to open late in June for a special party. Wilkins had a girl from Calgary lined up to take charge of it, to act as hostess, and this afternoon he got a wire from her that she couldn't come. So, when I heard that and remembered that you said you were quitting the place you were working, I figured . . . Well, I figured it might be a likely place for you to go. He needs to be sure of someone right away."

"But I've never been a hostess," Selva said.

"There's nothing to it. There will be someone there to cook. You just have to meet people, people from the city, and be nice to them and see that they have a good time. It needs someone with a good appearance who can wear clothes and meet people and talk to them."

Peter Wrogg had told her that in Montreal she could probably get a job as a model, wear expensive clothes and walk before people who had money to buy them. Now Clay Mulloy suggested to her that because she had a good appearance she could meet those same people in a mountain chalet, talk to them and entertain them. She had a quick vision of herself standing in a doorway, mountains above her. She would not wear jeans. She would wear jodphurs such as she had seen in magazine advertisements of eastern summer resorts. She would also be wearing a blue woollen shirt and a

112

white buck-skin vest and a beaded band around her hair. She stepped out of the doorway into the sun and shook hands with a gravely spoken banker just dismounting from his horse. Clay Mulloy, as guide, stood by the horse's head.

What would Peter say? She knew that Peter would advise her to take the chance. Now, instead of her going to the city, the city would come to her. She would no longer be a mere appendage to a house, or a piece of harried mobility behind a lunch counter. Now she would be meeting people on an equal footing, people who might find in her what Peter had found and — who knew? — who might offer her another way of life as he had done. She would have her small place in the sun and could hold her head high before the Wamboldts and Hank Barton and Slim and others of the town who thought that because today she was a hired girl she would always be one. Besides, the pay would be better. She might ask for as much as sixty dollars a month. She would be able to save it during the four months of summer and then, if she wished, she could go east or west, wherever fancy called her.

"But Mr. Wilkins . . ." she said to Clay Mulloy, "what will he think of meeting me in a beer parlour?"

The skin around Clay Mulloy's eyes wrinkled. It was as close as he had come to a smile. He said, "I've got something to say about it. I own an interest in the outfit. Besides, Wilkins knows who you are — he says he's met your step-father — and that you don't usually hang around places like this. He won't think about it. He's an oldtimer. He judges people for what they are and what they can do."

Selva followed him as he led her through the maze of tables in the room to Mr. Wilkins' corner. Smoke hung in a pall. Under it, as she passed, figures stirred, heads lifted, indolent as grass touched by the casual current of a pool.

Mr. Wilkins — he had come into the valley with his horses before rails were laid or the town was built — sat alone in his booth, a glass of beer by his elbow. Afterwards, Selva was to remember him principally as a pair of hands. The hands, rolling a match between their fingers as she approached, were wide and brown and gnarled. For some reason they recalled to her the branches of the willow in the beaver meadow from behind which Peter, following his fight with Slim, had appeared with the grimace of blood upon his face.

Then the branches of the willow had seemed to her like arms, and the forks in them beneath the leaves, like hands which called her on, yet bade her stay. The hands of old Bill Wilkins — he was old and bald but he was not grey — were like the forked branches of the willow because they too were brown and bent and gnarled. They too spoke of the soil and they spoke of toil close to the soil from which they took their shape. Hands like his grew in mountain valleys as surely as the willows they cut to clear a trail or the pines they felled to build a cabin. Throughout the short interview, Selva's eyes did not stray far from Mr. Wilkins' hands. She sat on his left. Clay Mulloy moved in on his right to face her across the table.

For half a minute no one spoke. Then Mr. Wilkins, leaning forward, locking his hands upon the table top and nodding to Clay Mulloy, said to Selva in a voice which rumbled in his great chest, "Clay here tells me you want to work for us."

Clay interrupted. "Not quite that. I said I would talk to her and ask her."

"Well?" Wilkins looked at Selva.

She said, "I don't really know, Mr. Wilkins. I've never . . ." Below the table top, she slowly rubbed her palms together. They were damp with sweat.

"What we need," Wilkins said, "is a girl who knows something about horses, who can take over if the cook gets sick and who isn't afraid of meeting people."

His brown bloodshot eyes turned to her, held her, looked through her until she felt that he could see the mole beneath her left shoulder blade.

"We're paying a hundred and fifty a month — with keep, of course," Wilkins said. "You think it over and come down and see me at the office tomorrow morning."

Selva's lips formed the words, "A hundred and fifty." She remembered the clothes she had that afternoon brought in from the line. In the morning she had ironing to do.

She said, "I can't very well get away in the morning."

"Well, come down when you can then. You know where it is. It's up by the corrals below the hill. Come in the evening if it suits you better."

Later, outside under the trees where the wind still blew, as Clay leading his black horse walked down the lane with her towards the Wamboldts' house, it seemed to Selva incredible that an issue so momentous to her could have been settled with so few words and only a dozen of them spoken by herself.

"A hundred and fifty dollars," she said to Clay as they passed the back of the pool hall, the horse's tread threatening their heels, his warm breath at her back. She had been prepared to ask for sixty.

"It's worth it. He pays well because it's only for the summer and it's not everyone that can do the job," Clay replied. Selva's cheeks glowed. She wished to thank him for what he said, for what he had done.

Instead, as they stood for a moment by the Wamboldt garage, he with his shoulder to her, his fingers testing his cinch, his left foot in the stirrup, she reached up and, without a word, put her lips lightly to his cheek. So she might have kissed an older brother. Clay Mulloy continued his swing into the saddle as if he had noticed nothing, his horse rearing until he loomed above her like a monument abruptly uplifted. He touched his heels to the horse's belly, his hand to his hat brim, and trotted down the lane.

Selva watched him go, heard the echo of iron shod hooves fade on stony ground. She looked down and at her feet saw a glove. It had fallen from his hip pocket. She picked it up. It was still warm from his body. It smelt of man and horse, of journeys and campfire smoke. It smelt of places he had been. It smelt of the High Valley where he had been packing in supplies, of the High Valley where a new chalet waited for its hostess.

nine

A week the following Saturday night — ten brutal days of spring cleaning at the Wamboldts' house behind her — Selva found herself lying under red Hudson's Bay blankets in a cabin beside Bill Wilkins' corrals beneath the hill at the back of town. Rain pattered on the roof and grey valley twilight sifted through the window beyond the foot of her bed.

The cabin was one used by hunters in the fall — hunters from the East and California — who put up there for a night or two before setting out for the northern hunting trails. It was new. It smelt of pine, of skins hung upon the walls, of the bear rug upon the floor and of wood slowly burning in the damped pot bellied stove in its centre. From the other bed on the far side of the stove, Rosie, the maid from the dining-room of the hotel, spoke. Together on Monday morning they were going into the High Valley — Selva to be in charge of the chalet as hostess and Rosie who had been hired, on Selva's suggestion, as cook. Selva wished to help Rosie, but even more she wished to help herself. As cook, she felt, Rosie would be amenable to her ideas. She would "keep her place" and her pale personality woud add lustre to her own.

"I can't get over it," Rosie said.

Selva, hands locked under her head, staring at the ceiling,

listening to the rain, asked, "Can't get over what?"

"Those roses. Think of him sending you roses, a dozen of them, and all the way from Vancouver. No one's ever sent me flowers that came in a box."

For that matter, Selva reflected, no one had previously sent flowers to her. Flowers grew beside the road, along the trail and by the stream. They could be picked, one by one, carried home and put upon the dresser top. These roses from Vancouver were of a different sort. They came cradled in the green of box and fern, delivered by the express man from the station to the back door of the Wamboldt house.

Mrs. Wamboldt had come into the kitchen as Selva was unwrapping the package. "Where on earth did they come from?" she desired to know. "A dozen roses . . . I never heard of such a thing."

"Someone sent them to me," Selva had replied.

"But whoever . . ." Mrs. Wamboldt commenced to speak again, thought better of it, turned and left the kitchen.

When, two days later, the Ford truck had come to take her valise and steamer trunk down to the corrals, Selva, reluctant to leave the roses for the new girl arriving to replace her, brought them with her. Now she could see them dimly in the half light on the table outlined against the window looking out into the corrals. At the Wamboldts' they had filled her bedroom with perfume, flooded it like a sunrise. Here in the twilight they scarcely could be seen and their perfume was lost in the stronger odours of hide and log.

They had come to her bearing no card, no note, but she knew that they had been sent by Peter Wrogg. They had come from a florist's shop in Vancouver. Besides, who else would send her flowers? Peter's letter the next day, written on the stationery of the Hotel Vancouver, though it made no mention of the flowers, confirmed her belief. He wrote in a small, round, careful hand, so light that the pen barely touched the paper. "Dear Selva," the letter began, "I hope you will not be surprised to hear from me. It seems a very long time ago that we talked upon the hill and later went down across the railway trestle to the beaver meadow where your friend in the chaps left me speechless, literally speechless. You see, after he had knocked you aside, he came close in to me. His head came up and caught my chin. Apparently my mouth was open because my jaw was snapped shut. My teeth cut into my tongue severing an artery. That was why I could not speak. Your town doctor sewed me up and I was able to take the next morning's train down to the Coast. In the diner I sucked cold soup through a straw."

"Here I have seen another doctor. There is nothing to worry about. I am first-rate now. You must not blame yourself in any way. I am the one to blame and I assure you I feel very much of a fool for letting such a thing happen to me."

"I remember our walk and what we talked of. I have more now to say to you than I had then, just as after dancing with you, I had more to say to you when later we went walking — though even so it now seems little enough. I have had time since to think and to remember. I will not say more than that. You might laugh at me if I did. Would you? No, I think you would not."

"I am leaving here today for Seattle and then for San Francisco and Los Angeles, in California, on business — my father's business, remember? On my return, I will be stopping off in Yellowhead — after all, I still might like to climb a mountain or two. Will you then let me take you walking again? This time we will go to another place than the beaver meadow. And, meanwhile, if you go walking alone, remember me when you are up on the hillside. Let your hair blow free in the wind and in that moment, wherever I may be, I will remember you." He had signed himself simply "Peter."

Peter would be passing through Yellowhead again, returning East, he said, in late July or August. In July and August she would not be in Yellowhead. She would be in the High Valley managing the chalet for Mr. Wilkins. Still Peter, if he so wished, could discover where she was. At the dance above the pool-hall, he had not known where she worked. He had inquired and found her. He could inquire once more and come to where she was if he desired to do so. She would step out of the door of the chalet to greet him and ask him, as she had asked him when he called for her in the kitchen, how he knew where to find her and he would tell her how he knew. Then she would take him, as she had taken him before, and show him over her surroundings — but now, instead of a kitchen and a house belonging to someone else, it would be a chalet where she was in charge and instead of the hilltop and the cemetery, there would be the High Valley with new mountains and strange names, and instead of a picnic lunch in the beaver meadow, there would be supper before a fireplace on a table at which she presided. He would see her there in a world of her own making.

A world of her own making? She wondered about that. Had she not met Peter at the dance, had he not gone walking with her, she would now be looking forward to nothing more than a summer in the Wamboldts' kitchen. If Mr. Winnie, the undertaker, had not talked, if she had not slapped Mr. Wamboldt's face, if Mrs. Wamboldt had not come into the kitchen and dismissed her, if she had not gone with Mrs. Weaver to the beer parlour and there met Clay Mulloy and Mr. Wilkins — if none of this had happened, she would not now be about to become the hostess at a mountain chalet. She would still be "the girl who worked for the Wamboldts." It was her world, but others had shaped it for her.

Yet the job in the High Valley was no final solution. It was only for the summer. In September the chalet would be closed and she would come down to the town again. It was so, she would by then have been able to save her money. At a hundred and fifty a month, she should have saved by that time close to five hundred dollars, a sum which would take her wherever she wished to go, and a greater sum than she had ever had. Where would she go and what would she do? Dimly she felt that the summer would reveal that to her. The summer, and perhaps Peter if he came. She was not in love with Peter. She liked him and respected him because he respected her and because doors that were closed to her were open to him and his kind. Through no fault of his own, he had failed her in the beaver meadow. His was a frail vessel, but one strong enough to contain her hopes for a while . . .

Across the room, Rosie stirred. Ashes settled in the stove. Freshened by the rain, the aroma of horse flesh and manure reached into the cabin. Horses stamped inside the stable. It was Saturday night. The men were up at the beer parlour. No voices sounded from the bunkhouse, only a bell, its tongue loosened from its keeper, clanged dismally from the corral where pack horses, heads down in the rain, were held. Closing her eyes, Selva could imagine that she was once more at the homestead in the foothills, for this too was man's abode — a territory of saddles and horses, of brooding silence with an ever present hint of violence. Here, unlike the Wamboldts' kitchen, a woman's voice did not command.

Yet the transition from one to the other, from being a maid in a kitchen to hostess in a chalet, had been easier than she would have believed possible. When she had seen Mr. Wilkins again, after the interview in the beer parlour, he had taken for granted her acceptance of his offer. They had talked of the clothes she would wear, of the linen and blankets needed for the four bedrooms at the chalet, of arrangements for bringing in by pack pony fresh meat and vegetables and fruit. Then, sitting back in his chair across the desk from her, polishing his brown bald head with a red bandanna handkerchief, Mr. Wilkins asked about her people. It seemed, indeed — at least he was convinced to his own satisfaction — that he had known her stepfather, Jed Williams, in the early days. They had met while hunting wild horses in the country of the lower Brazeau and once, he told Selva, he had stopped at the Williams' homestead on the Saskatchewan below Rocky Mountain House. He was one of the men then, she thought, who, when she was a little girl with her hair down her back, had come stamping and laughing into the kitchen to put their hands upon her head and call her "Sorrel Top." But no, he assured her, that had been before her time.

"The country was a small place then," Bill Wilkins said. "Everyone knew everyone else, not like it is today at all. That was why when Clay Mulloy — he's my oldest hand — told me about you, I listened. The name was familiar and I had heard that you came from the foothills. With that background, and because you looked the part, I figured you might be just what we were looking for, someone who could handle horses and look after people, take over by yourself if you had to."

He concluded with a word of caution, "This little trouble you've been in . . . I've heard Winnie talking."

"It wasn't my fault. It wasn't my doing," Selva interjected. Was she at the last moment to lose what was already within her grasp?

Wilkins had quietened her. "I pay no attention to Winnie," he said. "I wouldn't accept his recommendation, so why should I accept his gossip? I try to judge people as they are. But, remember, this summer you must be careful. Understand?"

"I understand, Mr. Wilkins," Selva had said. "I understand perfectly." . . .

"Are you awake?" Rosie, breaking into the revery, asked in a breath-filled whisper from across the room.

"Why?"

"You didn't answer me, that's why."

"What didn't I answer?"

"What I said about the flowers."

"There was nothing to answer," Selva said.

Rosie squirmed in her bed, was silent for a minute, and then asked, "Do you think he'll be coming up to the High Valley to see you?"

"Why should anyone come up to see me?"

"Well, he sent you flowers, didn't he?"

"Yes," Selva said, "but that's different."

"Why is it different? I don't think it's different at all."

"There's the matter of time," Selva said shortly. She did not wish to discuss Peter with Rosie and regretted now that she had offered any explanation as to whence the flowers came.

Rosie said, "I don't understand what you mean." She sighed. "Anyway, it's wonderful, isn't it?"

"What's wonderful? I'm tired. I want to go to sleep. Pretty soon they'll be coming back from the beer parlour and we'll get no sleep for a while after that."

"I mean it's wonderful — you and me and the chalet and all the expensive people we're going to meet."

"They're people, just like us."

"No," Rosie said, "they're not. You know they're not. They've got money. They come from the city. We go up to a chalet to work and they come there to have a good time." She was quiet before adding in a resigned tone of voice, "Of course, you being a hostess, you'll be able to go out riding with them and sit at table with them. I'll be working in the kitchen."

"That doesn't make any difference. I'll help you all I can."

"I know you will and don't think I'm not glad to leave

that old hotel and that Chinese cook. He used to say the most awful things to me and try to lift my skirts up. Really, he did. And some of the others too."

Selva wondered if Rosie spoke the truth. It was difficult to conceive of her as an object of desire — Rosie, who, in the beer parlour, had declared that it was quite all right for a man at table to pick his nose with his thumb so long as he did not use his finger. Yet for all that, she possessed a cute little figure and her voice, despite its shrillness, was appealing. It was more than that. It was avid and spoke of hunger.

Rosie continued quickly as though fearful of interruption, "Maybe up there we'll meet someone," she said.

"Up where?" Selva yawned.

"Up in the High Valley, silly! That's where we're going, isn't it?"

"Of course, we'll meet lots of people."

"But I mean, really meet someone. Someone nice, like your young Englishman who sent you the flowers and left the tips for me in the hotel. He's what I call 'nice.' Some of the guides are nice too, in a different way, I guess. I'll always have cake and pie baked in the kitchen and while you're out with the expensive people, the guides can come in to talk to me . . ."

As Rosie prattled on, Selva twisted wearily in her bed. Yes, she and Rosie, she and Rosie and Mrs. Weaver, she and Rosie and Mrs. Weaver and all the rest were hoping one day to "meet someone." She realized in sudden revelation that the High Valley represented as much to Rosie as it did to her. Rosie also had her "plans." She did not wish to return to the hotel where the Chinese cook or the guests reached for her skirt, nor did Selva herself wish to return to a kitchen where Mr. Wamboldt or someone like him, in his drunkenness, assumed to himself the right to put hands upon her. It was not that she objected to being touched by a man any more than Rosie, probably, would invariably object to having her skirt lifted. The point of objection was, she thought, that when a woman was a menial men took for granted that this gave them a peculiar advantage. A woman would not act towards a waiter in a restaurant as the men in the hotel and the Chinese cook had acted towards Rosie, nor would the men in the hotel address one another in the terms which they used towards the cook. She and Rosie, like the Chinese in his white apron, moved in a world of foreigners. The Chinese cook, if he saved his money and lived long enough, could go back to China, but where could she and Rosie go? As surely as he was, they were part of a minority, not because of their numbers but because of the womanliness which confined them and restricted them in what they did. The Chinese cook, if he stayed in Canada, might become a laundryman if he tired of his cooking. It would be unlikely that he would become anything else because, first of all, he was Chinese and, therefore, a member of a special group. What else could Rosie be but what she was, a maid at the hotel or cook at the chalet? She could become a wife which was, of course, what Rosie hoped for when she spoke of "meeting someone." Being what she was, she would then work longer hours and instead of working for wages would merely earn her board and room . . .

Selva was already dozing when men's voices from the bunkhouse aroused her. The men had returned from the beer parlour — from the beer parlour where women entered through a side door as though they were a species distinct from the men who came in by the front — woman, forever a transgressor in man's domain.

A horse galloped into the yard from the road. The rider pulled him up, shouted, lifted an oath against the teaming sky. Someone stepped out from the bunkhouse carrying a lantern whose bobbing glow fell upon the cabin window. Selva heard a loud "Shhh!" and knew that a head was being cocked towards where she and Rosie lay, which, with the word "Women!" demanded silence.

A loud and familiar voice replied, "Makes no difference. Give me that lantern."

A muttering followed. A man's form stepped between the lantern and the cabin window. There was a scuffle, then the lantern as though it were floating on the tide of night, bobbed closer.

Selva heard a tinkle of spurs and then hard, high heels upon the cabin porch. The door was slammed inward and in the doorway Slim stood holding the lantern high so that it lighted his long, sharp face, made pools of blackness of his eyes, fell upon the raindrops on his hat.

Rosie, alarmed, sat up, rubbing her eyes, clutching the red blanket to her chin. Selva raised herself on her elbow.

"Well!" Slim said to her, the upper part of his body swaying in a slow half circle. "A hostess, eh? And the High Valley. Say," he drawled, "you're getting up in the world, aren't you? I mean, going up two ways at a time. The High Valley's up and you're up too." He straddled his legs, put his head back and laughed.

Selva leaned over, picked up one of her new riding gaiters from the floor.

Slim, watching her, said, "I suppose you're going to take the tourists on picnics too, like you did that curly-haired Englishman I found you with down in the beaver meadow. And what a picnic that turned out to be!"

Selva lifted the gaiter. "Get out!" she ordered in a voice so tense and rasping that she did not recognize it as her own.

Then, past Slim's shoulder, over the threshold, taking shape from the shadows, lineaments and substance forming before her eyes from the night beyond the door, she saw the high cheek bones of Clay Mulloy.

He touched Slim's elbow and as Slim turned, moved his head in a backward gesture. "We'd better be going," Clay Mulloy said. It was the low, quiet voice of authority. It was not Peter Wrogg protesting in the beaver meadow.

Slim lowered the lantern, his face retreating into darkness as if behind a shade being slowly drawn. "Sure," he mumbled. "I just came by to see the girls having heard they were here. Selva and me, you see, are old friends, aren't we, Selva?"

"Do as you're told," Selva said, dropping her gaiter to the floor.

Slim looked at her, looked in surprise at Mulloy. "Sure, I'm going," he said. "I didn't come by to stay."

He went out and Mulloy followed closing, without a word to Selva or Rosie, the door behind him.

Rosie settled angrily back into her bed. "That fellow Slim," she said to Selva across the room on whose walls the glow of the receding lantern danced, "I never could understand what you saw in him. A girl with your looks who gets flowers sent to her can do a lot better than that."

Ignoring Rosie's remarks, Selva threw back her covers, reached for her robe, drew it over her shoulders and, on pale blue pyjama-clad legs, ran to the door. Opening it, holding her face against the night's chill breath, she called softly, "Clay! Clay!" It was the first time that she had addressed him by his first name — or by any name at all.

The bobbing of the lantern ceased, then she saw two feet wading towards her in its pool of light. When Clay stepped onto the porch she put her hand upon his arm. "Don't let Mr. Wilkins know about this," she whispered pulling the door to behind her. "I mean about Slim coming here. He's been drinking or he wouldn't have come near."

"Don't worry," Clay reassured her. "I understand. Wilkins won't hear a word. Now go back to bed." He patted her ever so lightly on the buttock.

Inside the cabin, Rosie asked, "What's the matter? What were you talking to him about?"

"Nothing," Selva said, slipping between her sheets. "Just something I wanted to say to him."

"Well, anyway, I hope that fellow Slim doesn't come up into the High Valley," Rosie replied through a yawn. "He'll make trouble wherever he is."

ten

Slim, as it happened, was no immediate problem or "trouble" in the High Valley — the High Valley to which, conducted by Clay Mulloy and a second packer, Selva and Rosie came after a two day pack pony trip over three mountain ranges broken by an all night camp in a mountain meadow.

They rode down into the valley from Crooked Pass in mid-afternoon of the second day out of Yellowhead. Clay who, on his tall black horse, was leading turned in his saddle and spoke to Selva following next to him. "Over there on your right," he said, pushing his hat back from his forehead, putting his hand on his horse's rump, "that valley to the west — that's British Columbia and the headwaters of the Fraser, grizzly country and caribou, and these peaks right ahead of us, they call them The Ramparts, and the lake at the foot of them is Amethyst Lake, and the river that flows out of it, the Astoria, empties into the Athabaska." He continued to speak, giving her the names of mountains and of glaciers. Then, facing forward, rising in his stirrups, he pointed to where the chalet stood, a thousand feet below in a belt of timber. Selva could not see it.

Nor indeed, as he spoke, had she listened well to him. Lulled by her horse's easy motion, by the thud of hooves upon the trail behind her, hearing, as in a dream, Rosie's occasional, piping voice from higher on the mountainside where she rode with the second packer at the tail of the pack ponies, she was absorbed, trying to grasp the valley, not as a series of names and units, but as a whole — this piece of meadow land set at the foot of rocky, snow-capped peaks where, for four months, she was to keep open house, a dominion towards which, in a procession of men and horses, she was being escorted like a queen upon a litter. It was hers, all hers, but only for the summer.

The valley, still patched with snow, ran east and west and she could see no sign of life in it, only the wind forever blowing, feathering the violet waters of the narrow lake and combing with a lighter green the dark green of the forest roof. Yet it did not seem to be an empty valley. It was a valley peopled by trees. The trees, the little trees, tapering spruce and balsam neighbouring the timberline, were like people. As the trail dropped down the mountain side, Selva passed rank after rank of them standing in the sunlight, lifting their spears to the sky as if they were men, sombre with lances. Farther away, across the valley, their columns mounted each mountain draw, assailed the ridges, pushing one against another in an unceasing endeavour to reach the heights above.

Taller, more opulent trees grew crowded on the valley floor. It was the lean, the starved, the scarcely living which scaled the rock and climbed the highest. It was these alone, clinging to their bare subsistence, who escaped the ruck. The trees might be people, but the forest was not mankind whose few were rich and apart and whose poor were crowded.

Later, when Clay Mulloy and the other packer had gone and for a few days she and Rosie were alone in the valley, Selva, walking by the lake, climbing the mountain side, was to feel a kinship with the trees whose place of living she had come to share. This was her first journey into the high mountains. The grey and towering peaks wrapped in the mystery of their clouds or looming arrogant in sunlight above the chalet at first affected her with a kind of terror, a sense of threat, disaster impending above her head and over the frail log chalet which men's hands that winter had built. The mountains at a distance, from the foothills or from the cemetery above the town, she could comprehend simply as territory or as a barrier to be surmounted. They did not otherwise involve her. But here in the High Valley, they were too close, too imminent, their shadows and the cold breath of their ice and snow upon her. They were not height. They were angry depth — the depth that she might fall — upthrust into the clouds against the sun, a trouble to the labouring earth which bore them.

At night behind the spruce logs of the chalet, enclosed in the arms of the forest, or walking during the day on the soft moss among the trees, for a time she could forget the mountains. The trees at her elbows were familiar things. They were brothers and sisters to the trees of the foothills where she had been raised — part of the great northern forest which, leaping rivers, encircling lakes, flanking mountains, lay over all the land that she had ever known sheltering bird and beast beneath its boughs and, beside running waters, giving man a home. When no wind blew, the trees stood intent as if listening for it, and when it rose suddenly from the valley, or forayed from the passes to lash against them, they bent and groaned, tossed their heads, flung their arms like a verdant and rooted humanity impotently protesting the storms of its destiny.

She spoke about her feeling to Clay Mulloy two mornings after her arrival. It was also the day that with the other packer he was to return over the divide to Yellowhead leaving herself and Rosie to ready the chalet for the season's first tourists due to arrive the following week. She and Clay had tied their horses, walked down to the shore of the lake and out onto a point beyond the timber.

"It's all so big," she said to him, "so big and strange, it makes me a little bit afraid." She spoke loudly because the wind blew howling and triumphant out of the western mountains, levelling the grass at her feet, drowning her words, folding a glossy, fine spun shawl of tawny hair against her cheeks. She turned into it, freeing her face with her fingers and the wind, pressing against her, shaped the blue-flannel shirt about her breasts.

"Here, come over here," Clay took her arm, led her out of the wind behind a rock the size and shape of an upright piano which, years before, had tumbled to the lakeshore from the mountain side. They sat there on the moss, close together, sheltered, arms locked about their knees.

"Tell me," Clay said to her gently as he might speak to a child, "what's there to be afraid of?" Slim, Selva knew, would have laughed at her fears. Peter Wrogg — remembering the roses and the letter, she realized with a quickening of her blood which surprised her, that in a few weeks he might be with her looking at these same mountains — Peter Wrogg would not have had to ask the question. And now, sitting beside Clay, watching him as he carefully filled his pipe in no hurry for her answer, she felt that there was little cause for fear. When he was close to her, she felt secure. He had come to her in the beer parlour, taken her away from the advances and rudeness of the bank manager's son and offered her a job when she needed it. Later, when Slim had forced his way into the cabin at the corrals, he had again interceded and Slim had left. Slim had not made a scene, she decided, because Clay's bearing suggested an untapped strength. In appearance he was not a big man — he had the large hands and small feet of a horseman and the narrow hips and tapered body that went with them. Yet he seemed big. It was as though he were a big man compressed into a smaller frame, as a coiled spring might be compressed.

"Come on," he said to her, "I asked you a question." His voice also had a similar quality, always low, subdued, as though more than came out were bottled within him. As he spoke, he turned away from her and again she had the impression that a part of him was hidden, listening to words she could not hear.

She looked at the dark waters of the lake furrowed by the wind and at the crested waves running over it. She looked above to the grim mountain walls from which, in banners, streamed the last night's newly fallen snow. Winter was not yet defeated. He had merely retreated and was encamped upon the peaks from which at times during the summer, in squalls of snow and driving wind, he would make sallies into the valley.

"I've noticed you've been quiet since we came up here," Clay said to her. "You've talked to no one very much, except to Rosie in the kitchen. Of course, people often feel strange when they come out into the mountains. Tourists are always

130

saying that they feel 'walled in.' And me, when I'm on the prairies, I'm afraid of bumping my head against the sky, it seems so low."

"It's nothing like that," Selva said. "I don't feel walled in. Maybe I shouldn't have spoken as I did. Maybe I should go back with you to Yellowhead and get another job."

"Nonsense — you can't let us down like that." Clay stared at her sharply. His eyes were not blue. They were grey and, for an instant, cold as glacier ice. In that instant, what she saw within them gave her pause.

"No, I wasn't really serious," she said, "but when I think of being up here alone with Rosie . . ."

"You won't be alone for long. We're sending up a boy to help with the wood and water and there'll be tourists in and out of here all summer. I'll be in and out myself, probably Wilkins too."

Selva considered for a moment. "You don't understand what I'm trying to say," she told him. He took his pipe from his mouth, pinched his lower lip, waited.

"What I mean," she continued, "is that I don't feel I'm ever alone. When I look up at that mountain, I feel that something is going to happen, something awful, I don't know what it is. It's as though someone were up there looking down. And all the time I know it's silly."

Clay looked up at the mountain, thumbing his pipe. He did not laugh as he might have done. "That's Mount Erebus. The Indians called it 'The Thunderer' because of its slides," he said. "You can be sure no one's up there. A man tried to get up there once three or four years ago. They've never found his body, his or the guide's either. Probably in a rock slide. You can see that mountain from the Athabaska valley." He pointed down the valley of the Astoria into which the lake drained. "We didn't come in that way because there's no trail, but you can see Mount Erebus from down there on the highway and that's right where his widow woman opened a tea shop for the summer trade. She comes there every summer. I never could figure it out."

As he finished speaking, Selva, still looking up at the mountain, felt tears in her eyes. She was disturbed, unnerved. She felt like crying, not for the widow, nor for the men lost in the rock slide, nor for the guide who had received death for his wages. She cried not for these. She did not wish to cry. Why was she crying? She did not know. Perhaps she cried for Rosie, working in the chalet kitchen, with pots and pans to deny her dreams, for Mrs. Weaver and her lost trapper husband and for all women bereaved by mountains. She cried for herself, no longer alone, but one of these others, for she also was bereaved by mountains of the life that called her and that was beyond them. Perhaps she cried for the sorrow in the wind which keened about the rock and for the sorrow of time itself which withered flowers, raised crosses whose muted words stilled the cemetery above the town, which swept before it men and women and little children as surely as the autumn wind swept leaves from the hill. Even this mountain rising before her, holding a glacier in its lap, bulwarked and turretted with rock, veined with ice and snow, flaunting its head in the clouds, one day would be humbled, whittled away by time until it too, like man himself, was brought kneeling into the valley.

Clay's arm around her shoulder gave her comfort. "It's nothing," he told her. "The altitude, a sort of mountain sickness. It affects some people. Depresses them. It will pass away. Tomorrow you'll be laughing about it with Rosie in the kitchen."

Selva blew her nose, dabbed her eyes with a flimsy lace-trimmed handkerchief. Clay rose, drew her up, then held her at arm length from him. "I like your outfit," he said.

"I must look awful." She touched the handkerchief again to her eyes.

"You look fine." She smoothed her hair, lifted her head. She was satisfied with her outfit. It suited the place and her duties. She had wanted jodphurs such as she had seen advertised in the fashion magazines where men and sun-browned girls stood beside horses, but unable to buy them in Yellowhead, instead had bought a pair of grey, tight fitting, whip-cord trousers such as the men wore. She had also bought a pair of neat black riding gaiters, flannel shirts, two blue and one grey, and a grey checkered mackinaw which was tied behind her saddle on the short barrelled sorrel mare which they had left in the timber. To complete her wardrobe, she had brought up to the chalet with her, her blue party dress and the black slippers, although it appeared that there would be small opportunity to wear them.

They rode the six miles back to the chalet through the timber, across the alplands, flushing a covey of ptarmigan still mottled with their winter white and seeing, high above on a mountain slope, a herd of caribou. Sometimes they rode abreast. Their stirrups touched or Selva's knee fitted momentarily into the bend of Clay Mulloy's as he rode on his taller horse beside her. The wind had fallen and the horses tossed their heads, twitched their ears, snorted to clear their nostrils of the swarms of "no-see-'ums," seemed to comment by gesture one with the other upon the countryside and upon those who bestrode them.

"You know," Clay said, "suppose a horse thought, had ideas. No matter how much he thought, he could only be a horse and we would never know a thing about it."

After a moment or two he added, "No, a horse doesn't think because he has no words. He only has a memory. He remembers, that's why he can be taught."

Selva asked him how long he had worked with horses.

"Not so long, ten years, eleven, but it seems I've always been in the mountains." He grasped his saddle pommel, struck out his jaw, hunched his shoulders forward, shifting with his horse's motion as if he walked on stilts.

"Go on. Tell me more," Selva said.

"Nothing much more than that, what I've already said."

She persisted in her questions as they walked their horses, she with a wall of timber to her left, he with the open alplands and mountains to his right and the mingled shadows of the horses, a dark, shifting carpet beneath them.

From a phrase here, an uncompleted sentence there, from a shrug of his shoulders or a muttered assent in this, and later meetings with him, she pieced together his story or, at least conceived to her own content, a background against which he moved. Now, she judged, a man of thirty-five or more, he had grown up, like herself, an intimate neighbour of trees. His father, a man of definite views and in his small way a rebel against society, had been a timber-cruiser working for the big lumber companies and at one time or another had walked over most of British Columbia and parts of western Alberta from the border north to the Yukon. He loved the forest and resented the necessity which made him an instrument of its destruction. Some of that resentment against working for others, against being dishonest with himself, he had handed on to his son.

Because, when he was twelve Clay's mother had separated from his father, he had for a time lived with his father's sister in the Crow's Nest Pass in southern Alberta. The boy had stayed with her until he was fifteen. Then his father had taken him with him on his summer journeys into the mountains. In the winter Clay had returned to the Crow's Nest Pass to go to school. But it was the summers which he remembered and looked forward to and the lessons which he quickly forgot. Selva pictured him — the boy now grown to manhood beside her — with his father who she imagined to be a tall man and lean with a long stride, walking up streams, by the shores of lakes and through the forest where sunlight shimmered in slanting curtains. There he had learned the softness of speech, the stealth of movement which had become a part of him. However, his father, himself the son of an Ontario farmer, was determined to give him more than this. He wanted him to be able to stand alone, to have to call no man his boss. Labour law, he thought, was an open field where he would be on his own and doing good and not merely be making money for others.

"And so," Clay said, "when I was nineteen and I had matriculated, he sent me away to McGill University in Montreal. I took Arts. You have to take Arts before you enter Law. I took three years. Of course, I worked summers to help out, mostly as an axe-man on survey parties. Then someone dropped a tree on the Old Man and I didn't go back to college. I never had wanted very much to go in the first place. I drifted around for a while — survey parties, lumber camps, a trip on a tramp freighter to Australia, and then I came to Yellowhead on a hunch, and — well, I've been here ever since. It's good enough, I guess."

"And you never got married?"

"No — maybe I lacked the initiative." He smiled.

Later, as they forded a narrow stream, Selva asked, "But didn't you like Montreal?" She wished to hear of Montreal.

"I liked the beer."

"Beer — I don't like beer so well, but I think I'd like Montreal."

He regarded her quizzically, ducked his head beneath a spruce bough, leaned over to pat the glossy black neck of his horse.

"Maybe you would at that," he replied. "Maybe you would like Montreal. I can see you in a silky dress with furs on your shoulders going into the Mount Royal Hotel. Or maybe it would be the Windsor. I like the Windsor better. It's better for drinking beer."

"Who would be taking me to a big hotel?" Selva straightened in her saddle, held her bridle hand higher.

"Maybe I would. If I was there, maybe I would," Clay said, his voice falling to a murmur. "We'd make a good looking couple. Of course, I'd have to have a change of clothes and, with me, you'd have to wear earrings, long green ones, and little pink slippers with bows to match."

Selva laughed, put out her tongue at him, touched the sorrel mare with her heels, galloped ahead across a sunny forest meadow.

"I'm not just saying words," Clay said as he overtook her with a creak of straining leather. "I wouldn't like to live in Montreal again with all those strangers about and feeling lonely when I heard a train whistling for the West, but one day I'll be going back for a while to visit. I've saved my money and I've got plans. I'll be setting up my own outfit one of these days. Not here. Probably over in the Fry Pan Mountains. The Old Man used to talk a lot about the Fry Pans. I've never seen them, but they're west and north of Prince George, over in British Columbia. It's big game country like this, only farther back from the railroad. Maybe tourists and hunters could be brought in there by plane." He paused, thoughtfully rubbed the sharp, the slightly awry beak of his nose. "No, I wouldn't use a plane," he added. "Men shouldn't have to look down on mountains. They're meant to be looked up at."

"I don't believe there's any such place as the Fry Pan Mountains. I'ts a name you've made up," Selva threw over he shoulder at him once more urging her mare ahead and into a gallop. The mare stumbled, floundered knee deep in muskeg. Selva lifted gently on the bridle lines, pulled up her head. The mare struggled, freed herself and, splashing through water, tossing with her hooves clods of sodden earth shoulder high, galloped towards a ridge which under moss and grass and stunted willow rose like the back of a pre-historic monster slumbering head down and only half buried in the land. A mile away the ridge dipped into the timber.

Selva slacked her lines, gave the mare her head. Sitting her saddle like an Indian, elbows high, heels kicking, feeling strong muscles gather and heave beneath her, she squinted her eyes against the wind until forest and mountain blurred in the speed of her passage. Her hair, flashing in the sun, poured between her shoulders, a cascade of sullen gold. Behind her she heard thudding hooves as Clay on his black horse followed. He called to her, but his words were whipped away by the wind. She did not know from what she fled nor why it was that he pursued her. Life was in the instant, surging between her thighs, holding her up to the sunlight, sweeping her on to the mile distant timber which waited below the mountains. Here was urgency, purpose that was blind and acquiescence that exalted. The timber as she approached became trees, separate and distinct, pushed up in sudden growth before her eyes. She realized then, near the end of the ridge, that her flight was not flight at all. It was no more than the wish to be overtaken.

The black muzzle of Clay's horse appeared beneath her right shoulder. "Pull up," Clay shouted. "Pull up or you'll smash your knees in that timber."

She pulled with both hands, sawing on the snaffle bit. The mare, neck outstretched, did not respond.

Clay's knee came against her own. His horse jostled hers, breaking the mare's stride. His right arm was around her waist lifting her from the saddle. He pulled his horse up so sharply that the horse reared, forefeet pawing the air. The sorrel mare galloped on, stepping upon one of the split lines which Selva had dropped, staggered forward on her nose, kneeled herself up, trotted a few more paces, then put her head down and commenced to feed at the timber's edge.

Selva suspended above the ground, her body crushed against Clay's chest, helplessly kicked her heels. "Let me down," she gasped. "You didn't have to pull me off anyway. You could have grabbed her cheek-strap."

"What you run away from always catches up with you,"

he said for reply. He did not loosen his grip about her waist. Breath whistling through his notrils, he swung his right leg over the cantle and grasping the pommel with his left hand, still pressing her to him, began slowly to dismount.

His toe slipped from the stirrup. The horse shied. Clay and Selva, arms and legs tangled, fell to the ground. She pushed against him, tried to free herself. His arm held her down. She tried again to rise. His gloved hand, smelling of horse flesh and ammonia, touched her cheek. She shoved it aside. The hand returned, now without the glove, and Clay's crooked forefinger raised her chin. As his lips touched hers, Selva shut her eyes. Her lips opened. She sighed. The tumult of the gallop, the pursuit, and at its end the fright of the approaching timber, had taken all strength from her. In its stead, the tender compliance of weakness was about her like a garment. She yielded herself, not to the man, but to the time, the moment, the place of brooding mountains of which he was a part.

And she did not protest when, rising, he stooped, picked her up, cradling her in his arms, and the sun, a glowing red through her closed eyelids, carried her the few steps to the timber's edge. There at last he rested her on a warm, dry slope of moss. Nearby she heard the clink of bits, the crunch of jaws as the horses grazed. From a spruce tree top a golden-crowned sparrow called, newly come to nest in the High Valley from lower parts and from far lands which knew no snow.

As Clay undressed her, pulled the riding gaiters from her feet, slipped the whip-cord trousers from beneath her buttocks, she murmured, "The chalet — we're too close to the chalet." She would have said more but her throat was dry, her thoughts misted. She had no speech. She knew only that this which she had no power to resist — somewhere in the mad gallop along the ridge she had shed the power — was not what she had intended.

"They can't see us. It's beyond the timber," was the guttural answer from above her. The voice was a stranger's voice and the words were uttered as in agony.

The wind shook a tassel of hair upon her forehead and in the sun her eyebrows were sprinkled with copper, and the down upon her cheeks was golden and her freckled eyelids, fringed with deep lashes, were pale in submission. A little pulse beat beneath her ear and the fingers of her right hand were intertwined with blades of grass.

She waited, passive, blind as the moist earth which takes the plough. She waited for the Incorrigible, the Never-to-be-Denied, the Always-to-be-Conquered, the Victorious-in-Defeat now within the creamy narrows of her thighs.

"Easy," she whispered, "easy." Tossing her body, rolling her head from side to side, showing her gritted teeth, she said, "Hard, hard. Hurt me hard."

Then it was as though she were falling, falling through hours and hours, through months and years of limitless night, through all the levels of darkness to a deeper and farther dark, and she cried, "Take me, take me! Hold me! Don't let me go!" And that which she gave up and which flowed from her, came into her.

She opened her eyes to the wisp of her white pants flung upon a balsam vine while above, beyond the tree tops, a white cloud, faceless as God's beard, roamed the empty sky. She heard far off the whish of a waterfall among the rocks. Overhead a raven flapped by, the very shape of the black ghost which had escaped her body.

Clay had gone to find the horses. Returning, leading them, he put his hand to his neck, took it away, looked at his finger tip. He grinned, "You drew blood," he said.

Riding again towards the chalet, she was aware of him speaking, but his voice came to her vaguely, from far away, as though he called to her from across a lake. He was asking her about herself — where she had been before she came to Yellowhead. She answered briefly. And then, as though he were speaking to himself, he was saying, "And up there in the Fry Pan Mountains, the Old Man told me he's been awake all night listening to the whistling swans and the grey geese and the wild duck, all of them winging northward underneath the moon, and when he looked out there were so many the night was dark around." Then he added, "One day I'd like to take you up there and show them to you."

Reaching the chalet, Selva, without a word, left him to unsaddle and to put the horses into the corral. She ran indoors, through the front room with its bearskin rugs and its fireplace of field stones, to the kitchen where Rosie stood above the great flat range hauled in in sections the previous winter on toboggans.

Rosie glanced up from stirring a kettle of soup. "Why, Selva!" she excalimed, "Whatever's happened? You're late, and you look . . . you look different. Your skin's so smooth."

"I don't look 'different.' And nothing's happened."

Selva brushed by her to the adjoining bedroom which they shared together. She slammed the door, bolted it. She did not come out for lunch, nor until, two hours later, she heard Clay Mulloy and his second packer pull out for town with the horses.

eleven

That night there was no moon and the stars were hidden by low lying clouds. Under the clouds, behind them, the mountains stood unseen but palpable as the walls of a room where one sat alone in darkness waiting for the door to open.

Clay and his second packer, an older man with a black moustache who several times had been about to speak but had thought better of it and instead had spat tobacco juice, before pulling out for Yellowhead had sawed and split a stack of wood and at ten o'clock as it grew dark, Selva and Rosie, tired after their day's work, were seated before the great stone fireplace which, rising to the vaulted ceiling, made an informal division between the dining room and the front half of the chalet. Rosie, legs folded, was on a blanket covered couch, eyes drowsy against the flames. Behind her, in disorder, were another couch, chairs, two tables, all built of knotted and twisted pine wood, each piece carefully chosen for its purpose in a lower valley. Upon the table and upon the floor were piled more blankets, pillows, rugs of wolf and bear, mounted heads of caribou, sheep and goat to be laid and spread and hung in the later settling of the room. The men had carried mattresses and beds to the two two-roomed sleeping cabins which adjoined the chalet proper.

Indoors was warmth and light. Outside, wind buffeted the

log walls. The forest moaned and breathed in great sighs of suffering. From the heights above came an occasional rumble and roar as an avalanche loosened by snow lately fallen or by the noonday thaw hurled its might into the valley, tossed echoes to the peaks, as though up there, far above the tree tops, giants haphazardly disputed using rocks for words and mountain crests for phrases. The chalet shook. The flame of the single candle upon the table top trembled, crouched, then reached again, clear and steady for the ceiling and the chalet with its burden of light, like a ship on the sea, like a thought in the night, rode on into the vastness of time.

"Did you hear?" Rosie asked.

"Those were rocks sliding."

"It sounded like thunder."

Selva's musings, before the crackling fire of spruce logs, had strayed far away. They were with her half brother and sister now asleep in the homestead in the foothills and they were in the Wamboldts' kitchen and in the beaver meadow where Peter Wrogg lurched from behind a swaying willow and they marched with her into the lobby of a Montreal hotel. Nearer to her, they were on the ridge where in the morning she had galloped and at the timber's edge where Clay's arms had been around her. Then she found herself recalling an afternoon of years before when she had gone walking in the woods with her half brother, Robert. The poplar leaves had turned and shed a yellow glow upon his freckled face and burnished the auburn of his tousled hair. She and Robert lay for a while on a slope of grass and stared up to fleecy clouds drifting under a high blue sky. In the clouds they pointed out to one another the forms of bears and wolves and horses. Then they fell silent, each seeing what was his alone. Selva had seen great castles rise and ships full-sailed and armies triumphant with banners and choirs of white robed angels singing — all drifting by on the wind above her. Cities grew there, tall with turrets, and perished in their building, and again, faces of men appeared with beards like God, and she had held herself very quiet and felt the earth turning beneath her and looked up into God's face and seen that it was her own.

Rosie's question broke into her musing, brought her thoughts back to the chalet, into embattled loneliness where mountains contended. But only for a moment until they went forward from her. There she could not see. Today that was passing, yesterday that was gone, these she could see for they were before her. The future which she could not see was behind her, hot against her shoulder, yet she could not turn her head to see into it. Like all mankind, eyes fixed along the narrow corridor through which she had come, she was forever backing out the doorway of the instant. As she moved, doorway and threshold moved with her. The corridor stretched farther, grew dimmer, while backward she pressed against the dark and urgent tumult of tomorrow.

"I know it's not thunder," Rosie, on the other side of the fireplace, was saying. "Still, it shakes the house and sounds like thunder. It makes me scared."

Selva replied, "You'll get used to it. There'll be lots of slides during the summer."

"Thunder reminds me of things I want to forget," Rosie said.

Rosie had been twelve when her mother died. The little girl with her pale cheeks, her faded, straggling hair, had been taken by her father and lodged in a convent in Edmonton. He had then gone down north to the Yellowknife where finds of gold were being made. The last she knew of him, he had been working as a bridge builder in the Yukon. She grew up in the convent in the fear of hooded nuns and priests and a vengeful God, having as reward when she was older, the washing of pans in sculleries, the scrubbing of floors in hallways and kitchens, the cooking of meals on farms, the making of beds and the waiting on tables in two storeyed, frame built hotels on the prairies and in the mountains.

"And then," she said to Selva, raising a timid voice to be heard above the gust of wind which beat against the chalet, "this night I was telling you about in Red Deer. It was two years ago. I was only seventeen and I didn't know anything — you know what I mean. Still, it seems lots longer ago than just two years ago." She paused, stared wide eyed into the fire.

To the hotel in Red Deer where Rosie served on table, four men drove up one late afternoon from the south. They were young, but they all wore beards because High River, where they came from, was celebrating an anniversary and with beards and gunbelts and high heeled boots they were out to represent men of the early days. "Of course," Rosie said, "I ought to have known better and when one of them, he seemed younger, his beard was so fair and sort of golden, when he asked me in a whisper when I was bringing in the coffee to meet him on the north edge of town, I didn't say no and I didn't say yes. It was a warm night though and it seemed it would be nice to go for a drive in the car."

But when Rosie, after her work was done, had walked the half mile to the edge of town and the car pulled up along the dusty road, she saw that four men rather than one were in it. She drew back, she turned away. The fair bearded man and one other got out, took hold of her arms, talked to her persuaded her. They would not go far, they said, only as far as the lake, then they would come back. "And the way they had hold of my arms," Rosie said, "I knew they weren't going to let go in a hurry. And, anyway, with four of them, it looked safer to me than if there had been only one."

At first in the car, which had turned off the highway along a side road to the lake, Rosie, who had not drunk before, refused the whiskey bottle. The two men in the back seat with her, the fair beard on her left, a dark one on her right, persisted. Just a sip, they urged, to taste it. It could do no harm. Then suddenly one man held her and the other tipped the bottle into her mouth. As she swallowed, half choking, and the liquor scalded her throat, she heard distant thunder, like empty wagons rumbling over a loose corduroy road. The day had been sultry. Now it was coming on to storm. They forced another drink and then another down her throat until in the bouncing, reeling car, the prairie reaching out on every side, the sky overhead scarred by blue lightning, she was singing with them the chorus of "Hallalujah! I'm a bum, bum! Hallelujah, bum again!" Then later she passed out, bearded lips imposed upon her own.

She awoke in a field by the roadside. The thunder had awakened her or the rain and the hail on her upturned face. Her gingham dress was soaked. "But it was more than just being soaked," she continued, speaking to Selva. "I was sore. I was bleeding. It was the first time and I didn't even know which one or how many had done it. There were those four men, all with beards. It was like one face with four men

144

behind it."

Rosie spoke dispassionately as though what she related had not happened to her at all but, perhaps, to a friend known to her grandmother in her grandmother's youth. Yet Selva felt her hurt, felt the outrage she could not express and rose with her from the field — the car had doubled back and left her less than a mile from town — rose with her and walked with her beneath the thunder and through the storm along the road and crouched with her by a hedge and took shelter with her for five minutes by a storekeeper's window before she crossed the street and groped her way through the back door of the hotel and up the stairway to her room.

"Of course, in the morning," Rosie said, "the men weren't in the dining room. They hadn't even registered. They had only stopped for supper. They had gone on to Edmonton or back to where they came from."

Nor had Rosie herself been able to go into the dining-room. She had been sick to her stomach and the upstairs maid, an older woman, to whom she told her story, had forced her to go to bed and the next month lent her money to go into Edmonton where, in a shack on the flats by the Saskatchewan River, a midwife, practising below the town and beyond the law, had given her the care she asked for.

"My God!" Selva gasped as Rosie finished her story. Involuntarily she rose from her chair, stepped over to the couch, sat down and put her arm around Rosie's shoulder. Rosie held herself from her, rigid, unyielding, "It's all over now," she said. "It was two years ago. I cried about it then. I don't cry about it now and I would never have told it to you at all except for us being up here all alone and hearing those slides that reminded me of thunder. I'll never forget the thunder that night as long as I live. A farmer was hit going from his barn to his house. Burned to a crisp, they said."

Selva gazed for long moments into the fire, watching the slow growth of glowing caverns beneath the logs, aware of night, an auditor beyond the window. Shame and pain, as if Rosie's experience had been her own, were deep within her and she remembered with an added pang her own first time. It had been with Slim the previous fall after a dance above the pool hall. They had stopped in the grove of pine trees in the Wamboldts' yard and she recalled the experience now as a struggle not so much with a man as with a force, tangible and excessive, born of the night and the rage of music at the dance. And afterwards in her bed, like Rosie, she too had cried because she had expected more than she had received, a revelation that had been denied her. Always with Slim that revelation, that light which would throw no shadow, that mingling with the rhythm of wind and rivers, of losing herself, becoming less that she might become more — always that had remained just beyond her touch, her body reluctant to surrender its secret. Now in the High Valley, after the gallop along the ridge, and Clay's arms holding her, she had experienced, if not all, at least what she had never known before. He had brought her to the entrance of the valley.

Rosie had been raped by four men behind a beard. Slim had worn no beard yet, for all the time she had been with him, he moved within his own anonymity, invulnerable to her touch, impenetrable to her further knowledge. Rosie had knocked upon a midwife's door in the flat below the foothill town. Selva felt a qualm, a tightening of her bowls. She was like a climber precariously poised upon the mountain side. Below her in the timber where she might fall were Rosie and the four bearded men. Behind them, underneath a tree, was Slim, a grin upon his face. Above, on the heights where clean winds blew, was Peter Wrogg. He called her on, pointed out to her the path of her ascent, but his words coming to her were spent, their meaning spilled on the air, and he himself, when she looked up, was only a figure shrouded in swirling mist. Ahead, level with her, on the edge of the forest's upmost reach, where beyond, illimitable and green, stretched the rolling alplands, stood Clay Mulloy. He did not beckon. He did not call. He merely waited for her.

As the fire burned low, as the chalet chilled, she and Rosie went to their bedroom off the kitchen and in the morning she awoke to hear Rosie singing by the stove. The night of thunder and violation and of four bearded men was behind her. Her tears were dry and she sang "Ave Maria," a song learned in the convent. Here in the High Valley, she had attained a freedom and a joy of doing that she had never known before. Instead of walking, she ran or skipped. Rather than be silent at her tasks, she would sing. As she sang, her voice no longer thin or timid, her throat swelled and the song she uttered was a portion of herself surrendered in gladness to the world like the song of a thrush on a bough. Selva in the bedroom envied her her song, envied her her well being, her imperviousness to injustice, her acceptance of today and forgetfulness of tomorrow. Like a rubber ball tossed down a hillside, Rosie would bounce until she hit the bottom.

She was still bouncing, going from table to stove to sink in the kitchen, humming to herself as she did so when, a week later, Selva called her out to the front steps to watch the approach of the season's first tourists from over Crooked Pass. In the chalet the fire was again laid in the fireplace. In the kitchen, Jimmie Bright, the sixteen year old boy sent up from Yellowhead as a helper, had stacked split spruce and balsam by the stove, filled the moisture beaded pails with clear cold water from the nearby creek. On the stove the kettle simmered and the kitchen was sweet with the smell of Rosie's newly baked bread. In the dining-room the table was set with linen and light white china for afternoon tea, for its centrepiece, a cluster of sprawling and shiny leafed kinnikinic cut that morning by Selva in the forest. On the chalet walls the mounted heads had been hung and pillows and blankets distributed on the couches. In the two cabins set apart among the trees, the eight twin beds were made and in one of the rooms, white sheets were turned back over red blankets. On the wash-stand the heavy china pitcher was full to the brim and new towels, freshly laundered to remove the stiffness, were hung upon the rack under the window where the morning sun would enter. A soft wolf rug lay on the floor between the two beds and above it, against the wall, a table, fashioned from native wood, bore two tall candles in a branched and varnished holder. Selva thought that the chalet offered soft comfort after mountain journeys.

"I hope everything is going to be all right," Rosie, now beside her, said, squinting up toward the pass. "Anyway, we've worked hard to make it all right."

"It'll take them an hour to get here," Selva said. "Be sure that your buns are hot. And don't put the jam on the table in its tin. Serve it in the little cut glass dish I showed you. And don't make your tea so strong. Make it with fresh boiling water, not water that's been boiling all afternoon in the kettle and bring the teapot to the kettle, not the kettle to

147

the teapot."

Speaking to Rosie, she was only repeating instructions given many times by Mrs. Wamboldt, so many times, indeed, that she had grown weary of their repetition. Now it was as though she did not speak to Rosie at all. She merely addressed herself of former days.

"You told me all that before," Rosie said, "and that I'm to serve from their left at supper and take away from their right. I learned that anyway when I was at the hotel."

"You didn't learn to serve in rubber sneakers. You'd better go in and change your shoes and put on a clean apron and tidy up your hair. It's crawling all over the back of your neck. And don't bite your fingernails all the time." Selva, recalling Rosie's story of the night before, rebuked herself for her harshness. She would be more gentle with Rosie.

"I won't. I mean, I was going to go in and change, but there's lots of time. You just said so yourself. They're up there so high they don't seem like people at all."

The riders — Selva counted three of them, one in advance with three pack ponies and the others following — were just now dropping down below the snow line. Up there so high they did not so much resemble animals and people as a minute trickle of life inexplicably manifest upon the mountain. Soon they would be swallowed by the timber after an hour to appear, perhaps with laughter, with calls to one another and with the whinnying of horses, the striking of an iron shoe on rock and the creaking of saddle leather in the clearing before the chalet, bringing with them a breath of the outside beyond the passes and a sense of surprise that they should appear at all, seeming not to have travelled but rather to have lost their identity for a while in the forest, to have been dormant in its greenery, and then to have been magically re-created and given the arms and legs and faces lacking to them on the slope beneath the snow.

"I wonder what they'll be like," Rosie said.

"I showed you the note Mr. Wilkins sent up with Jimmie. It's a man and his wife from Minneapolis. They're only going to be here four days. They've got a boat to catch in Vancouver."

"But I mean, really like, not where they come from. Maybe they're old and maybe they're young. Maybe they've got lots of money for tips and maybe they haven't."

"They've got enough money to come up here at fifteen dollars a day apiece."

"And maybe that fellow Clay Mulloy's bringing them in," Rosie said with a quick glance at Selva before turning to run up the steps into the chalet.

Selva followed and in the bedroom changed from her work dress into a blue flannel shirt, shoving the long tails into the top of her grey whip-cord trousers. She combed her hair, the comb pulling at strong roots, making her scalp tingle. She combed it back loosely, letting it fall lightly in a reverse roll over her forehead so that, in the mirror, her brown eyes appeared withdrawn and secretive. Around her neck she tied, in the horseman's style, a white silk handkerchief, tucking its ends into the open collar of her shirt. Then, for fifteen minutes, she cleaned and polished her fingernails.

She was agitated, at once shy and expectant before the advent of these two strangers from over the passes, people from the city accustomed to good things who knew their way about big hotels and department stores, who had money and had come so far to spend it and to look on trees and mountains. At times she had experienced the same excitement wearing a new dress to a dance. But now she was not going out. She was receiving. She was receiving in the greatest house she had ever been in, in the High Valley, with the blue sky for ceiling, hanging glacier and lofty rock for walls and at her feet, the green carpet of moss and grass. She went here and there in the chalet, settling the fold of a curtain, touching a cushion, flicking with a duster at a polished table top. Finally she ran down to the cabin, smoothed again the bed, set matches by the candle holder and in the outhouse behind, still unused and smelling of the earth, hung a roll of virgin white.

Later as she stood by the hitching-rail in front of the chalet and the tourists, led by Clay Mulloy, rode from the forest into the clearing, she saw that they were not at all the people she had prepared for. Their appearance did not bespeak wealth nor position, nor did their faces reflect the gaiety in her own. Mr. and Mrs. Arnold Prior of Minneapolis, Minnesota, were grey haired and past their fifties. They were hatless and wore high laced boots, khaki breeches and jackets. She was short, thin, prim, her lips snapped shut like a purse. He, dismounting, was tall, erect and reserved as a grandfather's clock. When Clay, after helping his wife from her horse, introduced him to Selva, calling her "Miss Williams," Mr. Prior hesitated, made a whirring sound in his throat, as though, instead of speaking, he would strike twelve o'clock. at last he accepted Selva's outstretched hand, mumbled a greeting. When she turned to his wife, realizing that it was she to whom she should have been in the first place introduced, Mr. Prior said gruffly, "Deaf. She won't hear you." But Mrs. Prior took Selva's hand. Her face unlocked and crinkled as though she were about to cry. She said, "How are you, dear? I'm so happy to meet you."

Selva said quickly to Mr. Prior who stood rubbing his long jaw, "I'll show you and Mrs. Prior to your cabin. You must be tired. You can wash up and then come over to the chalet. We have tea ready for you. Clay will bring your dunnage down to the cabin."

She looked across to Clay, found his travel driven face with its moist outthrust lower lip above a rumpled pack cover which he was slipping from a horse's back. He arrested his gloved hand, left it there before him. The grey eyes that seemed older than the rest of him did not glance. They penetrated. In the instant they held her, saw through her, and Selva felt herself impaled, revealed for inspection like a butterfly pierced by a pin. The eyes reminded her that he had not forgotten, that he would not let her forget, and she was again on the moss by the timber beyond the meadows with a white cloud above, the wind chill between her thighs and her white pants, her secret part, pressed against a balsam vine. A tremor ran through her. She shook herself and with an effort took her eyes from those beyond the rumpled pack cover. She moved away, called over her shoulder, "Clay — did you hear? Bring the dunnage down to the first cabin, the one with the pink curtains in the window."

"Yes," he said slowly, "I'll bring the dunnage down." She went with the Priors, left him with his horses, his pack covers, his hooks, his tangled ropes, heard him grunt as he set a loaded pannier on the ground by the hitching rail.

Afterwards, during tea, tea with sugar, and buns fresh from the oven served with butter and raspberry jam, Selva, between Mr. and Mrs. Prior, sat at the head of the table by the window, her tawny head of hair framed by snowtopped mountains. Clay came in on moccasined feet, fringes of his buckskin jacket quivering, tossed his hat upon a chair and, like a man setting himself down to his own table after work, took his place opposite to her. Selva was about to tell him that Rosie had his tea ready in the kitchen which was where she had supposed the guides would eat. She thought better of it. He would not have moved. He would have smiled ever so slightly at the suggestion. Also she remembered that it was due to him that she was where she was. The Priors too looked upon it as a matter of course that he should sit with them. They had camped and eaten together on the trail. During the summer Selva learned that Clay and the other guides ate at the table with the tourists and not standing up in the kitchen. Horsemen were a proud people.

Mr. Prior was interested in winter travel and in how a man cared for himself outdoors in snow and cold. Clay answered briefly. He seemed preoccupied, concerned, his bronzed forehead ploughed with thoughts.

Then he said with sudden interest, "I'm planning a winter trip myself this year, into the Fry Pan Mountains. I'll go in in the fall. I'll build a cabin. I'll stay the winter to look things over."

Mr. Prior raised a heavy eyebrow. "Fry Pan — it's a queer name for mountains."

"They're on the map," Clay said, "up north in British Columbia. They're real enough, big mountains waiting for someone to go in and look after them. A good place, I figure, for a man to set up an outfit of his own. It's new country, big game country." Now he no longer addressed Mr. Prior, nor had he tried to include in his remarks Mrs. Prior who sat, stiff-backed, impregnable in her cell of silence. His eyes caught Selva's.

She met their challenge grimly. She would show him. He would learn, he and his Fry Pan Mountains. The very name carried insult within it. It brought back to her the grease of the station restaurant, the stout, bullying cook by the stove, the glint of nickel and the imposed order of the Wamboldt kitchen until she saw the Fry Pans as only a vaster kitchen, more vastly steaming, with higher and darker walls which brooked no scaling and herself, a lost and forever diligent morsel of life contained within them. But the man was as imperturbable as his fabulous mountains. He would take for granted — she was sure that he would take for granted — that for which he lacked even the privilege of asking and regard as a beginning what at its most had been a moment of thoughtfulness. Besides, other people would be coming over the pass during the summer and it was with them that she would pass her time. They were people for whom the mountains were a holiday, not labour and sweat and the worry of straying horses. She would go riding with them, sit with them beside the trail, talk at table and before the fire, talk of cities and the opportunities there for a girl who knew how to wear her clothes, conduct herself as she should in company, a girl whose eyes were alight with hope and, in a later minute, sombre with its shadow. She thought again of Peter. Peter would come. He must come soon, Peter with his curly hair, his reluctant smile and his soothing words of promise. Somehow, in some manner, when he came, if he came, Peter would have the answer.

The Priors rose from the table and passed into the front room. Selva went to the kitchen to speak to Rosie about supper. Rosie had gone out to the root house. Selva, thinking to return in a few minutes, turned to go back to the dining-room. Clay Mulloy blocked the doorway. He came closer to her. The furred back of his hand, hanging at his side, touched her own.

"You heard what I said about the Fry Pans," he said to her.

"What's it got to do with me?"

"You know what it's got to do with you. I'm not going up there alone and begin answering back when I talk to myself. Besides, you'd like it. You like country. Most women don't. You'd like it up there."

"Suppose you let me decide what I like and what I don't like."

"Would you like to go for a walk then?" His hand pressed closer at her side. She drew her hand away.

"You know I can't got for a walk. I've got things to do, the Priors, and to help Rosie with supper."

"After supper then . . ."

"Say, what are you two whispering about?" Rosie's voice

came sharply. She had returned from the root house and — a head of cabbage in her hand — was closing behind her the door.

Clay, without a pause, said, "I just came by to see how you girls are making out — and to sample one of these." he reached over to the sideboard to a plate of ginger snaps. He put one into his mouth, bit into it, munched. "Good!" he exclaimed.

"You leave those where they are," Rosie said, approaching him with upraised hand. "You've had your tea. Those are for the people."

"What the Hell do you think I am — a kangaroo?" Clay took another ginger snap and retreated into the dining-room, one hand jingling coins in his pocket.

"He must think he owns the place," Rosie muttered. "And I don't like people in the kitchen when I'm starting to get supper."

"All right," Selva said. "I'll come in later then to make the coffee."

"I know how to make coffee," Rosie retorted. "Put it in cold water and bring it slowly to a boil and add a pinch of salt. You told me that when we first came up here. That's how Mrs. Wamboldt made it. You'd think you were still working for her."

"I'm just nervous, I guess. I want everything to be all right so that there won't be any complaints from the people." Selva left the kitchen. She went to ask the Priors what they would like to do while they were in the High Valley.

Not that evening, nor the next, nor the one following, did she go walking with Clay. Mornings and evenings he walked out to the meadows scattered here and there through the timber to look at his horses, returning to sit, whittling a stick on the chalet steps or to lie in his bedroll in the tepee set up behind the chalet for the guides and Jimmie Bright, the chore-boy sent in from town. Selva kept close to the Priors. They desired no program of activity. They did not climb mountains and they were still saddlesore from their ride coming in over the passes. They planned to stroll, to take pictures. They were well able to care for themselves.

The second evening, after having walked with them down to the lake, Selva stood with Mr. Prior on the porch of their cabin into which Mrs. Prior had entered to find a warmer wrap. Mr. Prior, looking over Selva's head, over the tree tops to the lakeshore where they had been, said slowly, "You see, it's a promise I made long ago." He was old. Time had run through him and his dark eyes were weary. His voice, recovered from its preliminary stutterings, was measured as though he could use only so much of it for any occasion.

"Long ago," he continued, "when we first were married. That would be almost forty years ago. The years go by very quickly, you know. And business too. We did not realize how quickly until the boys were married and had children of their own. But I had not forgotten my promise, nor had Mrs. Prior forgotten that I had made it. Now, on our first long vacation together, we are on our way to Burma."

"Burma?"

"Yes, across the Pacific, and I thought we should stop off here so that she could get used to it. I mean, by riding horseback first."

His eyes dropped, rested tolerantly on Selva. "You see, in Burma she is going to ride in a howdah chair on an elephant's back. That is the promise I made to her because when I was a boy I read somewhere that elephants there wear tiny bells and that they tinkle on their harness as they go along through the jungle."

Mrs. Prior came up beside them, a plaid shawl over her shoulders. "I suppose," she said to Selva — speaking loudly from behind her wall of deafness — "he's telling you about Burma. He's been telling everyone all the way across on the train — and I don't even know where Burma is, except that you get there by boat from Vancouver." She added in a lower, confidential voice, "Of course, I could find it on a map, but Mr. Prior doesn't want me to. He wants it to be a surprise." Once more her face crinkled into a smile, closer to tears than mirth.

Then she was silent and her husband's hand, with its knotted veins and its skin, brown and wrinkled like used wrapping paper, rose as of its own volition and gently stroked her grey head without, however, disturbing the little nest of velvet violets which, before supper, she had tucked in above her ear.

Selva, regarding them, felt an urge to stamp her foot, to

cry out to Mr. Prior who wished to surprise his wife with part of the sub-continent of Asia, "But she's deaf. She won't be able to hear the bells in Burma. You've waited too long. And the bells, even if she could hear them, will come to you now from far away, from long ago." The Priors would return to Minneapolis having discovered only what was forever lost. Even as they stood on the cabin porch, horse bells were tinkling down in the meadow, making mountain music for all horsemen who could hear them. But they were too close. The Priors did not hear them. They had ears only for the sound of a *distant* bell . . .

Selva left them in the gloaming on the porch, but she was to remember them through the summer, to remember them as they walked hand-in-hand beside the timber, along the lake, diminutive beneath the peaks, two children searching for a dream beneath a blade of grass or seeking God within the forest's gloom, within the vaulted, the untenated cathedral of the mountains. She was to remember them plodding back towards the chalet while the lowering sun shone pink on snow and glacier, sparkled on a waterfall and on the lake laid its evening benediction. Mrs. Prior, face flushed against it, paused for breath. She and her husband had gone down together, hand-in-hand. They returned up the slope separately, their backward shadows stretching long as memory, without speech to spare their wind or as if, down by the waters, each had found a truth to meditate upon.

The Priors were neither the "expensive people" of Rosie's imaginings, nor of the magazine advertisements. Undoubtedly they had money, though they made no show of having it. They were simple people, old people, inquiring for the bells of their youth, bells in the jungles of far off Burma.

twelve

During the next two months, Selva was to stand behind the chalet window on the chalet steps and watch many others climb up to supper from their afternoon by the lake or ride down to tea from the passes. She was to stand at the hitching-rail and greet them when they came in from town and again to wish them a good journey when they left to return. Indeed, the summer was to be but a series of beginnings, a life lived between arrivals and departures. She was to become familiar with the names of other guides than Clay — George, Sam, Dick and Harry, and with their strings of horses. Slim Conway did not appear. He had gone south to ride in the Calgary Stampede. When his prize money was spent, he would come back. Nor, after going out with the Priors, did Clay return until more than six weeks had passed. He was packing for a party of climbers far in behind Mount Robson.

A week after the Priors had left, one of the other guides, the older man with the drooping black moustache and the tobacco-bulged cheek, bringing in three women school teachers from Boston, delivered to Selva a package tied with a rawhide thong. "Clay told me to give it to you," he said.

The package held a beaded caribou hide vest bleached white and pounded by an Indian woman until it was soft as kid. Folded in its lower pocket was a note pencilled on a piece of wrapping paper. The letters were blocked and pressed so hard into the paper that in places the pencil had cut entirely through it. The note read, "To temper the wind when you go riding." It was signed "Clay." Selva hung the vest in her bedroom. For two weeks she did not put it on.

The school teachers went away, their beds in the cabins, their seats at the table to be taken by others — by tourists who came from Philadelphia, New York and Baltimore, from the Mid-West and from California, singly, in pairs, in threes and fours, in family groups until, by the middle of August, close to two hundred signatures were scrawled upon the pages of the guest book on the table inside the chalet door. They came, the young, the old, the middle-aged, though the young were few and none of the tourists was so old as the Priors. Most of them were middle-aged. The young lacked the time. They had not made the money. They had still to hear a bell receding into the distant past.

Middle-aged, those who came were also, for the most part, of middle means. They were well off, but not wealthy. The wealthy generally hired their own outfits, guides, horse-wranglers and cooks and went farther back into the mountains. Man and woman, young and old, with an exception here and there, came to the chalet wearing khaki breeches and shirts, high laced boots with upturned toes, uniformed for their holiday as though, if necessary, they were prepared to do battle for it. Canadians for the two months of summer had abandoned their mountains to the invader from across the border who arrived armed with money, with reservations and, above all, with cameras with which to carry off the scenery. Tourists were mass produced in the cities for the purpose of using up rolls of film whose yellow boxes and tin-foil soon littered the trails and the chalet clearing. Memory of where they had been, perception of what they saw, were provided for them, factory-made in a small black box, strapped to their bellies, stowed away in their pockets, to be taken out or banished at their will.

They snapped pictures. They asked questions. Under the peaks whose icy summits sparkled with sun kindled fire, they played bridge before the fireplace in the chalet.

In late July a man came through alone who carried no camera. Instead of a camera he carried an ice-axe and instead of the tourist's high laced boots, he wore ankle length boots with Swiss climbing nails around the edges of their thick soles. He was a New Zealander, the only one to appear during the summer, and his general bearing of aloofness, the intonations of his voice, the clipped phrases, reminded Selva of Peter Wrogg. But Mr. Branchflower, short, thick-set, was a man in his late forties or early fifties, a narrow line of darkness grasped between his busy eyebrows, head outthrust as though he were in search of, and in despair of ever finding, what long ago had fallen at his feet. Those feet with their armoured boots were heavy. Coming in the door he stopped, stamped once, twice, three times with his heels, rasped a wide calloused palm over his short cropped steel grey hair, took off his gloves and looked about as if for someone he could toss them to.

He went for long walks by himself, sometimes overnight, missing his meals. At other times he would sit for hours studying with his glasses the slopes of Mount Erebus which lifted almost five thousand feet above the valley floor. One Saturday evening he was absent from supper, nor that night did he sleep in his bed. But then he had been away at night before. On Monday noon he was again at the table with Selva and a shoe merchant and his wife from Philadelphia. He had bathed, shaved, changed into tweeds and soft brown shoes. He seemed refreshed, the crease gone from between his eyebrows, his cheeks burned brick red with the sun.

Selva said to him, "We were worried. I was going to ask one of the men to go out and look for you."

Mr. Branchflower smiled. He usually smiled just before he spoke, showing small and worn yellow teeth tight beneath his trim moustache.

"To look for me?" he asked.

"We missed you at meals yesterday and this morning at breakfast."

"Oh, that!" Mr. Branchflower waved his right hand as if a fly had come between him and his beef stew. "I went for a stroll," he said.

Selva waited. He did not add to his remark.

However, Mr. Scoreby, the shoe merchant from Philadelphia, a man with a round red and perspiring face which looked as though it had been boiled and then set aside to simmer slowly, was inquisitive. He moved his thick legs under the table and inquired bluntly, "Where did you stroll to?"

Mr. Branchflower put back on his plate the piece of meat which with his fork he had been lifting to his mouth. He studied the man across from him, then turned to regard Mrs. Scoreby. Apparently finding little there to hold his interest, he addressed himself once more to his questioner, opened his mouth to speak, thought better of it and went on with his meal, his teeth crunching a piece of gristle.

After lunch he called Selva outdoors. He took her a few steps away from the chalet, bade her sit with her back against a gnarled spruce tree. He gave her his field glasses, showed her how to adjust them and to hold them with her elbows on her knees.

"Now," he said, "I want you to look up on that peak and see what wasn't there before." The peak was Mount Erebus below which she and Clay Mulloy had sat in June, the peak whose rocks four years before had dashed to their death a climber and his guide.

"I don't see anything," Selva said. "Anyway, no one's ever been up to its top."

"Look more closely. You will see a cairn."

A white cloud lay pillowed sleeping against the mountain. Above it at last, she saw the cairn, a dot, no more, a period set by man's endeavour in the sky. She took her eyes from the glasses, looked up at Mr. Branchflower. Lips drawn back from his teeth, breath hissing as though he still were climbing, he gazed up at the mountain.

Mr. Branchflower's "stroll" had taken him to the top of Mount Erebus. He had simply put his bed roll, his sweetened chocolate bars, his raisins, his flask of brandy into his pack and climbed to where no man had been before him. "Not too difficult at all," he said to Selva. "That is, of course, if you have had experience. But for no one else. Remember, for no one else. One bad pitch just below the ten thousand foot level. After that . . . not bad at all." He said no more. No more remained to be said. Selva rose. He patted her shoulder several times quickly with his heavy hand as he might have patted a horse's withers. Looking up at the mountain, neighbour to the sky, Selva conceived that the man beside her was not ordinary flesh and bone. He was strung on a frame of steel and for nerves he had piano wire.

Mr. Branchflower stepped back a pace. He took from his jacket pocket a stubby briar pipe and pushing its head into a leather pouch, commenced to fill it, slowly, methodically, but without taking his eyes from Selva's face, head lowered, regarding her from under his thick eyebrows as if, with the ram of his broad shoulders, he were about to charge.

"What is your name?" he asked.

"Williams."

"I know that. I refer to your given name."

"Selva."

"Selva," he repeated. "Selva. Hmm. Odd sort of name. Like Sylvia. Means forest too. It is the Spanish word for forest."

Clenching his pipe stem grimly between his teeth, he lit the pipe, took it from his mouth, exhaled and waving the pipe to indicate the surrounding mountains, asked, "How long have you been here?"

"Not very long," Selva said. "I was brought up in the foothills."

"Hmm, I see. Like it?"

For answer, she looked away.

"I see," Mr. Branchflower said, "Usual thing. Want to get away. The city. Bright lights. People. Glitter. They come up here. You want to go there."

After a pause, he inquired, "Father?"

"I don't understand," Selva said.

"Your father — what does he do?"

Selva did not take the question to be unkind. She answered steadily, "I have never seen my father. The man my mother married is named Williams. He has a homestead in the foothills below Rocky Mountain House."

Looking away again, she bit her lower lip.

Her father, she thought, might have been a man very like Mr. Branchflower whose hand now touched her shoulder, this time lightly, lightly. "I am sorry," he said, "very, very sorry. I do not intend to intrude, nor to be rude."

Selva, groping for words, seeking to return the conversation to its former impersonal level, said, "I have a friend who likes to climb mountains too. He is a young Englishman."

"He does, eh? And what has he climbed?"

Selva did not know what Peter Wrogg had climbed. He had told her only that he had climbed in Switzerland. She explained to Mr. Branchflower that they had met at a dance in Yellowhead and that Peter had subsequently gone down to the Coast. "I'll probably see him," she said, "on his way back east." Hope, but not assurance, was in her voice.

Mr. Branchflower had stepped back a pace and, as he looked at her, the little blue bags under his eyes seemed to puff out and when he spoke it was as though he addressed not her, but himself.

"Met him at a dance, eh? Keen on him, are you?" he asked. His eyes, accompanying his thought rather than his words, moved up and down, measuring her, assessing her worth as if she were on display in a store window.

"Peter is very pleasant to be with," Selva replied, flushing under Mr. Branchflower's gaze. She turned now to go back to the chalet.

He touched her arm. "No hurry, is there?" he inquired. "Stupid people, that shoe merchant and his wife. They'll be quite all right by themselves for a time."

He coughed lightly. He came closer. He said, "Tonight — let us say about ten o'clock — I will be in my cabin. If you should come down that way, we might have a spot of whiskey together."

Selva drew back. She said, "Really Mr. Branchflower, I . . ."

He interrupted, "Nothing wrong with it, is there? A little drink. Quite above board. You can tell me more about this young English chap. No harm in that, is there?"

When she demurred, he touched her arm once more. It was more a nudge than a touch and aroused her resentment. "Ten o'clock, then it is," he said. "No need to knock. I'll be waiting there for you."

Mr. Branchflower's cabin was the farther of the two from the chalet, the first being occupied by the shoe merchant and his wife. At midnight from her bedroom Selva saw his candle flame still glowing through the window.

In the morning to avoid meeting him at breakfast, she left the chalet early. She walked a mile down to a little pool rimmed by moss in the timber by the meadow where the horses grazed. She took off her clothes, stripped herself even to the signet ring her mother had given to her when she was young, piled the clothes, the signet ring on top, on the moss, and with only the spruce trees watching, immersed herself in the cold water.

When she returned to the chalet, Mr. Branchflower had left with his guide for town.

Weeks later, in the Sunday section of a Vancouver newspaper discarded on a table in the chalet, Selva was to learn that Cornelius J. Branchflower of Christchurch, New Zealand, to whom was credited the first ascent of Mount Erebus in the Canadian Rockies, was known internationally for his solitary climbs. Alone, disdaining the help of an alpine guide, he had made first ascents in the Austrian Tyrol, the Russian Caucasus and in the New Zealand Alps. Leaving the Rockies, he had now gone south to climb in the Andes of South America, one of the race of men who find the earth forever hot beneath their foot soles.

On the day of his departure from the chalet, he had written four lines of verse beneath his name in the guest book:

> "Wanderers eastward, wanderers west,
> Know you why you cannot rest?
> 'Tis that every mother's son
> Travails with a skeleton."

Mr. Branchflower had come to the High Valley, taken what he referred to as a "stroll," and won a mountain and gone away as happy as it was given to him to be. He had come with an object in mind. Achieving it, he had left. What was the object of the others who preceded him, who came after him, tourists who did not climb mountains? Perhaps they rode the trails and suffered in the saddle. They fished in stream and lake. They sat in the sun and looked up at the mountains. They felt the lack of running water. Here it ran in streams and not in lead-joined pipes. Mountains, they complained, were higher in California and there they could be reached by car. Yet they came. They came, they signed the guest book and they went away. Wanderers eastward, wanderers west, they came, they went away.

Little man with your camera, your upturned boot toes and your carefully nourished rotundity, with your toothpaste

163

and your brushless shaving soap and your wife who in the dark cabin snores beside you, your wife with her Kleenex, her three kinds of facial cream and her sleeping pills — little man, what brittle skeleton stirs within you to bring you here? In San Francisco you have an office. You are in the advertising business. You are there in your office, adding your piddle to another's flow. You sit behind your desk, behind your glasses, your uneasy eyes shifting now here, now there, ready to see far into the future or, as the case may be, to scrutinize with an air of profundity the obvious and the close at hand. "P. R. Wurpering and Associates Limited," is your firm's title. They call you "Public Relations" Wurpering because of your initials and that, of course, is good for business. There at your desk you have buttons to push, secretaries to command and callers who read *Fortune* and wait patiently beyond your door. But here in the High Valley, it is you who wait beyond the door. It rains. Mist hangs low. There are no buttons to press, no secretary to respond. The mountains do not emerge for your camera at your summons. The mountains are in conference. They are busy. They have their heads together. They must not be disturbed. You will have to wait, like the callers beyond your door in San Francisco, for it is you who are now beyond the door. You will have to wait for an hour, for two hours, for a day, for two days, for a week or a month. And when the mist lifts, even then the door will not open. Here where winds are sired and rivers born, where mountains pillar a stubborn sky, where men ride long stirruped, tall growing in the saddle as though God's fists upheld them by the armpits — little man on horseback, your pudgy legs stick out, your feet flail the air. You will go away, back to your city with a purchased sunburn, a picture in your camera and a wife whose ass has been scalded red in the saddle. You will go away and you may wonder why you came at all to the High Valley and to the door barred against you.

And if it opened — what do you seek beyond the door? And if beyond the door, in the darkness or in the light, you stumbled upon what you seek, would you remember it from your mother's womb? And what is the door? Is the door what is beyond the door? And you there by the fireplace standing tall and gaunt and from Connecticut — is the riddle the only answer? Has the skeleton the answer deep within us? You now teach morals and philosophy in an eastern university. No buttons are yours to press. Rich in hours because your summers are long, you feel the skeleton stretch his limbs, you whose farm boyhood was on the prairies, who went East to learn, who returned West in the summers to work. Your work took you up into the mountains, chainman on a survey party. Your party climbed, built cairns upon and named the peaks along Alberta's western border. You knew this very valley. You come back now in retrospective pilgrimage after twenty years. And with you, your wife, the woman in the chair staring into the fire whose eyes are two black pools, whose cheeks, like twin pincushions, are puffed, are satin, and through whose brown hair time has once stroked his finger. Your wife has come with you. You wish to show her — what? The campfires that you used to sit beside? The boy who sat beside them? The dreams he had? All these are gone. Now she is the dream and you, you are the dream that then she had. The dream is now and here. There and there or here again. Between are twenty years. Is that the riddle, the door that will not open? It may be that, instead, you wish to divigate, to explain, to say, "But on the other hand . . . that is, if you look at it this way . . . And there are, of course, two sides to any . . ." After all, you left your boy who is studying to be a doctor — you left your boy at home. You did not bring him with you up to the High Valley of your boyhood.

And you, Miss Vera Wigglesworth, you who sit by yourself on the rock by the lakeshore in the twilight. It is chill. Tomorrow morning, frost, the age of the year, will be silver on the moss that is here around you. Still you sit. Like Mr. Branchflower who climbs mountains, you travel alone and, like the little man from San Francisco who is an advertising man and whose mouth with its fringe of moustache — he never shows his teeth when he smiles — uttering the obscenities, lies and brittle half truths of his business, is merely a Japanese or thwart-wise version of what it resembles — like him, you are an executive, but from New York and of a different sort. You produce. You make things that did not exist before. You are, let us say, a designer of women's clothes. You are no longer young — forty, perhaps a little more, but slim, erect and well preserved. You are always well dressed. No one could find fault with what you are at present wearing — the soft, hand-tooled boots, the breeches with their flare, the neat, silver buckled belt, the long brown tweed coat and the pink flannel skirt beneath it. And your hair, still blue-black, is swept carelessly up, combed meticulously back. The wrinkles in the skin beneath the earlobe, as though spiders had been working there, in the twilight are not easily discernible. Yet you sit alone. Not long ago in New York you sat across from the man in the ticket office with the yellow roar of Fifth Avenue beyond the window. His finger, lately manicured, held the pin pointed pencil with which he traced for you your journey across the continent. Then he showed you on a map of larger scale the High Valley and the surrounding country. The contour lines of the mountains ran together, making a solid black, indicating how steep they were. Now those contours are before you, are above you, crimsoned by the sun which has set. You know — everyone knows — that a mountain chalet such as that whose lights you see through the trees, is "a good place for men." But, you did not come to find a man precisely — not precisely, in the usual sense. That is a quest you abandoned some years ago. You do not need a man — in the usual sense. Your business is your own. You have money, twenty people working for you, such security as insecurity can give. No, you were brave enough to accept what would not last, an afternoon, perhaps part of a night beneath the stars. You thought it might be a guide — tough-sinewed, smelling of horse and sweat. Such a man, for instance, as he who brought you in from the railroad. He was not particularly tall, though he seemed tall. He told you his name was "Sam." He was lean as hunger and knew how to wear a hat. The clothes these guides wear are functional. They wear them well. Down there by the railroad, Sam adjusted your stirrups. He told you how he had his own. "Just so I can take my weight on them," was what he said. He commanded you to stand in yours to see that you had the proper clearance and not too much, holding his hand for a moment upon your knee. Then he mounted his horse and you followed behind the pack horses. During the trip into the High Valley he addressed you as "Ma'am." You were unable to break through this impersonal formality. Tomorrow you will ride back with him into town, over the passes. Meanwhile you sit here by the lake and no one, not Sam, nor one of the tourists — there are, it is true, only three married couples at the chalet — no one has come to sit beside you. You wonder why it is that you sit, as it were, before a door that does not open. Still, you have sat here before in other places. The experience is not a new one. Your bones, the skeleton within you, stir again with hope. You will get up now and go back to the chalet. There are people there, women and men, though they are married, and on your way you may meet Sam walking out to look after his horses. You remember too that there is another summer coming, always another summer, and other ticket offices on Fifth Avenue where next year you will call to make reservations. Next year, who knows, you may go to Alaska, to Mexico, to Jerusalem?

And you of the wondrous name, Mr. and Mrs. Robert Mountjoy. You come from Montreal and you are on your honeymoon. You have not been out West before. Your friends have always gone to England, "abroad," because that gave them "prestige" and more to talk about when they came back. You came West because Robert is a railroad lawyer and may travel on a pass. Now, in the morning after breakfast, you have broken away from the others who were going for a ride up to Barbican Ridge and have climbed up on the mountain side above the chalet. You can see the buildings, the wood pile, the little creek, and, below the point where drinking water is taken out, the outhouse behind your cabin. The whole is in miniature, like dolls' houses, and apt to perish with the kick of a careless foot. You, Mrs. Mountjoy, think of that. It gives you pause. What you and Robert plan to build, not the house alone with its white picket fence in Outremont, but what you will build around the house, and within, will it be so fragile as that seems to be which is below you? Will it bear up under the winter snow? Here in the mountains, man is small, his works impermanent. He lives in crevices. You see him walking here and there near the chalet, to the woodpile, to the stream, riding in a group across the valley, and each man you see is alone in time, alone in the mountains which are time visible and frozen before you. You turn from the mountains. You grasp Robert's arm. "Oh, Robert!" you exclaim. He smiles. He squeezes your waist. He squeezes you again. But you are remembering, Martha Mountjoy, what the hostess, the slim girl with the high hips, who, speaking to a man, leans back from him with her shoulders, yet stands close and pushes her hips towards him — the girl in the white skin vest and blue woollen shirt, with meditative brown eyes, whose low voice recalled another voice you had one time heard, a voice now forever beyond your memory. You are recalling, Martha, the story she told you when the two of you were sitting apart from the others after supper in the corner by the window with the new moon coming up over the mountains, walking with Venus across the sky. She told you of a Mr. and Mrs. Prior of Minneapolis who had passed through the High Valley early in the season on their way to Burma. Mr. Prior, an old man now, had read of Burma when he was a boy. He had read that elephants there wore bells on their harness which tinkled through the jungle. He was taking his wife across the Pacific to hear them. But his wife, Martha, was deaf. She could not hear the bells. She would see the elephants, but she would not hear the bells, nor would he hear the bells that he would have heard when he was young. And now you yourself are listening, listening, listening. Horses are down there in the meadows, small as mice among the trees — bays, blacks, whites and buckskins. You listen and you can hear, ever so faintly, the distant sound of their bells. Again you grasp Robert's arm. "Do you hear what I hear?" you ask, as though you were letting him in on a secret which, as it turns out, you are trying to do. He listens. He has good ears, young ears, but he does not hear the bells. He hears only the wind, low in the grasses. And you know that he will never, never hear the bells, nor now be able to remember them, these particular bells of this particular morning in the mountains which are not so much sound as a tremulous silver which spreads its lustre over the landscape. Already there is a door between you. You know. Robert does not — as yet. You know because you have knocked upon it first. Or is the door the skeleton beneath Mr. Branchflower's name in the guest book and are the bells tied upon the skeleton and is the skeleton hung upon the door and will the bells tinkle each time you knock? The bells, the door, the skeleton —

168

they are perhaps all the one and same. They weigh nothing, still man bends beneath their weight. So now you go down the hill through the spruce trees and in moss that is ankle deep, and tomorrow you will say good-bye to the hostess who sits at the head of the table in the chalet and who told you about the bells in Burma and who will stand in the doorway as you leave and stand behind it closed, facing the obdurate wood when you are gone.

Selva closed the door. She stood behind it. She opened it again. She had talked with the executive from San Francisco, with the professor and his wife from Connecticut, and she had felt compassion for Miss Wigglesworth from New York and been unable to help her. She lifted up her eyes towards the pass through which, not Peter Wrogg, but only other tourists came until the summer was no more than a succession of sunburned faces showing in the afternoon at the clearing's edge and of shoulders and bobbing heads on horseback leaving in the morning on the trail for town. Each face was strange and each in its strangeness was familiar. She had seen it, she had seen them all before. She began to feel that she was not riding the trail with people, nor sitting with them at table, nor talking with them after supper by the fireplace, nor arranging the details of their comfort at the chalet. No, she was in a Presence, demanding her attention, absorbing her every minute from seven in the morning until eleven at night, taking from her so that she felt with each tourist's going she was that much less, as the valley seemed to grow smaller with each picture taken of it. Sometimes at night she would start up, wide awake, with a half-stifled cry and when Rosie from across the room would enquire for the trouble, she would reply, "Someone asked a mountain's name and I couldn't remember." Or she would say, "I dreamed there was something to do and I didn't know what it was." Or "I dreamed that a mountain was falling down upon me and I was caught and couldn't get away." Her eyes sank deeper under the heavy eyebrows speckled with copper and the Wamboldt kitchen became a haven of quiet which she had needlessly forsaken.

At times to avoid the tourists for a few minutes after supper, she would walk out to the fire the guides had made by the tepee behind the chalet. They would be squatting on their heels, hats cocked back, chewing a piece of grass or smoking. They would be scratching their ribs, talking and spitting, or lying on an elbow staring moodily into the flames. What did they find to talk about? They were seldom without words. They gossiped more than women ever gossiped. They gossiped about incidents on the trail, horses, or other guides in the outfit who were absent. They boasted. At her approach they fell silent and soon, sensing their unease, she would leave them. She did not wish especially to talk with them. She wished merely to be with them. They were of her world. The other world was around the fireplace in the chalet. Yet, though of her world, they were apart. They were men. She was a woman. What they talked of among themselves, they would not share. They had one speech for themselves, another speech for her.

Nor by the fireplace with the tourists was she easy. They too talked of what was beyond her, but openly and before her. They talked of the cities they came from and had visited, of good hotels and bad, of food, of trains, of mountain trips in other parts. Often they discovered they had friends in common. Selva, who had not stayed at their hotels, nor travelled on the trains they mentioned, who knew no people of their acquaintance, and who considered that the food at the chalet, fresh meat, fruit and vegetables brought in by pack pony from town, was as good as any she had eaten, sat on a stool, chin cupped in her hand, on the edge of the circle. She was there because she was expected to be there. She now usually changed for supper and wore a simple blue cotton dress ordered through the catalogue of a Winnipeg store. The dress had a row of imitation Irish lace down its front and a fringe of lace around its round collar and on the sleeve ends which reached halfway to the dimples in her tanned elbows. No one had commented upon the new blue dress. These were the people from the city she had longed to meet. Yet, before her, they seemed jealous of their life at home. They excluded her from it. The questions, the remarks addressed to her were of local reference: the name of a mountain, the species of a tree, the time for meals and what did she do in the winter. She was a part of the chalet, as the chalet was part of the valley. She was an adjunct of their accommodation and, like that accommodation, rented to them for a time.

What would she do in the winter? The summer was too urgently with her for her to ponder much what might be beyond it. Even the image of Peter, once so clearly before her, had drifted farther and farther into the distance, fading from her like a cloud on the sky line frayed by the wind into trailing tatters, until at last, where a voice had spoken at her side and a smile had called her on, only memory and doubt stayed with her. Peter was as far away as the Priors and his promise as elusive as their bells in far off Burma.

This, despite the fact that she had, early in August, received a further letter from him. It was a note, no more, written on straw coloured paper, a foreign stamp upon the envelope which had been mailed in Mazatlan in Mexico. Peter wrote that he would be stopping off in Yellowhead on his way back to Montreal. He would be later than he had planned to be. He had been "detained." He did not say what had detained him, nor why he was in Mazatlan. He wrote also that he had "something of importance" to say to her. "At least," he added, "It is important to me." But that had been three weeks ago and now, at the end of the month, Peter remained far away, lost in the green and distance of an exotic city, farther from her than if he had not written.

So that, following four days of rain when, due to that rain, the flow of tourists into the chalet had temporarily stopped and the two cabins were empty, Selva on an afternoon in late August heard a champing of bits by the hitching rail and Clay Mulloy speaking softly to a horse — "Easy, boy, take it easy" — she rose to meet him from the fireplace where she had been reading a eulogy of a bulging eyed man named Mussolini in an old copy of *Time* left by a tourist. She rose quickly and gladly, with a swirl of skirt.

Clay, after his trip into the north country, was tanned an even darker brown. The skin of tourists' necks was pink and thin. That of the men who worked with horses was creased and thick, like old leather. Tourists' hands hung flat and open. A guide stood with his hand half closed. Clay stood like that now for a moment, his back toward the chalet, then, throwing the bridle lines of his black horse over the hitching rail, he stepped quickly to the side of a rangy roan with a grey-black mane, the fringes of his buck-skin shirt quivering on his shoulders, giving him the air of tenseness and expectancy Selva so well remembered. The girl on the roan, who had had ample time to dismount, had waited for him to help her down.

His hand under her elbow, she lit on the ground with a little bounce. Their shadows had pooled beside the horse. The simple and explicable happening caused Selva to ruminate, to recollect. She remembered then the hillside above the town. Peter was beside her. The lowering sun from behind them cast their shadows down the hill and merged them and it had been to her as though for a moment their bodies had mingled. That was long ago, three months ago. Of more immediate concern was the circumstance that the girl dismounting below her by the hitching rail wore trim black riding shoes and that the jodhpurs, which a brown gloved hand was smoothing, spread wide above her knees, and that her tight, brown woollen sweater served to reveal only how much of her lay hidden. Her fair hair shimmered. It was not like hair at all but rather a nimbus, cobwebs and gossamer that had become entangled in sunlight about her head as she rode through the forest. Her dark eyes were small and quick and her face, with its cheeks of rose petal, had surely that morning been washed in dew.

She lifted that face to Selva, raised a hand, wiggled delicate fingers. "Oh!" she called in a voice drowsy as the evening note of a bird, a voice that was no voice but only the memory of a voice. "Oh!" she said, "You must be Miss Williams! Do come down! Clay has been telling me about you and I do so want to meet you!"

Selva stood hesitant, then she went down.

Miss Natalie Summers was from Pasadena in California. This was her first journey into the Rockies and the night before had been the first in all her life that she had passed under canvas. She and Clay had stayed at the overnight camp in the meadows where a cook was permanently stationed to care for the trail parties. But she simply loved horses, was "crazy" about them! Her father for as long as she remembered had kept a stable. Thoroughbreds, of course, and English saddles. These saddles were different. They took a while to become used to. In what Selva guessed to be her twenty years, Natalie apparently had been deprived of nothing that she needed and little that she desired. Walking with her to her cabin, Selva wished only to tie a bow of pink ribbon under her chin, to tie it very tightly, and send her back whence she came wrapped in cellophane.

"And," Natalie continued, in her fainting voice, "I might not have got here at all — that is, if it hadn't been for Clay. Last night, two miles from camp, my horse, young Baldy there, shied and ran away. We would have crashed into the trees, but Clay came up alongside and caught him by the cheek strap."

"I thought you said you were used to horses," Selva said.

"Oh, but I am. But he took me by surprise — Baldy, I mean."

Selva looked at Clay dropping the dunnage bag inside the bedroom door. "It was nothing," he said. "A gopher popped out of his hole and Baldy — he's just a colt — took fright." Selva, lifting her chin, saw his neck, broad based as though it had roots between his shoulders, redden under its tan.

Turning to Natalie, she said, "You've got to be very careful about gophers. They pop up in the most unexpected places. There have been times when Clay has had to gallop after a girl when her horse ran away and pull her right out of the saddle. Isn't that so, Clay?"

Clay licked his upper lip. "I'll see you after a while — up at the chalet," he said to Natalie.

Later, as Selva by the fireplace waited for Natalie to come into supper, he came up and spoke to her. "It was nothing," he repeated. "The horse shied and I caught the cheek strap. That was all. We rode right into camp."

Selva said, "You'd better go down and look after your guest. She's waiting, probably in a corner, for you to escort her into supper."

"Nuts!" Clay replied. There by the fireplace, he moved towards her. She pushed him rudely away as Natalie came up the steps.

The next morning Clay rode in the rain back to town with Natalie. She had reservations on the train two days later for the East. From the steps, Selva watched them go, Clay, the pack horse, the girl in a yellow slicker. Having rebuffed him, now she wished to call him back. Already she regretted her atttitude of the previous evening. If he looked around, she would wave to him, call him back to say good-bye alone. He did not turn in his saddle. After him, as they disappeared into the timber, a tree branch moved and was still. Rain pattered in the clearing, drummed upon the chalet roof. A girl's voice, Natalie's voice, again like a bird's cry, rose from the forest in laughter, in comment, its meaning lost in distance.

Rosie came from the dining-room. "He told me in the kitchen he was coming back next week," she said to Selva. "They're going to start packing up in the chalet because the season's almost over."

Selva stamped her foot. "I don't care if he never comes back! And they can dump the chalet in the lake so far as I'm concerned!"

She turned away, eyes suddenly brimming with anger — anger at Rosie who had become a second conscience, reminding her of when she too had been attentive to stoves and the pots upon them, reminding her that what she had been, she might become again. She felt anger at Clay, at the universe around her, but, most of all, she was angry at herself.

Yesterday, when Clay had arrived at the chalet, she had risen at the sound of his voice and gone eagerly to meet him. Because he was with a girl who represented all that she was not and who had what she would never have — and doing no more than his job as a guide required him to do — she had been short with him and rude, thereby revealing her true self to him. She was amazed that her reaction had been so marked, her feelings so deep. What, after all, had she expected of Clay? Only that they would sit down and talk and she would tell him of the summer and now that the summer was nearly over, look with him beyond it. Of course, he would then have mentioned again the Fry Pan Mountains. Or he might not speak at all when silence would remain as his co-conspirator. But she was no longer the hired girl in the Wamboldts' house. Today she had money in the bank. She was not dependent on Clay, nor on his mountains, nor on anyone else. Now she was able to go East or West as she preferred. yet, deep within herself, she knew that she would make no decision. She was one of those for whom decisions were made by others or by events. Eighteen months ago, she had not willed to leave the homestead in the foothills. Her

174

mother had died and she had had to leave. In Edmonton, she had not searched for an employment bureau and gone there seeking work. No, she had happened to walk by it and had followed a blowzy woman indoors who trailed from her hand, as though he were a half empty satchel, a whimpering five year old boy. The employment bureau had sent her to Yellowhead. In Yellowhead, she had not left the station restaurant. Mrs. Wamboldt had come one night to her room and persuaded her to leave it. Nor, of her own volition, had she left the Wamboldts' employ. Again, events had dictated to her. And finally, she had come to the High Valley for no other reason than that Clay Mulloy had called her from the table in the beer parlour and brought her before Mr. Wilkins.

And now, at the season's end, when Clay had gone up the trail with Natalie Summers of Pasadena, she wished, when it was too late, to call him back — and why she wished so to call him back, she did not know. With him beside her she had once felt secure, yet his strength, which had been her security, at the same time threatened the security it gave. Like herself, he looked beyond the place where he immediately was. His was not a vision of a city in the East. He looked west to the Fry Pan Mountains. His vision, because more practical, she feared might be stronger than her own. At any rate, in its shadow the hotel lobbies, the busy streets — and not the hotels, the stores, the streets alone, but the wider, fuller life they bounded — were more remote, less consequential, not as they had been when Peter Wrogg had spoken about them to her on the hillside above the town. Then they had appeared so close that had she stretched out her hand a little farther, she would have had them in her reach. But it was Peter who would have had to sustain that hand. Peter had gone away. He had sent her flowers. The two letters he had written, worn with many foldings, were still in the square wooden box where she kept her handkerchiefs on the shelf behind the mirror in the bedroom off the chalet kitchen. His letters had been a promise that he would see her again, urge her another step along the path which they saw together. All summer she had waited, humble below the pass, but Peter had not come. She waited, needing a word, a touch, an arm behind her.

thirteen

Three saddle horses remained in the High Valley and as usual, when no guides were on hand to tend them, Selva, on the morning of September the second, walked down to the meadows to see that they had not strayed. Sometimes she brought a cake of salt with her and, earlier in the season, had built smudges into the smoke of which the horses would gratefully poke their noses to escape the flies.

On this morning she found only two horses, a buck-skin and an old swayback bay mare. The black and white pinto, Paint, who should have been with them, had pulled out. Perhaps he had gone towards Crooked Pass and town for it was his first trip into the valley and, being barn-fed, he still hankered after his hay and oats. Selva decided that later in the day she would walk up under the pass to look for him. She was not worried. If she failed, Clay Mulloy, returning, or one of the other guides would come upon him along the trail. Clay who, so the story was told in the outfit, had once for three days in the drear valley of the Moose tracked and caught and broken single-handed the black horse, Midnight, with the Roman nose, which today he rode.

Approaching the chalet again, seeing the woodshed outside the back door, Selva stopped abruptly. It seemed that a man stood there, waiting for her. Then she remembered that what she saw was what she had seen before: Two months previously, Clay had hung on a nail in the woodshed and apparently forgotten an old grey and black checkered mackinaw shirt. No one had bothered to remove it. It had remained there through the summer and, going out the kitchen door, she would brush against it and it would remind her of the man himself, as if, though far away over the hills — he had been with a climbing party north of Mount Robson — he had left his shape behind in token of his return. All summer, with unending patience, Clay had appeared to be standing by the post close to the kitchen door. Now Selva passed by the mackinaw and into the kitchen.

After lunch she went out once more to walk up the trail to Crooked Pass, four miles away, to look for the pinto horse. She was restless, her energies pent-up. Since Clay had returned to Yellowhead with the girl from Pasadena, time had been pretty much Selva's own. No tourists were at the chalet. With the coming of September, as though an order had been given, a gate shut and latched, or as though a bridge over the always necessary river had fallen, tourist travel had ceased. Schools were opening. Children called to their parents. Those who had no children were bound, nonetheless, by the same calendar.

Earlier that day Selva had observed the change of season as she had walked down to the meadow. She saw it in the leaves of buckbrush and stunted willow burned by the frost and in the horses' breaths rising misted from their nostrils and in the fringe of ice brittle around the lips of shadowed muskeg pools. She felt it in the sharpness of the air and in the silence now upon the land, as after a great word spoken. The silence was a pause, a waiting for the answer. Like the country, she too waited for an answer to the summer's promise.

May was a maiden, knee deep in grasses. September was a yellow and red bloused strumpet, setting up house for Old Man Winter who would come in, drunk on a blizzard, and tear it all to pieces. From the hillsides he would rip all tasselled splendour. He would freeze the song of stream and the splashing of the lake. Then under his hoary mantle he would lie down, grumbling, to sleep and the snow-studded winds which scoured the valley and beat upon the empty chalet's

178

walls would be his breath lifting, troubled from his dreams.

A sudden, cold wind which caught her as she neared timberline, was but a premonitory puff of winter's coming. For a minute, after scanning the alplands above for sign of the missing black and white pinto, she took shelter from the wind behind the wall of an old trapper's cabin which, on a little rise, stood a few feet off the trail.

She had visited the cabin before. It affected her with a sense of desolation and abandonment which at once repelled her and called to her. Now, as she swung wider the door on its leather hings, and as the grey smell of pack rats assailed her nostrils, she knew what she would see inside. To her left was a rusty tin stove and against the farther wall a bunk, its wooden legs gnawed through by porcupines, had sagged to the earthen floor. In one corner, through the caved in roof, a ray of sunlight fell, and at her feet, entering through a chink between the logs, pale strands of kinnikinic were intertwined, reclaiming with stealthy fingers what man had abandoned.

The wilderness was a presence. Man fought against it. He built walls. They would be pierced. He cut trails. They could be overgrown, but never, except with the plough or the roadway, obliterated. He spoke his words, but they were lost on air, while always the wind blew and the river flowed. Selva was depressed by this place where man had been but was no more. The scattered boughs of balsam that had been his mattress, the double bitted axe head lying rusted on the floor, the old woollen sock hanging from a nail — these were the relics of defeat, what he had left behind him in his flight.

As she turned to leave, she was arrested as always by the pencil scrawl where at eye level an axe had shaved white and flat the surface of a log abutting on the doorway. The letters, large, crude and shaky, read: "Bill, I've gone on ahead with the horses." Grim finality was in the sentence. Bill had been left behind. Someone had gone on with the horses. Who was he? Where had he gone? Why had he left without Bill?

Outside again, Selva breathed deeply, as if to cleanse herself of the air inside the cabin which, on its prow of land jutting over the treetops, was like a vessel strangely foundered and tossed aloft, in a moment to subside and be immersed in the green and wind-combed waves of the forest. Had she stayed there another minute, she felt that she would have gone down with it into the womb of that past where men went on alone with horses. She would have been the one left standing before the empty cabin's door while beyond her a blizzard roamed the valley.

Now, outside the cabin, no blizzard blew. Only the wind howled and stamped. Walking another half mile to the timber's edge, Selva studied the barren reaches of the alplands. She saw nothing except a herd of caribou in a high basin. She looked back and down to her right. There she saw a man walking. He was off the trail. She repeated to herself that he was off the trail and it seemed to her a personal affront, a flaw in the rightness of things, that a man should have missed the trail to the chalet marked by blazes in the timber and by the hooves of hundreds of horses on the alplands where no trees grew. And he was walking. In the mountains, except in winter, a man should be astride. There he was, off the trail, a straggler from the herd, a piece of flotsam left upon the mountain by the summer's receding flood.

Leaving the trail, she commenced to run, to overtake this stranger who was striding, pack upon his back, across the wind, head twisted into it as though with ear horizontal he listened for the ground to speak. In his right hand he carried like a staff a bladed and pointed ice axe such as Mr. Branchflower had used when he climbed Mount Erebus earlier in the summer. He was bare headed and instead of the mountain man's mackinaw, Selva saw the sleeves of a heavy grey tweed jacket. Seeing this stranger who had not seen her, wandering lonely beneath the peaks with no trail to guide him, Selva felt, in the instant before recognition, that he was a being just now created by her vision. Should she close her eyes, he would sink again into the earth whence he came, leaving no sign that she had ever seen him. Only her vision held him within man's eventful scheme. It was a feeling she had been told common to men who hunted.

Then, when she was only a hundred yards away, he stopped, shook his head as if within the wind's blast he fought for breath. Under the pack he shifted his shoulders. He looked down at his feet, at the untutored moss and sod. He saw no trail. No mark of man was there before his own. A lock of black hair fell across his forehead. With his free left hand, he brushed it impatiently aside.

The quick gesture, the pink cheek which it momentarily showed, came to Selva as a revelation and she was again over the pool-hall in Yellowhead during an intermission in the dance. A young man in a grey flannel suit stood alone in the middle of the floor. Nervously he brushed curly black hair from his forehead and, sensing her glance upon him, blushed as if in shame of his solitary stance and moved into the crowd by the head of the stairs. There, as now, seeking the trail which he had lost, he seemed not only solitary, but defensive to what was around him. "Peter!" Selva shouted. "Peter . . . Peter Wrogg!" She shouted into the wind. He did not hear her.

She was gasping now, stumbling downhill in her high heeled gaiters and her hand reached out and touched his pack before Peter stopped and turned to confront her. They stood wordless, the cold wind between them, she fighting for breath, he with a rim of sweat around his brow.

Tenderness such as she had never known, a desire to nourish and protect, welled up in Selva's breast and she remembered with a twinge of conscience how, after the dance above the pool hall, Peter had come the next afteroon, a Sunday, to the back door of the Wamboldts' house and she had opened the door and from the stoop looked down upon him, on to these same round, apple pink cheeks and into these dark blue eyes with their long, thick lashes, eyes which had seemed to be floating in their own luminosity so that she had then been reminded of a tramp's body reported that spring to have been floating in a log jam in the Athabaska river, eyes open to the sky. She had asked Peter to come in and he had come in. And now, on the windblown alpland she recalled too how, following his fight with Slim in the beaver meadow, he had appeared from behind the waving branches of a willow, blood on his shirt front and a gurgling in his throat. The last time she had seen him was as he had climbed wearily into Mr. Winnie's sombre motor car and been whisked away into the deepening dusk. Thinking of Peter's coming during the summer, she had remembered principally their meeting at the dance, their walk upon the hill above the town, the hope that his words about a job as a model in Montreal had brought to her. Now that he was here before her, she remembered first the instances when disaster had cast its shadow at their side. Hers also might have been disaster of another sort if she had not seen him and he had continued to wander with no trail to guide him, into the forest and below the lake, to discover himself in the muskeg and pathless timber of the Astoria valley.

At last she spoke. "You're off the trail," she shouted against the wind. It was all that she could bring herself to say. She wished at once to embrace him, to hold him to her. More than that perhaps, she wished that his arms would open and enfold her in their circled magic. Yet Peter stood as if rooted and the words that she sought for were beyond her reach. He was off the trail. It was important to her that he was off the trail, that she had come to him when he was off the trail. Eventually, of course, he would proably have found the chalet, seen the smoke from its chimney above the tree tops. Still, to miss a trail — though for a stranger it was easy enough to do — was a comment upon the man himself, as if in life he lacked direction to his goal.

Peter nodded, smiled feebly. Yes, he was off the trail.

Why, Selva asked herself, was he alone, without a guide and horses? Why was he carrying a pack, wearing boots with climbing nails around their soles as if he had come in to climb a mountain? And why, yearning for him, did she wish now to reproach him?

Peter began to speak, hair flattened, temples frayed, features thinned in the wind as if he were gradually being whittled away from before her. Selva touched his arm. They walked down into the timber.

Peter explained as they walked, that Mr. Wilkins, when he went to see him in Yellowhead, had had no guides nor horses immediately available for the trip into the High Valley. Horses were being re-shod and many of the guides were preparing their outfits for the season's northern hunts. However, a guide with a pack horse and an extra saddle horse was to go in as far as the halfway camp in the meadows below Crooked Pass to close the camp and to fetch in the cook to town for a hunting party. Peter had ridden that far with the guide and then this morning come on alone over the pass.

Before going to see Mr. Wilkins in his office by the corrals under the hill, he had called at the Wamboldt house. The Wamboldts had recently gone away.

Selva, at his side, asked, "You mean they weren't there?"

Peter nodded. Other people were in the house and another maid came to the door. Yes, Selva thought, that was the sort of house, that was the sort of door which would always have its maid as surely as a certain sort of wooden clock which she had seen in the jewellery store window had its doll-like man and woman to step forth to predict the weather. She had had no intention of going back to the Wamboldts to ask for work. Yet the fact that they had gone away was to her as incredible as though she had been told that in her absence the town, of which they were an integral part, had itself been swept off the map, leaving only a vacuum for her to return to.

Peter had inquired further. The clerk at the Chaba Hotel recalled that Rosie had gone with Selva into the High Valley. He directed Peter to Mr. Wilkins.

"I was surprised," Peter said, "delighted too, that you had found other work to do. But then I knew, we talked of it during our walk that Sunday, that you would not be long where you were. You were so obviously cut out for something better."

"I might have been there still," Selva said. "It was just a piece of luck." She might have been there still, she thought, if she and Peter had not gone walking together down to the beaver meadow across the river from the town. It was in that that Mrs. Wamboldt had found an excuse to dismiss her.

"That I do not believe," said Peter. Angling over towards the trail, they dropped down until they were below the wind. "Anyway, I was impatient to come in to see you. Mr. Wilkins asked me to wait a day or two. One of his men — odd sort of name, Clay something or other . . ."

"Clay Mulloy."

"Yes, that was it. He would be coming in here in a day or two with horses, Mr. Wilkins said. I decided not to wait and to walk in from the halfway camp. I had telegraphed my mother earlier to send out my climbing gear — this rucksack, these clothes and boots. It was waiting for me at the station, so I really had no need to wait. Remember I told you, I had walked and climbed in Switzerland?"

She remembered, and that he had said that he would like to climb in the mountains around Yellowhead on his return to the East.

"Your mother?" She asked in slight surprise. Peter, she supposed, was twenty-six or seven.

"Yes," Peter said. "She does not approve of my climbing, but she did as I asked her to."

"I guessed your mother would be in England."

"She was. She has come over for a few weeks to see that I am properly set up in Montreal — house and cook and all that. She writes that she has found a house in Montreal West and is furnishing it."

Peter paused to light a cigarette and Selva noticed that the knuckles on the back of his hand were dimpled. Changing the subject, he told her that he would have returned earlier from the Coast but, while in California, he had been invited to go to Mazatlan with some friends who owned a yacht. There he had been laid up for a few weeks with a low grade infection. Now he felt himself quite fit again.

Selva wished to hear no more of Montreal, of his mother, nor of Mazatlan. "Peter," she said, coming closer to him, "you must be tired, hungry." Already she was planning the supper she would give him. She would care for him, tend him after his long journeys. Later, in the warm chalet, they would talk.

"Peter," she asked, "do you know, I thought you would never come?"

"I've been coming to you all summer," he replied. "Even going away from you, I was coming towards you."

He paused, threw his cigarette away, stamped it out. "I've lots to tell you," he continued. "We'll talk tonight of the blue dress you wore the night I met you at the dance over the billiard room and of our walk on the hill above the town and we'll talk of what we talked of then."

"Really, you haven't forgotten?"

"Forgotten?" He laughed softly, put his hands on her shoulders. "Give me a kiss then so that I can never forget."

184

fourteen

That evening after supper, sitting with Peter before the fireplace in the chalet after Rosie had left them and gone to the bedroom off the kitchen, it occurred to Selva that the moment was at hand. Peter now would reveal his purpose. He would speak and tell her why he had come into the High Valley. His speech would fashion a picture of some sort for her — speech which in itself was a thing of wonder and the seed of magic. In all the High Valley, only in the chalet would speech be heard that night. She remembered well how, after Slim had ridden down to the beaver meadow outside of Yellowhead the Sunday evening following the dance above the pool hall, Peter had staggered out from behind the willow bush. Then he had been unable to speak. Instead of speech, a gurgling came from his throat and red froth, like madness, showed upon his lips. Wordless, he had stood before her and had seemed to her to have been trans-formed into another being, one stuttering and incompetent, offering for her comprehension the gibberish of an idiot. She had led him away and back to town. The incident, not mentioned, appeared to be accepted by common agreement as closed between them.

Tonight Peter would speak. Earlier he had said to her, "You told me when we were out walking that afternoon in Yellowhead, remember? You said that you had spent all your life in the mountains and the foothills." It was a question and she had replied to it as such in a few words. She spoke of her stepfather, Jed Williams, and of the homestead, but referred to him as a "rancher" and to the homestead as a "ranch." She might have gone away to school or college, she said, but after her mother died, she had preferred to be on her own and had gone to work. This, of course, was not strictly so. Her schooling in a loghouse school, a ride of eight miles from the homestead, had been limited. It would not have qualified her to enter college even had that opportunity come her way.

Now, Peter demurred about the idea of college. For a man, yes, but for a woman he was not sure that it was so essential.

"Why not?" Selva asked, bridling. Here again, as at the beer parlour where women had a separate entrance, and as at the campfire behind the chalet during the summer when the guides became silent at her approach because she was a woman, she was being excluded, if only by implication, from man's wider field of privilege.

Peter mentioned his mother. She had not had a university education. Schooling, of course, and of the very best, but at her parents' home with a tutor. He had spoken of his mother earlier that day when Selva had found him wandering off the trail and she suffered resentment anew against this older woman who from across the ocean and the continent so persistently intruded, and listened with impatience for Peter to come to the point. Time was precious. Tomorrow might be too late. Tomorrow Clay Mulloy with a gang of men might appear to pack the furniture, blankets and staples of the chalet and seal it for the winter. When Clay came she wished to meet him armed with whatever promise Peter had to give her.

Until now, since coming in from the trail, showing him to his cabin and afterwards having supper, she and Peter had had no time alone. Rosie, telling him that he was "one of the family" — Selva had spoken of him to her — had set a place for herself at the table for supper and proceeded thenceforth to talk for the three of them.

Over the canned beef and the boiled carrots and the mashed potatoes, she had said to Peter, "I remember you from the hotel in Yellowhead."

Peter looked up, surprised.

"Yes," Rosie said, "I was waiting on table there. It was away back in May and you asked for fish for breakfast."

"Probably I did," said Peter.

"No one had ever asked for fish for breakfast before. Herrings, I think it was you asked for. But then I would have remembered you anyway."

"Really?"

"Yes, because your eyebrows aren't neighbours."

Peter glanced at Selva in astonishment. Then, holding his face in profile at Rosie, regarding her warily as he might a strange form of life seen for the first time through the bars at the zoo.

"I mean," Rosie said, "that your right eyebrow rides higher than your left one and it's curved and your left one is straight."

Peter did not take offence. "I am probably a very curious appearing fellow," he said.

"Oh, no! It's just that something like that, what I was saying, makes a face that much more interesting, that's all."

With Peter on her right, Selva had Rosie on her left, nearer the kitchen door. She kicked her foot to still her prattle. Rosie said, "Selva, stop! You're kicking me!"

Selva blushed. She was embarrassed. In the limited time at her disposal, she had gone to pains with the supper. No fresh meat was on hand, but she had tried to make amends with a dessert of huckleberry pie which, over Rosie's protests, she had insisted upon baking herself. No one, she thought, could make a crust as light, as white, as flaky as her own. While it baked, she had gone into the bedroom and put on her blue crepe dress, the one she had worn to the dance over the pool-hall the night she had first met Peter. It was the first time she had taken it out during the summer and, observing herself in the mirror, she had been happy with its touch and the narrow trimming of lace, heart-shaped upon her throat and breast. It was all of the dress which the small wall mirror permitted her to see. She had combed her hair back tightly and made it into a bun over her left ear, a fashion copied from Mrs. Mountjoy, the bride from Montreal who had been at the chalet in early August. She had rouged her lips, pinched her cheeks. She took the mirror down, held it before her, and two brown eyes, half lidded, looked out at her, drowsy, but with a kernel of yellow light thrown from the wall lamp burning deep down within them. She replaced the mirror, took several long steps about the room feeling the grateful swirl of the skirt about her legs.

In the front room, hands behind his back, head outthrust, legs straddled, Peter was already waiting for her before the fireplace. She thought he was very handsome with his thick, black curly hair, his ruddy cheeks, his grey tweed jacket with a green silk scarf tied loosely about his throat. He had taken off his climbing boots and instead wore a pair of pliant leather slippers. The leather slippers were a home-like touch and Selva, entering the room, imagined for a moment that they were not in the chalet, nor in the mountains. Outside was no hitching-rail, no clearing, no forest, no lake. Outside the window was wide, smooth lawn. Around the edges of the lawn ran the half circle of a gravel driveway. In the driveway, by the steps leading to the oaken door, a low black motor car waited. Peter had come home to supper and afterwards they would take the car and drive down to the theatre in the centre of the city. Before going in to supper, they would sit by the fire and he would tell her of his day in the office . . . Or they were entertaining. A man and his wife were passing through Montreal on their way to the Orient from Buenos Aires. He was a business acquaintance of Peter's and Peter had asked her to take pains with the dinner. She had been most of the afternoon in the kitchen with the cook watching the cooking of the roast and the baking of the pastry and afterwards watching as the maid set the dining-room table with tall silver candlesticks and sparkling glass. Now, as they waited for the guests to arrive, Peter was telling her once more of his good fortune in having a wife to whom he was always proud to introduce the people he knew . . .

A log sparked loudly in the fireplace behind Peter, a flame leaped high and threw his shadow across the lamplit room and Selva found herself crossing the chalet floor towards him. He did not speak. He came up to her, held her at arm's length, appraised her up and down, slipped his arm about her waist and, humming, waltzed her around the room. His mouth against the bun of hair above her ear, he whispered,

"Lovely girl. Lovely dress. The same dress, the blue dress. That's how I think of you — the girl with Titian hair, the girl in the pale blue dress." He kissed the lobe of her ear. She smelt liquor on his breath, but when he asked if she would take a drink — he had a bottle of rum in his pack sack in the cabin — she said no. "Let's dance again," she said. Then Rosie had called that supper was on the table.

Selva preceded Peter into the dining room, repeating to herself the words which he had spoken. "The girl in the pale blue dress." Not the maid in the Wamboldts' house. Not even the hostess in the High Valley. She was simply, "The girl in the pale blue dress." And that, she supposed, was what she most wished to be. When he came home from work in the city, she would be wearing a blue dress when she went to meet him in the doorway and afterwards going with him as now into the dining-room.

Then coming to the table where Rosie was already seated, she smiled a little sadly. Her fancy had taken an even further flight than usual. After all, the most that Peter had once suggested was that she might, perhaps, if she came to Montreal, secure a job as a model in one of the big department stores. It was true, he had a house there. His mother was fixing it up for him. But it was his house. She had no reason, no reason whatever, to think that it would ever be hers.

Still, for all that, the pretense that this, their supper in the chalet, was a supper in a house of their own, lingered with her until Rosie's presence and then her awkward questions shattered the illusion beyond repair. She and Rosie, when they were alone in the chalet, ate together, but this was the first time that Rosie had presumed to sit at the table when another was there. Until the last moment, Selva had been unaware of her intention. She had had to concur in it to avoid a scene. The least that Rosie could have done being at the table, it seemed to her, was to sit quietly and not attempt to command the conversation. Certainly her remarks on Peter's appearance were in bad taste.

Of course, one of his eyebrows rode up higher than the other, especially when he smiled or was about to speak. The right eyebrow was also curved, as Rosie had said, while the other was straight. More than that, studying him now, Selva noticed that his right eye was wider, rounder than the other. The left eye did not have a cast. Nothing as definite as that, but the eyelid dropped ever so slightly, giving to that side of his face a thoughtful, even a secretive expression. It was as if with his right eye he met her fully and frankly, while with the left eye he avoided her. The disparity of which, until now, she had not been conscious, affected the entire cast of his face so that she wondered what it was that lay hidden behind those dark blue eyes, those smooth pink cheeks and those lips which, before he spoke, opened and shut tentatively showing small, very white teeth, as though he were practising beforehand what he was about to say, or merely murmuring to himself what would forever remain unuttered.

Selva was perplexed during supper not by anything that Peter said, but rather by what he did not say. He was reticent. He replied to questions but seldom ventured a remark on his own. Rosie complained, as she had complained throughout the summer, about the draft in the kitchen stove. "The chimney needs to be higher," she said to Selva. Peter raised his head, looked from Selva to Rosie and back to Selva again, as though he watched the flight of words between them. Then he gave himself once more to his food, cutting his meat into small pieces, picking up each piece separately with the prongs of his fork, eating with appetite, but, strangely following his long walk, not from hunger.

After supper, before the fireplace, Selva was even more perplexed when he commenced to speak of his mother. While she had been in the kitchen telling Rosie that she and Peter wished to be alone, he had gone down to his cabin and returned with the bottle of rum. It stood now on a chair beside them with two tumblers and a pitcher of water. Selva had blown out the lamp and taken from the dining-room the three branched candlestand and put it on the table behind the couch where the three white flames stood on tiptoe against the darkness. Peter leaned forward, poured rum from the dark bottle into a tumbler, added water and handed it to Selva. She took a sip, set the tumbler back on the chair, while he poured a drink for himself. It was, she thought, the third drink he had had since supper.

Turning to her, tumbler in hand, the flame from the fireplace laving his cheek and the back brushed hair on his temple, he said, "You'd like my mother."

"I would?"

"Mmm." He sucked his lip, nodded. "I think you would."

"Perhaps she wouldn't like me."

"No reason why she shouldn't." His lips opened as if he would embellish the remark, then closed again in silence. the left eye, next to Selva, under its slightly lowered lid, gazed contemplatively into the fire. The other eye she could not see.

His mother — what had his mother to do with Peter or with her tonight in this chalet in the High Valley ringed by mountains where far, far away, under the night's cold, blue stars, a wolf's howl was a lost soul yearning for the flesh?

"Remarkable woman, my mother," Peter continued after a pause. He took a swallow from the tumbler, held the glass in his hand upon his knee. Selva smoothed her skirt, crossed her knees, lifted the black toe of her slipper until she saw the light of the candles from behind her reflected in its shiny leather.

"We get on well together," Peter said. Looking up, Selva at first thought he referred to themselves here before the fireplace, but his distant expression warned her that he still spoke of his mother.

"You do?" she asked.

"Famously. See eye to eye, so to speak, except for one thing."

"And what is that?"

"What I mentioned this afternoon. She is opposed to my climbing mountains. It is an interest we have never shared."

"I think your mother is quite right. I never could understand why people wanted to climb mountains. We had a man here this summer, a Mr. Branchflower . . ."

"Branchflower?" asked Peter in a higher tone of voice. "He's a very well known alpinist."

"He climbed Mount Erebus. We were looking up at it this afternoon."

"Think I read something about it," Peter said. "A first ascent, wasn't it?"

"That's what the papers said and he took me out and showed me the cairn he had built right on the very top. He let me look through his glasses."

Peter sighed. "I've never made a first ascent — you know, virgin peak idea. That's what I like about the Canadian Rockies. Any number of virgin peaks."

Selva regarded him sharply. "And what would your mother say?" she asked.

Peter lit a cigarette, flicked the match into the fire. He shook his head. "She wouldn't know about it until afterwards, and then she would be very much put out — as she was once years ago when we were travelling in Switzerland. I have no brothers or sisters, you know, and we have gone many places together. My father was always held down by his business and when he did go away he seemed to prefer to go alone. Anyway, my mother particularly liked the Continent and this summer I speak of — I was just past my nineteenth birthday — we stopped at a little inn in the valley below the Weisshorn."

"The Weisshorn?"

"It's a peak in Switzlerand. And in the inn we had adjoining rooms. I would always call good-night to her and knock against the wall when I was in bed and she would answer back. Not many people there in the inn, you understand, a private sort of place — an Indian army officer and his wife, a couple of German climbers, a Scotswoman with heavy boots and a stick in her hand. Then there was this American girl who was alone. Hardly a girl though, closer to thirty, I would say, but quite attractive, tall, with blue-black hair — and well-spoken too."

Selva remembered Vera Wigglesworth who during the summer had come to the chalet from New York. She also was tall, with blue-black hair and she was alone, very much alone, indeed, wandering by the lakeshore, in and out of the chalet as though she searched for something precious that was lost and needing someone, anyone, to help her find it.

"Her name," Peter said, "was Geraldine. Geraldine Spalding, I believe. At any rate, she and I decided one afternoon that that night, because the moon was out, we would go walking after the others in the inn had retired. It was a completely innocent expedition, I assure you. I went from my room on tiptoe shortly after eleven o'clock. I met her in the parlour downstairs and we set out. We followed a path — you would call it a trail — until we came out of the forest on to the alplands. Then, before one o'clock, we returned to the inn."

Peter raised his tumbler, took a long drink. He shook his head again, slowly, ran his fingers through his hair. "Yes," he said, "we returned and the proprietor of the inn, a little man with a goatee and a white nightcap on his head — the proprietor and my mother, in her dressing gown, were waiting for us by the desk."

Selva inquired, "How did they know you had gone out?"

"Oh, that!" Peter turned to her. "That was my fault. You see, I had forgotten to knock on the wall to tell my mother that I was in bed. She had waited. Then she got up and looked in my room. Afterwards she went to the proprietor. It was not the first time we had stayed at his inn and he was what might be termed 'co-operative.' My mother had even surmised that I had gone out with this Geraldine. Don't ask me how she knew. She knew. That is the thing about her. She knows. And she had discovered beforehand what I learned only during our walk, that Geraldine Spalding was a married woman living apart from her husband, who was an oil man in the United States."

"Well," Selva said, "you came back into the inn . . ."

"Yes, we came back into the inn. I was miffed, indeed, I was angry at having a reception committee to meet us. No words were spoken. I went at once to my room, my mother to hers. We did not knock on the wall then or ever again. In the morning before we came down to breakfast, Geraldine Spalding had left the premises. My mother had told the proprietor that if she did not leave, we would."

"Your mother told him that?" Selva rose from the couch, walked to the side of the fireplace, turned, her blue skirt swirling, leaned her shoulder against the stone and looked speculatively down on Peter.

Hunched forward, elbows on his knees, he said, "She told him that. According to her lights, she acted in the only way she could. A married woman, you see, and then I was hardly more than a boy. But I was very upset about it, I assure you, and the day after, without seeking my mother's permission, I engaged a guide and we tried to climb the Weisshorn. It was a trifle late in the season, about this time of the year, possibly a little earlier, and we failed to make the peak because of a storm. I came back to the inn to find my mother prostrate with grief and shock."

Peter gulped, blinked his eyes. "But we did not merely come back to the inn," he said, "we ran back to it as though we were pursued and it, a refuge. My guide was too young, hardly older than I was, a man of twenty, twenty-one, no more. The storm had held us on a ledge. There had been thunder and loose rock. It was as though we were being bombarded. When we could we hurried down the mountain. We were trembling. Each looking at the other, saw fright in his face. Of common accord, with no words, we turned and ran into the forest. Ran until we were exhausted. Panic." Peter clipped the word from his mouth. "The Greek god, Pan," he mused, "who inhabits forests and dwells in the caves of hostile mountains."

He leaned over to pour himself another drink. His hand, holding the tumbler, shook ever so slightly.

"Peter," Selva said, "you've had quite a few drinks already."

"I've had nothing very much and I rather like to drink when I talk."

What had prompted Peter to talk as he had? She had waited for him to talk of themselves, of his coming to the High Valley. She had waited for him to put his arms around her and tell her why he had come. Instead, he had talked to her of his mother and instead of there being only the two of them in the room, the mother now sat between them on the couch. And the girl, Geraldine, the oil man's wife — why, above all, had he mentioned the incident of the night below the Weisshorn? To show her, Selva, how close he and his mother were to one another or to emphasize to her that other women had found him attractive too? Also, she was surprised that he had drunk so much. The rum had set loose his tongue. Perhaps it had muddled his thoughts as well. Selva was vexed. Cold rather than warmth was in the room. She looked up at the forty inch sheep head over the fireplace. The sad brown eyes, the loot of windy heights, gave her no token.

Peter, as though reading what passed through her mind, looked up too. Then he stood. He walked towards the door as if he were forsaking the room entirely. At the door he swung about, facing Selva across the width of the room.

194

"I suppose," he asked, "you are wondering why I am speaking at such length about my mother?"

When Selva made no response, he said, "I will tell you then. It is this: she wants to meet you. She wants you to go East so that she may meet you."

"Your mother wants to meet me?" Selva pointed a finger to her breast in unbelief. She would not have been more surprised if a glacier had come down the mountain and poked its cold snout into the door asking to be fed.

Peter nodded, he sipped from the tumbler which he held in his hand. Coming closer, until he stood behind the couch, he said, "You may think it strange, and I am sure you do, but as you have probably gathered, there are few secrets between us, between my mother and myself. From Vancouver I wrote her about you. I said simply that we had met at a dance. She assumes that your home is Yellowhead."

"You didn't tell her I was a maid, a hired girl in someone's house?"

"Of course not. Of what importance is that?"

"Your mother would likely think it was very important."

"You are not a housemaid now and my mother knows how much I think of you. That is what is important to her — and it is a feeling of which you seem to be unaware. Why do you suppose I broke my journey to come up here? Why? Why?" He leaned over the couch, his body suddenly a weapon, thrusting, his teeth showing, eyes wide, yet glazed, not meeting hers.

"Why? I'll tell you why!" he exclaimed. "Because, since the night of the dance, when I saw you sitting by the wall in that blue dress you have on, you have not been out of my mind for more than a minute at a time." He straightened. He put a hand just below his ribcage. "It is a pain, an emptiness, don't you understand?" he said. "It affects me here, here. It is with me, you are with me, every waking moment." He walked around the couch, sat down upon it, hung his head.

Selva spoke slowly. "Why," she asked, "did you never write and tell me. In your two letters you said nothing like this at all."

"I attempted to write — several times. I was unable to put the words on paper. It seemed inane to write them out."

From her stance by the fireplace, Selva moved over to the fire. Turning, dusting her hands, looking down on Peter she saw that the hair on the back of his neck was twisted into small, tender curls above his jacket collar. She was tempted to put her hand upon it and to smooth it. Instead, she asked, "Have you ever been in love, Peter?"

He raised his face, pale now, drawn, older, touched with the agony of his longing. "In love?" — his nostril twitched — "What do you fancy I am speaking of?"

"But before, ever before, really in love?"

He clasped his hands, then spread them impatiently apart, fingers extended. "Oh, before!" he said, "The usual thing. Dances, the seashore, moonlight and roses, that sort of thing."

"How do you know it's different now?"

He did not reply directly. He said, "It's like famine, the cholera. You read of it happening to others, foreigners. You never expect to have it happen to you."

"Cholera — that's a funny thing to say. Poor Peter, you are unhappy, aren't you?" Selva came forward, sat beside him. He leaned back, stretched out his legs and her breast touched his left arm. He reached for her hand, held it on his leg.

She felt a thrill of authentic power. Here she commanded. With Slim Conway and with Clay Mulloy she had felt herself to some extent the victim, but Peter was a complex of forces which she had summoned and was moulding to her desire. For her, he had stepped from the train in Yellowhead and walked into the High Valley. She had found him off the trail below Crooked Pass and brought him, as one might bring a trophy, with her to the chalet. He was the shape and substance of dream, the lustre of her hopes, an emissary from that world where she wished to be. As such, she had created him, fashioned him from loneliness and hunger as surely as tonight he sat beside her. Here, before the fire, he had revealed himself to her and shown that, as she needed him, so he needed her. His need was even the greater. He spoke of his mother who had come from England to set up house for him in Montreal. Vaguely, in the back of her mind, failing of conscious expression, stirred the idea more felt than thought, that his mother was part of that need. His mother expected that she would go to Montreal. Selva did not trust this mother. The vision rose before her of another Mrs. Wamboldt, also a woman of possessions, and one who had a son by her first marriage who had gone to Australia — but this was a taller, a leaner, a more calculating and polished Mrs. Wamboldt. Old woman, she thought, ruthless old woman who in other mountains turned another from her lodgings, of what are you scheming? What are your plans? I know your plans. In your fine dress, among your linen and your silverware, with your servants, in the house which you have furnished, in the security of your station, you would have me come, a stranger and a suppliant, awkward in my speech before you, stumbling in my efforts to be at ease, until you could point without pointing and nod without nodding, until you could say without saying to Peter beside you: "I told you so. Now you are able to see for yourself that I always speak the truth, that I always know what is best and that what I do and what I suggest is always for your good.

Old woman, you would say to him when I had gone, you would say, "You ran away from me once, you remember, many years ago in Switzerland, only because I had done what I could to protect you. You ran away with a guide up the mountain and you came running back. You have run away at other times. You have climbed mountains against my will. Everytime you have climbed a mountain, you have run away because you have done it against my will. And now this last time, you ran away again into the mountains and you brought back with you this girl with the tawny hair, the long legs, the rude, western accent — or is it that she lacks an accent? Now she too has gone and you have come back to me. You will run away again, but always you will return. I am the Eternal. I am in you. From me you will never escape because I am you, yourself. I gave you and, giving you, guard you deep within me. When you run from me, at the farthest turning you encounter only yourself."

On the couch Peter reached for his glass of rum. He took a long swallow.

"Peter," Selva said, "you've had enough to drink." He answered by putting the tumbler back on the chair.

Old woman, Selva thought, your Peter, while you are far away in Montreal, is now beside me, pliant in my hands.

Tonight I am the strong one, my magic stronger than yours. Tonight belongs to me. It is mine, mine, all mine.

She said aloud to Peter, "Peter, your mother means a great deal to you, doesn't she?"

"Of course, naturally, as I've tried to tell you. But that's quite different. It has nothing to do with you and me."

Selva lifted her hand, ran her fingers through his hair, held herself close to him. "What soft hair," she murmured, "so glossy, soft. It's like a girl's hair . . . But, Peter, if your mother has nothing to do with you and me, why do you want me to go East to meet her?"

"Because I wrote her about you. The suggestion comes from her."

"And if I go — and then?"

"Selva, do you mean . . . ?" He jerked himself upright, turned until his breast was against her own. He took her face as he had done when they had stood on the porch outside the dance hall in Yellowhead, cupped her chin in his hand. Now he pressed his lips on hers, gently, gently, pushing her head against the blanket thrown over the back of the couch. He took up her hand and into the white, satiny bend of her elbow put his lips. Light as a butterfly's wings, they ran up her arm to her shoulder, touched her neck, the lobe of her ear. "The forehead and the little ears," he quoted softly, "are from where Saturn keeps the years." Then he kissed her mouth. His right hand cradled her breast, stroked her flank, carressed her thigh. Selva lay back, closed her eyes, opened her lips. Her body one tremulous ecstasy, she floated, swooned, as upon a smooth river endlessly flowing. She twisted her head, freed her lips, opened her eyes, saw above on the vaulted ceiling, probing fingers of shadow from the fire. "Peter," she whispered, "dear God, dear Peter."

The next moment she had flung him from her, so that he staggered back against the fireplace. She stood up, settling her skirt, touching fingers to her hair.

"God's Truth, what's the trouble!" Peter exclaimed, rubbing the back of his hand across his mouth.

Selva gestured with her head. "Someone's out there at the door. I just heard a noise." On the couch, turning her face again towards Peter, she had heard beyond the door, the creak of the steps leading up to it.

Now she moved towards the door, but before she reached it, it opened giving her a glimpse of frosty stars above the tree tops, of shadowy mountain masses and letting into the warm room the cold, biting breath of the out of doors. Clay Mulloy, eyes shining, teeth gleaming, hat tilted off his forehead, saddle bags over his shoulder, slowly shut the door behind him, stood hesitantly, poised on his toes, looking from Selva to Peter, then back again to Selva. The candle-light tinted his brown throat. The fringes of his buck-skin shirt rustled as if a little private breeze coursed about his shoulders.

His voice vibrant, deep, filling the room, he said, "I'm sorry. I didn't know. I mean, I didn't mean . . ." He looked in question at Peter, in the act of pouring himself a full sized drink from the bottle of rum.

Selva, following his glance, said, "Peter, perhaps we should all have a drink." Then, "Peter, this is Mr. Mulloy, Clay Mulloy. Mr. Mulloy, Mr. Wrogg."

fifteen

Peter, the tumbler half full, red as blood in his hand, stood with his back to the fireplace. "How do you do?" he said to Clay Mulloy. Clay nodded, muttered. The men did not shake hands.

Selva walked between them across the room to go to the cupboard in the dining room to fetch a tumbler for Clay. On her way, she picked up the pitcher from the chair. It was empty and needed to be refilled. She looked at Peter's glass. He had not poured water from the pitcher into it. He was taking his drink neat, a half tumbler of Hudson's Bay over proof rum.

She went through the dining-room and into the kitchen, where the wall lamp burned low, to the water pail. She returned with a full pitcher of water and the extra tumbler for Clay. In the two minutes she had been absent, the men had not shifted their positions, Clay still standing by the door, Peter with his back to the fireplace. Clay had dropped his saddle bags to the floor and Peter, in what must have been a mighty swallow, had drained the last drop of rum from his glass.

Yet returning to the silence of the room, broken only by the the stuttering of the fire, Selva felt that a subtle change had taken place within it. It was as though a moment before

201

the two men had had their heads together and had drawn hastily apart to stand at a distance from one another the instant of her entry. A whisper seemed to float in the stillness. Then outside, in the forest, a great horned owl hooted.

She set the tumbler, the pitcher of water, on the chair. She glanced at Peter's empty glass. "You might have waited," she said, "until I came back."

Peter, his speech thick, cheeks red as the rum he had drunk, the lid of his left eye, the secret eye, drooping until it was almost shut, said, "Yes. Rude of me. Simply wasn't thinking, didn't think. Apologize." He gulped, swayed, put his free hand behind him to touch the stone of the fireplace.

Selva said, "And a full half tumbler too."

Clay Mulloy said, "It's all right. I don't want a drink right now."

Peter lifted a weary eye.

Clay waited, shoulders hunched forward, hands hanging half clenched at his side, his face, as always, taut and driven with travel. When he moved, it occurred to Selva, he moved in only one direction — forward. Peter moved forward, it seemed, only that he might take another step back.

She said to Peter, "I think I'll have a drink then, if no one else will."

"I'll pour it myself," she added as he looked towards her beseechingly in what she conceived to be his inability to function further as a host.

He fumbled at the skirt of his grey tweed jacket and at last extracted from the watch pocket of his trousers a small, gold watch. He held the watch at arm's length, squinted at its insatiable face.

"Late," he said to Selva, "Think, with permission . . ." He bowed slightly to her, squared his shoulders and, vacating the field, marched with the dignity of a regiment on parade around the couch and across the floor to the door and out the door to his cabin. Clay stepped aside to let him by.

"Well!" he said to Selva when the door had closed behind Peter.

"He shouldn't have had that last drink," Selva said.

"I read somewhere," Clay said, "that one drink is good for you, two are too many and three are not enough."

They heard the door slam in Peter's cabin.

Head down, adding water to the spot of liquor in her tumbler, Selva asked, "What were you two talking about while I was in the kitchen?"

"Talking? We weren't talking. He asked me if I minded about him taking his drink alone. I told him to go right ahead, it was all right with me."

Selva sighed. Wearily, she sighed. Holding her drink of rum, she sank upon the couch before the dwindling fire. She felt exhaustion in all her limbs. Flesh itself was tired, dropped so suddenly from the height of emotion in Peter's arms into the valley of frustration. Peter's every effort seemed doomed to failure. He had failed before. She was ready to believe that he would fail again. Events conspired to cause his failures. Yet the failures bound her to him, awoke tenderness and longing, a desire to overcome and master what it was that kept her from him.

Clay said, "Maybe I will have a drink." Selva made no response. She heard him come around the couch and at her shoulder heard the gurgle of the liquor from the bottle and the splash of water from the pitcher. Then in his moccasined feet he passed again around the back of the couch with a slight shuffling sound, like a shadow wearing overshoes. Clay set himself down at the far end of the couch from her. The rim of the tumbler clicked against his teeth.

"You called him Peter," he said quietly.

"Yes, I called him Peter." Selva drew herself farther into the corner of the couch. With Peter the couch had seemed long as a corridor. Now, alone with Clay, it was cramped.

"And I've never seen you in that blue dress before," Clay said. After a pause he added, "I like it. It's you."

He took another swallow of rum. "Mr. Peter Wrogg," he said meditatively, "the mountain climber."

"He's not a mountain climber," Selva said. She felt that this talk of mountain climbing was imposing upon Peter a character not truly his own. He had climbed mountains. She had the clothes he wore and his word for that. But mountain climbing was not a primary function with him as it was, for instance, with Mr. Branchflower who had climbed Mount Erebus. Peter, as when he had attempted to climb the Weisshorn, after his mother had had the oil man's wife evicted from the inn in Switzerland, had had mountain climbing forced upon him.

"That's what he told Bill Wilkins anyway," Clay said. "He said he wanted to come in here to do a bit of climbing. Those were the words Bill repeated to me. He could have waited and come in with me. But he was in too big a hurry. Too big a hurry even for a mountain climber, it seemed to me."

"I didn't expect you to come in until tomorrow or the day after," Selva said.

"The boys are coming in then, maybe a day or two later, to pack up here and then, this week, we're going to start to build another chalet over in Geikie Meadows on the other side of Thunder Ridge. Tourist business is booming. I've got to see if we can take horses over the ridge or if we have to go in by way of the Fraser which takes a day longer. That's one reason I came on ahead. I left at daybreak, I made it in a day's riding."

"What's the other reason you came on ahead?" Selva remembered the old trapper's cabin she had visited that afternoon and the message by its doorway, "Bill, I've gone on ahead with the horses." Clay had come on ahead. He had come on ahead to the chalet. He was of that breed of men who always went on ahead — alone into darkness, into storm and, finally, of course, into silence. He was a mountain man, a hall-forgetter.

Now he leaned forward, slowly stirred the fire with the poker sending sparks up the chimney, causing the flame to wash his face in its glow.

Settling back in the couch, he said, "Your friend Slim is coming in with the boys. He got back two weeks ago from riding in the stampedes down south."

"Slim?" Selva puckered her brow. Slim was far away and long ago. His name touched her only with indifference.

"Slim Conway," Clay said.

"You didn't come on ahead to tell me about Slim. Besides, you know he's no longer any friend of mine."

"No, I didn't come in ahead to tell you about him, nor about finding a horse trail over Thunder Ridge."

He regarded Selva quizzically. "And I didn't come in to talk about the Fry Pans."

Clay put down his glass, got up from the couch, and going behind it, commenced to pace forth and back, letting his phrases fall one by one, with impact, over Selva's shoulder. "What this country needs," he said, "is a horse. It's full of horses, but it needs a horse. It needs a native horse, a horse that can be born here, thrive here, grow here and be bred here. Our horses come from Kamloops or the prairies when they're two, three or four year olds. Those from the prairies when they first come in don't know how to step over a log. Those from Kamloops don't winter well."

He stood still. Selva could hear his heavy breathing. "I'm the man," he said, measuring his words, "who is going to give the Athabaska valley the horse it needs. I'm going to import a blooded stallion and breed him with the native cayuse — the closest thing we have to a native cayuse, mares that have lived here most of their lives."

"That costs money," Selva said.

"I've got the money. I've got the ranch site out on the Little Hay between the mountains and the foothills. I've told Wilkins I'm quitting next spring. He's all for what I'm going to do."

"You've got the money?"

"A man I had out hunting on the Smokey two years ago — he's putting up the money. We've been in touch ever since our hunt. We talked my idea over then. He's an easterner, but he likes horses and he likes the mountains. This way he'll have some place to come to in the summers and fall."

"You came to tell me that?" Selva asked without turning her head. She was moodily watching the logs in the fireplace. A face appeared there and slowly before her eyes split into a fiery grin and fell apart with a slight shudder of coals and ashes.

"I came in to tell you that — and more." Clay stood before her now, above her, eyes intent, staring, the shape of the enduring skull pushing against the tight and wind browned cheeks. He had become a man with a mission.

"I came in to tell you more than that," he repeated. "The Fry Pans — that was a dream, something my Old Man would talk about on winter nights. But this on the Little Hay is real, it's there, waiting — for me, and for you."

"For me?" Selva straightened herself in the couch, tossed her head. "You take a lot for granted."

"For you — that's what I said. You knew I was going to

say it."

"I did not know. And anyway, I couldn't."

"Couldn't?" Clay stood back, lips slack. The possibility of her refusal apparently had not occurred to him. This was the end of the season. She was simply waiting for him to come to her as he had come to her in the beer parlour in Yellowhead when her job with the Wamboldts had run its course and was finished. His effrontery angered her. She wished to hurt him.

"No," she said, "I couldn't — and I wouldn't." She looked away towards the window beyond which was the cabin where Peter slept.

Clay followed her glance, his puzzled expression that of a small boy who had had something snatched from his hand. "What are you looking out there for?" he asked.

"I can look where I want to, can't I?"

'"Sure. There's no law against it, but I'm beginning to wonder if he came up her to climb mountains after all."

"If who came up here?"

"Him, out there. This fellow that you call Peter." Clay moved back against the fireplace, laid his arm along the mantle. "You must have got acquainted awfully quick to be calling him Peter so soon. Unless you knew him before — but how could you know him before?" He came forward, stood close to her so that Selva smelled the smokey, forest-wild smell of his buck-skin shirt. "Did you know him before?" Clay asked. His voice grated. Threat was in it. Selva expected his hands to reach out and seize her. Instead when, lowering her head, she did not reply, he stepped back again. "So," he said, "you did know him?"

Selva said, "I never said that I didn't, did I?"

"Where did you meet him then?"

Selva, her voice rising, faced him fully. "What right have you to ask me when I met him?"

Clay did not immediately answer. He came over and sat on the couch, at the far end, away from her. He put his elbows on his knees, cupped his chin in his hands. "Selva," he said in a changed, soft tone, "I have no right, none at all. I wondered about him when he was in such a hurry down there in Yellowhead. If he had waited a day he could have ridden all the way in with me. I guess I had a feeling. I guess that's why I rode in ahead of the boys. Old Midnight was pretty tired when I rubbed him down and grained him out there behind in the corral before I came in here tonight. Then here were you and this fellow sitting around a bottle of rum. Tell me, does he mean anything to you?"

"Maybe he does," she said.

"A great deal?"

She answered slowly, "Maybe he means a great deal. I don't really know." She turned from Clay, hiding her face.

He moved closer to her, took her hand. She let it lie in his.

"A great deal, eh?" Clay echoed as if talking to himself. Then he asked, "And what has he said?"

"He wants me to go East to meet his mother."

"Go East to meet his mother?" Clay rose, lifted a log from the wood box, threw it on the fire, then squatted on his heels before the flames. "His mother, eh?" he said over his shoulder. He whistled through his teeth.

"Are you going?"

"I don't know. I haven't had time to think about it yet."

"You mean he asked you that tonight — that's all he said, to go East to meet his mother?"

That was all Peter had said. She would go East, there to meet his mother. Beyond that, he had not committed himself. It was she who, if she went East, would commit herself. Instead of the job as a model, the shop windows, the theatres, the gay parties and dances, at the end of the rail line Peter's mother was waiting, grim and unscrupulous antagonist, in a room of her own furnishing, a room like the Wamboldts' front room, but larger, with a higher ceiling and with more expensive fittings.

Now beside her again, Clay said, "Selva, you'll never do it."

"Why won't I do it?" Who was Clay to tell her what she would or would not do?

He continued without heeding her interruption, "You won't do it. You won't do it because you're not in love with the guy. You're not in love with me either — yet. You're not in love with this guy Peter, because if you were, you would know it and you would be on your way East to meet his mother."

"But I am going East. Now I've made up my mind," Selva said. She stamped her foot. "You've made it up for me."

The low voice insisted at her side, relentless in its pursuit as water running over pebbles. "No," it said, "you're not going. It's not Peter what's-his-name you're in love with. You're in love with where he comes from, the big city and the dances and the parties. That isn't him. That's a part of yourself. Part of you is away out there beyond the mountains. Part of you is right here beside me. I got a hint of that the morning in June we went riding here down by the lake. We were talking about Montreal. I saw it. It came alight in your eyes."

Clay paused. Then he asked, his voice scarcely above a whisper, but husky and closer to her, "Remember that morning, Selva?"

She was silent.

Clay said, "And we were riding and we talked of Montreal and I told you about my Old Man and the Fry Pan Mountains and then you galloped ahead and I let you go away from me until you were only a dot that moved under the mountains. And then I caught up to you and your hair was flying in the wind and I knew, riding close behind you, that there before me was something I would always remember — that hair and the wind and the mountains. I knew that it would come to me in the morning after sleep and that it would lie down with me at night when I went to sleep. And then . . . and then I caught up to you." His voice trailed away and was still.

Clay rose from the couch, walked around it and paced forth and back across the room, forth and back, four paces towards the window, four long paces back towards the dining room, unceasingly, regular as the swinging pendulum of a hall corner clock. "Yes," he said, "I caught up to you. And do you know what I remember? No, you don't know. I remember a little white flower. I don't know its name. It had five white petals and it was growing just by your ear where your head lay on the moss. It was no bigger than a snowflake. It wasn't there at first. Anyway, I didn't see it but afterwards, when you moved your head, it was there, growing in the sunlight as if it had sprung up in the minute. It was as if we had come there to that hollow by the timber just to make that little flower grow."

He hesitated in his pacing. Then, beginning again, restless as a beast in a cage, he said, "That afternoon I pulled out with

208

the horses back to town. A few days later I came back with that old couple, the Priors. He told me he was taking his wife away off to Burma. Something about elephants and harness bells. I never could get it straight in my mind what he was talking about. I came back up here with that old man and his wife. I came into the chalet after putting the horses away and you were sitting over there in the dining room giving the old people their tea. The window was behind you and out the window were the mountains. You wore the mountains like a crown about your head. And I had the feeling coming in and throwing my hat on a chair that this wasn't a chalet at all. No, this was our house, your house and mine, and I was sitting at your table and you were sitting at mine and with us we had guests for tea. And then when tea was over and the Priors had gone into the front room, this room where we are now, I went out to the kitchen and asked you to go walking and you wouldn't go. No, you wouldn't go."

Clay came and sat on the couch. He said, "And that, Selva, is the story. I guess that's what I came in to tell you. When I was riding in here along the creeks and over the pass, it was singing through me but now that I've told it, it seems little enough to have said. Peter Wrogg, maybe he's got more to say to you than that. I don't know. From the looks of him, he's got money. He's probably got a good job, a motor car and a big house. Me, I'm a working stiff who until now never thought he would get married, a pair of hands who wants to raise horses. Peter's got a family too. You say he wants you to go East to meet his mother."

For minutes now, Selva had not looked at Clay. She held her head averted studying a ragged and wandering crack in a floorboard revealed by the glow from the fireplace. She felt his shift and stir on the couch as he said bitterly, "Huh, I had a mother too, once a long time ago. I told you when we were riding about my Old Man and that they had separated. Even afterwards he always said that she was a beautiful woman and I suppose perhaps she was and others besides the Old Man thought so as well. She was tall and straight and fair and had one of those low voices which made you lean forward, closer to her, to listen."

"I remember one afternoon — I was about eleven then and we were living in one of those little towns on Vancouver

Island where Englishmen go to retire when they're no more use in this world. Moss grows well down there. In thirty years you might find Peter near this town wearing flannels, carrying a walking stick. And a pain in his kidneys. Anyway, we were living in a cottage close by a beach. The Old Man was up the Island cruising timber. I was going to school. We had moved around so much that my schooling was irregular and because of that I never did have many friends when I was a boy. However, I had made a good friend here at Qualicum where we were living. He had a funny name, Randolph McPherson, and we called him Randy. It was a Saturday afternoon and Randy and I were walking down the beach, digging clams. It was just sport for Randy. His father managed the big hotel, but I knew my mother and I needed those clams to eat. Randy, as I said, was the first good friend I ever had, a year older than I was. At that age, a year makes a lot of difference. I was proud of having a friend older than I was. When we were out together we didn't have to talk. Each did what he wanted and we usually wanted to do the same things. Randy knew my mother by sight, but he had never seen my father."

"Where we were about two miles down the beach from our cottage, it seemed deserted. It is a long beach, the longest on the east coast of the Island. And this afternoon in April the tide was far out. Randy was a bit ahead of me. He called to me and I lifted up my head from my digging. A pile of driftwood, high as a man's shoulders, was there beyond him and he pointed to it. Something was there and he wanted me to see it. A man and a woman, he told me as I came up to him. He held a finger to his lips and we approached the driftwood cautiously. We got up to it and looked beyond it. There was a stretch of sunny beach — I remember how blue were the sea and sky that afternoon — and an old heavy log with roots flung up like arms that had been left there by the waves. On the other side of the log was the woman and the man. Their faces, as they looked at each other, were turned sideways to us. The man had short cropped curly brown hair and a moustache. He wore glasses. The woman, her honey coloured hair coiled in a braid on the top of her head, was my mother. Backs against the log, she was talking and he was listening, leaning closer and closer to her. It wasn't that he had to. Her voice carried well enough, but it had a quality which drew you to her."

"Randy looked at me startled. 'Golly!' he said. 'It's your mother. I didn't know it was your mother and you didn't tell me your old man had got back from up the Island.'"

Clay coughed. He stood up, sat down again. "Of course, Selva," he continued, "the man was not my father, but I couldn't say that to Randy and as we watched — I was dumb of speech and tied to the spot — he, the man there on the beach, moved nearer to my mother. He embraced her. I heard her sigh. I heard a bird twitter in the bushes above the beach. I saw white gulls wheel. Then my mother's head fell down below the log and her knee and white thigh rose above it against the sea. Randy looked at me. He was frightened. I was sick to my stomach. Randy turned and ran. I walked away."

"That night at home, my mother and I did not have clams for supper. She told me, without my asking, when I looked and saw the sand on her shoes, that she had been up on the hotel golf links during the afternoon walking with old friends who were passing through. When at the table I began to cry, she came and put her arms around me and asked me why I cried. Later that night she came into my bedroom and when I began again to cry, she put her cool hand on my forehead and told me that some day when I was older, I would understand. Perhaps she knew, perhaps she guessed. I never knew. I know I cried for my father. I cried too because Randy and I would be friends no more, and he was the first real friend I had ever had. He would speak to me, but I would never be able to speak to him again. You see, soon my father would be coming back. Shortly after he came back, my mother went away. She went away late one night in a motor car which called there at the cottage for her. The Old Man and I moved up into the Crow's Nest Pass in the Rockies."

Clay's voice died away to a whisper. He shook his head. "Words," he said to Selva. "Too many words. Too many shadows. She died next fall in the hospital down in Vancouver. Something she had swallowed, so they said."

With thumb and forefinger Clay pulled pensively at his lower lip, then he took out a big, nickel plated watch. He said, "It's late now, almost midnight. I didn't mean to talk so much."

Selva said, "I'm glad you did, Clay."

Rising from the couch, she told him he might sleep in the room adjoining that of Peter Wrogg in the first cabin where Rosie earlier had lit the stove. It would save him the bother of kindling a fire in the tepee.

As she turned to go from the room, he held out his hands, palms down, studied them and said, "Remember — you may go East. You may stay here. Wherever you go, whatever you do, these are yours for the taking."

"I'll always remember," Selva said. "I'll always remember you and tonight."

She would always remember the two little boys behind the pile of driftwood by the sea and the white gulls wheeling. Yet the next morning when Clay came into the chalet it was as if the night before had not been. He entered with Peter. they had slept in adjoining rooms, and had met and now came in to breakfast together. They were laughing. Peter apparently had been telling a joke for as the front door opened, Selva heard him say, "then the Queen said to the King. 'George,' she said, 'don't give him no bloody medal!'" Clay laughed, tilting his head. Peter was about to laugh with him, then, seeing Selva across the room, his lips tightened and he came towards her.

"Sorry," he said.

"What about?"

"I had a bit too much to drink last night. I feel perfectly hellish this morning."

Before Selva could reply, Clay came up from behind him and addressing her said, "That's all right. Everyone has too much once in a while. He'll feel better after breakfast. Then I'll go out after the horses and we'll take a ride down by the lake."

"You're going riding?" Selva asked.

"Sure. We're all going riding. Rosie too, if she wants to."

"But I thought you had to climb Thunder Ridge to see if you could take horses across?"

Clay brushed her suggestion aside with a wave of his hand. "I'll go tomorrow."

"How about the men — won't they be coming in today?"

"Probably not till tomorrow or the day after. They've got some trail widening to do and some work at the overnight camp on the other side of the pass."

The men who were to build a chalet at Geikie Meadows — it would provide a pleasant day-trip from the High Valley if horses could be put across Thunder Ridge — did not arrive for another three days, Slim Conway travelling with them in charge of their ten horse pack-train. During the two intervening days, Selva found herself in the grip of an event which swept her along as the river sweeps away the uprooted tree whose roots its currents have in the first place undermined. Without seemingly making an effort to do so, Clay had taken complete command of the chalet and of everything which went on within it and around it.

In retrospect, she thought that the development stemmed from the incident of the axe. They had gone riding, all of them, including Rosie, the first morning as Clay had proposed. He gave Peter a tall white horse. Peter rode well, but with a short stirrup, posting in his saddle. He had good hands, though not so sure and, therefore, not so gentle as those of Clay, who never for a moment was out of contact with the mouth of the black horse beneath him, signalling with a touch of the lines on his neck what he would have him do.

Gradually, down by the lake, Clay and Peter drew ahead. Clay was interested in London and particularly in Ireland because of the horses which were raised there. Selva, riding behind with Rosie, heard the men's voices above the plop or thud of hooves but could not be sure of what they said. She spoke to Rosie, asked her what she intended to do now that the chalet was closing. The men who were going into the Geikie Meadows might be in need of a cook. Rosie was not certain of what she would do. Probably she wouuld return to the hotel. She had had enough of the high mountains.

Looking ahead at the shoulders of the two men, Selva sensed that in some way, dim and devious and beyond her comprehending, her own future, what she would do, had been taken from her hands where it had at best insecurely rested and was there being determined for her. Up ahead was a masculine fraternity from which she and Rosie were excluded.

At noon the four riders stopped for lunch in an open

patch of moss and grass above the falls where the waters of Amethyst Lake fell with a roar into the lower valley. After loosening the saddle cinches, Clay turned quickly and expertly to make a fire to boil the tea water, chipping with his axe from the trunk of a dead standing spruce a long splinter, making shavings from it with his knife — "Rocky Mountain feathers" they were called — laying them clustered on the ground, touching a match, then building tepee-like with twigs and larger pieces upon them, the whole performed with the precision of a ritual, with tenderness, an act of worship to evoke the reluctant flame.

Clay's back was turned as he bent to his task. Peter, seeing the axe, its blade embedded in the butt of a green balsam, lifted it free and, endeavouring to do his part in helping with the fire, swung wildly overhead at one of the tree's branches. He missed. The axe blade completed its arc and, avoiding his toe by an inch, clicked against a stone in the ground. Clay jumped, turned as if he had been stung. Fury was in his eyes. Then as quickly he restrained himself. He made a long step towards Peter, took the axe from his hand. "Never touch another man's axe," he said. He regarded the wounded blade which the stone had nicked, shook his head and spat.

"Awfully sorry," Peter said. "Really didn't mean . . ." He was abashed. He had transgressed a code and in so doing had shown himself less than the man who now rebuked him for it. Selva, hanging the billy on the pot-hook over the fire, knew that he felt himself humbled. He had marked himself as an outlander — tourists, male tourists, especially if a woman were nearby, invariably reached for an axe and as invariably nicked the blade if they were so fortunate as not to slice a foot.

After returning to the chalet, Peter came in alone from his cabin shortly before supper. Selva stood by the front window, looking down upon the lake rimmed with its sombre spruce trees, flecked with the wind, golden in the earlier setting sun. Rubbing the palms of his hands together, Peter, approaching her, said, "Topping ride, topping country . . . good chap, this fellow Clay. A bit on the brusque side, that axe business, you know, but underneath it, a good chap."

"You think so?"

"Yes, thoroughly good chap. You know, I think he's

rather fond of you."

"Really?"

Peter glanced away for a moment. Thoughtfully, he spoke. "Not anything he has said. It's the way he has of looking at you when you're looking in the other direction."

He touched his chin with a curved forefinger. "That would make two of us, Selva," he said.

Selva replied, "Clay and I just happen to be working for the same outfit. There's nothing more to it than that."

"Perhaps." Peter was unconvinced. "At any rate," he said, "you know how I feel. I do want you to come East to meet my mother . . . and I'm terribly sorry about the rum drinking espisode last night."

"Don't worry about the rum, Peter."

After an instant's hesitation, Peter said, "I know you would like her."

"Who?"

"My mother. And she will like you."

Selva waited. He did not embroider his remark except to say, "You will come, Selva, soon?"

She said, "But Peter . . ."

It was one of the few occasions during the two days when she and Peter could speak alone. Now Rosie came into the front room, interrupting them, setting on the table the Aladdin lamp which in the kitchen she had just filled with kerosene. Clay followed from the woodpile. He and Peter, it appeared, had discovered that during their boyhoods they had both been readers of *Chums*, an English published volume of adventure stories and now, before the fireplace, with Selva no more than a sounding board for what they said, they began to exchange reminiscences of characters drawn from long forgotten days. They mentioned "White Rep," an English gentleman-fighter, who had come out West and lived as a rancher and they spoke of other stories written about hunters and trappers.

Then and later, Rosie relegated to the kitchen after supper, the three of them, under Clay's guiding hand — as insistent, as persevering, as sure, as gentle as it ever was with horse-flesh — became a trio, a three-headed, six-legged embodied consciousness inhabiting the rooms of the chalet, passing from the front room to the dining-room and back again to the fireplace. *Chums?* This was the sort of country, the same sort of log building the very life that Peter as a boy in far off England had read about and Clay, perhaps eight years older than himself, was the prototype of those former heroes who rode horses and shot from the saddle. Clay did not attempt to keep Peter and Selva apart. Rather, he held them together, himself in the middle. So that it seemed natural that the next afternoon the three of them were sitting with their backs against the sun warmed logs of the chalet, while Clay pointed with his pipe stem across the valley. "That's Thunder Ridge," he said.

Thunder Ridge was a saddle in the mountains rising perhaps one thousand feet above the valley floor. Mount Erebus rose sheer on its left or eastern side. Another peak rose sheer on its right. Beyond it now sullen cloud masses loomed, piled one upon the other. Below them, the ridge was like a mighty threshold which a giant might have used to pass from the valley of light into farther darkness.

"I'll be afoot," Clay said, turning to Peter, who sat between him and Selva, "and the way I'll go tomorrow, will be to follow up that draw. It's just below the snow patch that looks like a beaver's tail. Horses could get up there all right and maybe farther up too, but higher there'll be loose shale and then big boulders. And then there's a ledge — you can see it there at an angle with the snow caught on it. I think I can follow it to the top. It's easy enough on this side. A horse might even make it up that ledge without any work being done on it, but on the other side there's a waterfall and we'll likely have to build a flying trestle around it. I'll leave early in the morning, camp beyond the ridge in the timber and come back next day."

Peter asked why it was necessary to put horses over the ridge.

"Tourists," Clay said. "Next summer they'll be able to ride over to Geikie Meadows in a day. That's where we're going to build the new chalet. Otherwise" — he waved an arm to the west, towards the Fraser valley — "they'd have to go away down there and then climb back along the far slope of those mountains. The round trip would take four days instead of two."

He added, looking across Peter to Selva, "Not that it will

matter much to me. Next year I'll be raising horses as I told you while we were riding yesterday. But Bill Wilkins asked me to do this before I quit."

Peter seemed not to be listening. He had addressed himself to the ridge. He turned to Clay, his face brightening. He said, "I daresay what you will be doing is known as trail blazing, like those old stories in *Chums*. Man against the wilderness idea."

"There won't be much blazing to do," Clay replied. "Most of the time I'll be above the timber. If the weather holds, it will be a nice little hike, about twenty miles round trip."

Peter stretched out a leg, wagged his climbing boot on its heel. Clay touched his arm. "There's a flock of goat up there now," he said. "Let's go over here. We can see them better." He rose, walked to a tree thirty feet away. Peter, dusting his trousers, followed. Selva remained seated. Though taking no part in the conversation, it had had interest for her. Tomorrow Clay would be up on the ridge. She and Peter would be alone.

The two men were staring up at the mountains. They moved farther away. Then they looked down as though they were discussing Peter's boots. Now, coming back to her, she heard Clay say, "Sure, they'll be first rate. I've got a pair of hobnails with me that I'm going to wear." The casual words sent a chill through her. She started to her feet. "Peter!" she exclaimed, "You're not."

Peter's right eye was as wide as though he were fitting a monocle to it. The lid of the left one drooped. He said, "Selva, it's not at all a difficult climb as it looks from here." "Besides" — he waggled again the toe of his boot — "I haven't done much with these, have I? And it may be a long time before I come back. Business, you know, and all that."

She saw through him as though he were transparent. He might be unhandy with an axe, but he had climbed mountains. There on the ridge he would assure himself and he would show her that what Clay could do, he could do. More than that, here was a chance — it might never happen again — to meet the wilderness of the Canadian Rockies on the terms on which the characters in his boyhood stories had met it. The incident of the axe, small enough in its way, had set loose a train of thought within him for which the climb over the ridge was the logical culmination. It had also given Clay an ascendancy which, to Peter's mind, could not go unchallenged. He was accepting that challenge by the only means within his grasp. Perhaps too — the notion flashed before Selva and was gone — he fled from the greater challenge of being left alone with her. Yet his purpose, so he said, in coming into the High Valley had been no more than that — to be with her. She remembered their defeat before the fireplace. She saw again the beaver meadow and Slim riding down to it and afterwards her leading Peter back to town. The first time they had met and Peter had taken her to the porch outside the dance above the pool-hall, he had moved as if to kiss her, then hesitated and the moment had been lost. Now he was here. Tomorrow would have been their own and he was turning from it. He would run away, but he would always return.

Clay came to stand between them, brow creased, studying the ridge. "Maybe," he said to Peter, "you might find the going a little tough."

"Nonsense!" Peter laughed. "My dear chap. I've climbed, you know, in Switzerland and other places . . . peaks." He looked up at Mount Erebus, scowled.

Selva frowned too. She glared at Clay. When he had spoken, he had said the last thing which, in the circumstances, he should have said.

"Well," he said now to Peter, "it's the weather I was thinking of. Might get snow. I feel sleepy. I always get sleepy just before the snow flies." He commenced to yawn, put his hand to his mouth to shield it.

Looking across at the wall of stubborn rock flanked by glacier and peak, Selva felt her stomach tighten. "Peter," she said, "you're not going."

"But Selva, I've already said . . ."

Clay knocked out his pipe on the palm of his hand. "We'll talk about it at supper," he said. "Lots of time. All evening to get ready."

That night, getting into bed, Selva looked out the window and for the first time in the season saw the green and golden banners of the Northern Lights stream across the sky.

sixteen

Into the deep and overpowering well of sleep, a voice called. On the bed, under the blankets, Selva tossed, spread her arms and moaned. Eyelids closed, darkness weighed upon her and doom impended. Sleep threatened once more and the voice, remembered but no longer heard, cried to her lonely from the wilderness of light.

It was morning and the voice was Rosie's voice singing in the kitchen. Still Selva did not rouse herself.

Rosie came to the door. "Breakfast," she said. "The men are at the table."

Selva turned her face to the wall. "I've a headache," she mumbled. "I'll have breakfast later."

Sometimes Mrs. Wamboldt had stayed in bed with a headache. It usually happened that she did so on a morning following a noisy row with Mr. Wamboldt, probably about a business deal in which he had failed to follow her advice.

Selva had had no row. However, she was angry. The men were leaving to climb Thunder Ridge. The previous afternoon they had stepped aside, beyond her earshot, to make their decision. The decision finally, she knew, had rested with Clay — but had Peter asked to go or was it Clay who in the first place made the suggestion to him? That she did not know. Clay's conduct throughout had been consistent. He had postponed to the last moment his exploration and conquest of the ridge. So long as he remained at the chalet, she and Peter, failing an overt stand, had had no time alone together. Peter had made no such assertion of himself. Clay had not taken her away from Peter. On the contrary, being obliged to climb the ridge, he was taking Peter away from her. He had shown himself to be a redoubtable opponent, nose to his purpose like that of a horse snubbed to a tree. She would not get up and sit at breakfast with him that he might further taste his triumph.

They were at breakfast now. She heard their loud voices, their laughter, their heavy boots scuffing the floor. They were exulting because they were fulfilling one of man's prime functions. They were going on a journey. Its hazard — every journey had its hazard — and its effort were the bonds of their union. Sometime during the summer, she had read in a tourist's magazine that man was so made that for his health and well being he should walk at least twenty miles a day. She began to doubt that a woman was fully equipped to keep pace with him. Early man had been a hunter. To hunt he had to travel. His woman stayed at home. This morning she too would stay at home. She would stay in the only home she had, in the chalet, deep as she could be within it, in the bedroom off the warm kitchen, in the bed which her hands had made and on the mattress shaped by her limbs and body.

In a while, she heard nailed boots tiptoe across the kitchen floor. They stopped outside her door. After two or three seconds of hesitation, knuckles knocked quickly three times upon the door. When she did not call out in response, after a further wait, the door creaked open. Selva kept her face to the wall.

Clay spoke. He took a step into the room. "Rosie tells me you have a headache," he said.

Selva said nothing.

"I'm sorry," he said. "I'm sorry for everything, but I can't back down now. I can't tell him he can't come with me."

Clay paused. Selva took a deep breath.

"It would hurt him," Clay continued, his voice low as though fearful that he might be overheard. "You see, he's never done anything like this before, travelled into new country, carried his own food, camped out under a tree.

220

Just now he's down at the cabin." As an afterthought, he added, "Maybe he thinks we don't believe he ever climbed a mountain." Then, enigmatically, "Maybe he's just interested in being a man. So am I — a live one." He said, "Hell, I don't really know. If I knew I'd tell you."

Then, speaking in a changed tone, Clay said, "Slim Conway will be in with the boys today or tomorrow at the latest. Tell them to wait right here until I come back. Tell Slim to turn his horses down from mine in the lower meadow."

Clay moved closer until she felt him standing above her shoulders. He did not touch her. Looking down upon her, he said, "That head, that head upon that pillow . . . I'll take good care of Peter Wrogg, Selva. He's yours. I'll look after him well. We'll be back by suppertime tomorrow night."

He turned to go. "Well —" he said, then he had gone and the door shut gently behind him.

In the kitchen, he took from Rosie the lunch and food she had prepared for the overnight trip. "Remember," Selva heard Rosie call to him, "the tea's in the sugar bag and the salt's in the pepper tin."

Then the front door opened and closed. After a few minutes the door from the cabin slammed finally shut. A shout shook the air. "Ho!" It would be Clay, she supposed, head back, face lifted to the challenge of the mountains above him. A horseman from the prairies would have given forth shrilly. Clay, who was first of all a mountain man, shouted. This was his home ground. There before him was work to do — a trail to find, if he could, by which horses would be taken over Thunder Ridge into Geikie Meadows.

In the kitchen Rosie moved among her pots and pans and dishes.

"Rosie!" Selva called. "I'm getting up now."

Rosie came to the door. "Feeling better?" she asked.

"I feel all right."

"There're pills you can take for those sort of headaches." Rosie said. "You see them advertised in the paper."

"It isn't that sort of a headache," Selva replied. "And anyway, I told you I was feeling all right."

"I'll put on some fresh coffee for you," Rosie said, "then I'll go down and tidy up the men's cabin."

"Never mind about the cabin. I'll go down and make the

beds and straighten it up."

"But you're not feeling well."

Selva spoke sharply. "I told you I'd look after the cabin. You've got lots to do. We're going to have a gang of men here on our hands to feed. You'd better do some baking."

Later, standing beside her at the table, regarding the bacon and eggs, the pile of hotcakes, Rosie said, "You're off your feed. You haven't eaten anything but a piece of toast and drunk three cups of coffee."

"It's just that I'm not hungry," said Selva. "I feel as if I had a cold." It was true. Her cheeks were flushed, her forehead hot.

After her breakfast, she went down to the cabin where the men had slept. This was the cabin in which the Priors, enroute to distant Burma, had stayed. She climbed the four steps to the porch. She opened the door, stood hesitant in the doorway. A tin heater stove, damped, but still warm confronted her, giving its heat over the partitions to the two rooms, left and right. The room where Clay had slept was on her right, Peter's on her left.

It seemed that the choice which she would make, as to whose room she would enter first, was important, as though the men, now walking through the forest to the ridge, would know what her decision had been. She put out her right hand, turned the knob of Clay's door, pushed it open.

The room at first glance seemed devastated as if, the night before, not one man but several had camped within it. The mattress from one of the two beds had been pulled to the floor. Apparently Clay preferred a hard bed. The sheets had been thrown on the top of the other unused bed, the two pillows flung after them into the corner against the log wall. Clay had no use for sheets and pillows. On the mattress at Selva's feet in the middle of the room, the red and blue blankets were snarled and twisted as though night long he had struggled with another to possess them. Of his own personal possessions, except the saddle bags hung over the back of a chair, nothing at all remained. Clay travelled light, carrying only what he could use. He wore hobnailed boots. His moccasins would be in his pack sack with him to wear around the campfire. The room, with its smell of saddle leather and the smokey smell which she associated with him, was a scene of accomplished violence as if, deep within the man himself, beneath the exterior of calm and purpose, a fiery turmoil smouldered. Selva folded the blankets, left them on the mattress on the floor.

When she crossed the hallway to Peter's room, it was to step from storm into quiet. Clay's room had had the air of having been irrevocably abandoned like the trapper's cabin off the trail above the chalet. Here, Peter's presence, on the other hand, still lingered, his brown leather slippers which he had worn when sitting with her before the fireplace set side by side for his return beneath his bed. He had made his bed, blankets neat, without a wrinkle. The room had no clothes closet and his grey silk pyjamas and tan silk dressing gown hung from a hook by the head of the bed. Beside them hung his grey tweed jacket. Selva stroked the silken dressing gown, put her nose against the jacket with its smell of peat and bog. The room itself was pungent with Peter's face lotion. She saw the green, squat bottle on the dressing table top, "Spruce — the manly lotion." Beside the bottle was a canvas shaving kit, unrolled, safety razor, brush and a round, wooden case of Yardley's shaving soap set neatly upon it. Just to its right was a pigskin case with the initials "P.W." in black stamped upon it, which held places for two military brushes, a comb and toothbrush holder. Peter had taken the toothbrush, the comb and one of the ebony backed brushes in his rucksack. Clay might have a comb with him. Most certainly he would not have carried a hairbrush.

To the left of the face lotion bottle was a book, *Poems — W. B. Yeats.* An envelope was in it, marking a place. Behind the book, against the mirror, was another envelope. On it was written, "For Selva." She opened it and read in the remembered, delicate handwriting: "Selva — I am waiting for Clay. We are about to leave. I had hoped to see you this morning. Rosie — who will take this to you — said you were unwell and I thought it best not to disturb you. We shall return tomorrow afternoon, so I believe. You will have two days free of me, of both of us, to think on what I have said. Perhaps it is best that way. Perhaps it is only a dream I have. But softly, Selva, tread softly on my dream." The single letter "P" was at the bottom of the narrow page of note paper.

Re-folding the note into its envelope, Selva noticed again the book of poems. She took it up, opened it at page fifteen where the envelope had been inserted. A pencil had been drawn vertically down beside several of its lines. They read:

"Had I the heavens' embroidered cloths,
Enwrought with golden and silver light,
The blue and the dim and the dark cloths
Of night and light and the half light,
I would spread the cloths under your feet.
But I, being poor, have only my dreams;
I have spread my dreams under your feet.
Tread softly because you tread on my dreams."

Poor? Could Peter be poor? Selva looked around the room at the tweed jacket, the silken robe and pyjamas, at the tooled leather of the travelling kit, recalled the house in Montreal West and the mother waiting there — was this then poverty? She reflected, who upon the ridge would find himself the richer man?

Tread softly, Peter said, for she trod on his dreams. Whose was the richer dream upon the ridge? She looked again at the tweed jacket. Odd, she thought, that Peter should leave behind his warm tweed jacket.

Returning to the chalet by the back door, through the woodshed, she noticed that the grey and black checkered mackinaw which had been there summer long reminding her of Clay, who early in the season had left it and forgotten, was not now hanging from its nail on the post.

She called Rosie from the kitchen. "Where's the mackinaw," she asked, "that's been hanging here all summer?"

"He gave it to the Englishman to wear," Rosie replied. "He came out last night before supper and got it. He gave him one of his woollen undershirts too."

The simple circumstance that Peter was now wearing Clay's old mackinaw brought a first shiver, a premonitory touch of apprehension with it. It was true — the black and grey mackinaw would be more serviceable than the tweed jacket for the climb over the ridge. It was warmer, looser. With the mackinaw, the woollen undershirt, his own flannel shirt and pullover sweater, Peter would be well provided for against the weather. But the mackinaw had hung there untouched throughout the summer and into fall, faded by the sun, blowing in the wind and barely protected from the rain. Forsaken, a thing cast off and forgotten, it seemed now to confer its qualities upon its wearer and to have been preserved through the long months for the purpose which presently and remotely it was serving.

Peter's note to Selva had said that she was treading on his dream. Perhaps, she thought, it was he who was treading on his own. She looked at the post, bare, smooth and upright, supporting its roof of shakes. She looked past the roof, past the tips of spruce trees, to the sky. There was no answer where she looked. No sun shone in the sky. The sky around the horizons was grey and overhead it was a dark and sullen blue, an unbroken dome of cloud. When she stepped out to look at the mountains, at Thunder Ridge, at the forest straggling on the slopes and crowded in the draws, at the lake quiescent below the chalet, the same blue mood persisted. It was not colour. It was rather the absence of the familiar colours of leaf and rock and water. A haze obscured the land and shadowed all events upon it. No wind blew. The valley listened.

The snow came that night. Selva heard it from her bed, over Rosie's slow and gentle breathing. She heard it rustle against the windowpane above her head, so faint in whisper that it was no more than silence falling. Later in the night it shifted on the roof as though that silence had briefly spoken.

"What's that?" Rosie asked, rising on her elbow.

"It's snowing," Selva said.

The snow was falling. It would fall on roof and mountain top and on the great horned owl bunched in his feathers on a spruce tree limb. The morning would show the snow white upon the ground and in it the pattern of little feet light as the touch of thistledown where mice had gone from bush to bush for fallen seed. Blotting out their slender tracings would be the pads of coyote, wolf or wolverine, sniffing nose down upon the trail, or perhaps the scooped out saucer with a curved grey feather rocking within it where the wakeful owl had swooped.

The snow would fall upon the forest and fall melting into creeks and on the surface of the lake. It would bead and mat upon the tails and manes and melt cold upon the backs of the horses pastured in the meadow, while on the backs of moose and deer and caribou, unmelting, it would form a blanket against the cold. The snow would fall upon Thunder Ridge and upon the camp of the two men beyond the ridge. It would not fall upon the men. Clay would have made a good camp, close in against the trunk of an old spruce or balsam tree, fire at his feet, protected under the low sweeping branches as if within the folds of a mothering skirt. For the night that forest tree would be a mother, the mother in the forest that men of long ago had worshipped, crouched in skins about their fires.

The snow fell throughout the night and in the morning as it still was falling Selva awoke to a new and windless world beyond the chalet door. She could not see far. She could see to the trees hooded and mantled in white, heads bowed, penitents appearing out of the dimness. She lifted her eyes. There, out of the grieving sky, from higher than she could see, in hundreds and thousands, in unnumbered twirling hosts, the winged flakes were settling. They lay four inches deep on the chalet steps and furred the hitching-rail and covered all the clearing. Beyond that she could not see and the world was no more than the narrow confines of her vision within which she and Rosie moved.

Yet it seemed to Selva that everywhere she had ever been it was snowing. It snowed upon the homestead in the foothills, and in Yellowhead the new maid, working for the new people in the Wamboldt house, would be sweeping the front walk out to the gate in the hedge of spruce. People would be passing the house, heads down, fresh snow steaming from their feet. Smoke would be coming from the town's chimneys and near those chimneys, in dark patches below the roof ridges, snow would be melting. The steeple of the Catholic church, too steep to hold the snow, gaunt and black over the town, would be a finger forever pointing to the sky. From the narrow door beneath it, the priest, like a marmot from his hole, would poke his head and wring chubby hands at the blessing of the weather. Above the church on the hill, where in the cemetery slept those who had learned the fearful worth of churchly promise, the snow would trim with lace the crosses and lie, a blanket of softest down, upon the mounded graves. And the waxen flowers over little Lucinda's grave, the section foreman's daughter, would seem to bloom again in the white spring of its coming.

Out on the prairies past the foothills, the snow would be falling as in the cities with their tall towers and their streets of shop windows where women in furs, breaths rising as though slow fire consumed them, taking short steps, were passing in procession. It fell on the seas and on lands beyond the seas where strange flags flew and on the whole earth wearily turning. And as she stood in the doorway, looking up and blinking, Selva felt it falling, slowly falling, on all the summers that she would ever know. The flakes brushed her eyelids, were a benediction upon her cheek. One fell and melted within the fold of her lip.

She turned to look towards Thunder Ridge. There the snow, like a swarm of grey moths fluttering, confused and then blinded her eyes. The rocks of Thunder Ridge would be wet, they would be slippery with the new snow falling. Clay, she thought, might wait, postpone for a day his and Peter's return. The snow was the first snow of the season and it would not last. But no, he would not delay. Slim Conway and the builders and the pack-horses were overdue from town. He would return, if he could, to meet them.

Later that morning she went into the kitchen to make a chocolate layer cake against Clay's and Peter's return. They would be hungry for sweets when they returned. Halfway through its mixing, she gave it up. She came back to the front room, paced before the unlit fireplace. Then, before lunch, she went to her bedroom, changed into her whip-cord trousers and flannel shirt, took off her shoes and, with a pair of heavy woollen socks, put on the blue beaded moccasins one of the older guides had given to her late in the summer. Over the flannel shirt she wore the caribou hide vest and a mackinaw. She bound a blue silk handkerchief about her head, carried white woollen mittens in her hand.

"And where do you think *you're* going?" Rosie asked as Selva came from the bedroom into the kitchen.

"For a walk."

"In this snow? You're crazy."

"It's not cold," Selva said, "and I won't be gone long."

"I know," Rosie said. "I've been watching you all morning, going forth and back. You're going out to the ridge to meet the men."

"Maybe I am."

"Well, you can't do them any good. They're all right. That fellow Clay knows what he's doing." Rosie looked at the moccasins. "Besides," she said, "you'll get wet feet. Besides, you're getting a cold, so you said."

"I'll change when I come back."

"Why don't you take a horse then?" Rosie asked.

"It's not worth while walking two miles down to the pasture and back again and saddling up."

Finally Rosie said, "You'd better stop and have some lunch first."

Selva took a piece of bread and butter, a slab of yellow cheese, ate standing before the kitchen stove, sipping a cup of tea.

The trail to the foot of the ridge would not be difficult to follow. It was marked by a line of blazes through the timber. She would not climb far on the ridge, its foot three miles from the chalet. She would meet the men when they came down from it. No purpose, she knew, was served by her going — unless it was that of release from the inaction of waiting inside four walls.

"Don't get a chill," Rosie called after her from the chalet steps.

Selva walked through the aisle of the forest. Occasionally, her elbow touched a down hanging bough and a flutter of snow fell beside her. The snow dusted her trouser legs above her ankles. On the smooth, unbroken trail she kicked it into little balls which rolled in runnels before her like tiny beasts with long and ever lengthening tails scurrying from her toes. Ahead in the tree trunks, the blazes glowed, lanterns lighting the way. It was not cold. She guessed it was close to freezing. Her breath rose yellow and her nose and cheeks were tingling. Snowflakes lazily fell.

After nearly an hour of walking, she came out from the forest and with a stick in her hand, on brown, emergent boulders whose snow sluffed into the water from her moccasins, crossed a westward flowing creek and began to climb towards timberline on the ridge. Then, after half a mile, she paused. Before her were tracks in the snow. A grizzly, fording the creek lower down, had passed up the slope. The claws of his front toes had made minute indentations in the snow four inches beyond the marks of his mighty paws while his hind feet showed as though a man had walked there barefoot. The tracks were fresh, for even as she studied them where they had pressed through the snow into the moist muskeg, a tiny trickle of water flowed. This was the Great Bear — shaggy, fanged and clawed, the hidden host of the valley.

Selva hesitated. She went on a few more steps. She stopped again. There at her feet was what had been a porcupine. His hide had been turned completely inside out, fat, flesh and bone devoured, and then it had been discarded like a glove cast off. She had heard an old trapper say that, were it not for the porcupine, the wolverine would be the ruler of the bush. The wolverine, the wolf, the coyote, attacked the porcupine with mouths open. The quills festered in noses, tongues and throats. Then they could not eat and perished. The bear knew better. He put a paw under the quilled wad-dler, turned him on his back exposing the vulnerable stomach, protecting himself from the quills.

Now at Selva's feet not a drop of blood remained upon the snow, only the white envelope, inverted, where once warm life had been. Beside it, the figure of a little man upright in the snow, stood a solitary quill. Removing her mitt, Selva picked it up gingerly, noted its barb, its dark point, its paling length to the root which had been lightly rooted in hide. She twisted it slowly between thumb and forefinger. Memory stirred, but at first its relevance eluded her. Then she stood in her bedroom in the Wamboldt house. Slim Conway had brought her back from the dance above the pool hall where she had that night met Peter Wrogg. As she combed her hair before the mirror, she was thinking that Peter had said as she was leaving the dance, that he would call for her "tomorrow." She had felt a stab in her finger. Inexplicably, a porcupine quill had been loose in her hair. Se had put it into the kitchen stove, returned to her room, sucking her finger.

At the time it had been a mysterious visitation. Now, standing in the snow below the ridge, looking backward through the months, it seemed to her that her first meeting with Peter had been like the prick of that porcupine quill which had brought a bead of blood to the tip of her finger. It was he and no other who until then had perceived her longings and had translated them to her in terms which she could understand and had put before her the hope that they might one day become fact. Afterwards, he had gone away, but the idea he had implanted, the little stab which he had given to her fancy, had stayed, had clung to her, had become a thing of subtle torment as the porcupine quill would have stayed and clung and festered had she not, that night of their meeting, plucked it deftly out.

She shook her head. She did not know. "Dear Peter," she thought, "kind Peter . . . Peter somewhere up there on the ridge beyond my seeing."

But now the snow was lifting. A patch of blue was in the sky above her and high above the slope, beyond the timber, 'she saw the grizzly's track and knew that he would not molest her. She turned and looked across the valley. She saw the diminished chalet, a brave plume of smoke showing from Rosie's fire. Above the chalet was the notch of Crooked Pass. On the white snow below, black specks were moving as foreign to it as a string of ants upon a sheet hanging from the line. Slim Conway and the boys were dropping down to the chalet and, as always, watching, Selva was touched with the wonder of life so quickly manifest, as though it had no past and would have no future, on the mountain side below the pass.

With the lifting clouds the wind blew cold from the west. She buttoned the top button of her mackinaw, turned up the collar. Looking down into the valley, she saw the tree tops bend before the wind and as its great hand stroked them, saw their branches shed wavering veils of snow until, no longer white, they showed green and new as if a sudden springtime rose before her.

But behind, above on Thunder Ridge, no springtime was appearing. There winter walked trailing banners of snow and there the pale, cold sun was already slipping behind a craggy peak. From the ridge, the lofty threshold between the mountains, a blue shadow descended by imperceptible degrees, like ink seeping through the snow. The grizzly had climbed as far as the shadow then Selva saw his tracks curving back and down until they entered the timber again half a mile away and below her.

She thought it must be three o'clock. At any moment now Clay and Peter would top the ridge, follow the ledge she saw above her and drop down to where she stood at the timber's upmost reach, unless, of course, Clay had decided, because of the snow, to delay his return for a day. She would not climb farther. She would build a fire and wait for half an hour.

She hunted in under the boles of spruce trees where, shielded by the branches, the ground was bare and no snow had fallen. She found dry twigs and hanging caribou moss and broke off several dead branches.

Over her fire she stood swinging her arms, feeling the blood sharp in her finger ends as warmth returned once more.

Selva looked up to the peaks above the ridge. They were old and worn with time. They were strong. They had out-gazed sun and weather. For long ages, before man began, they had known the moon and stars. They were the ages regarding her. She stood solitary among them, suppliant, below the pass at the edge of timber, the first being in a world newly made or the last one on a planet fled by its people.

Above her, higher than she could climb, on the rock, in the cold, deep snow, was Peter — Peter in a borrowed mackinaw, shaped by another man's use. Peter of the apple rosy cheeks, the deep blue eyes, the curly hair, the soft hands with dimples in their knuckles. Peter was up there because of her, as certainly as though she had sent him. Peter had talked to her of Montreal, showed her a world beyond her attaining. She, a woman, hungered to be what she was not, to have what she could not have. All her life she had sat looking out a window. She remembered her mother, sitting against the train's coach window, going into Edmonton from the homestead, into the city where she might visit, but would never stay. She was like her mother and her mother was like the mother before her. Her mother had given her a name, "Selva." It meant "forest" in another language and it had served to remind her mother of the first happiness she had known. The name of her daughter, she had thought, would in some way perpetuate that happiness. Now Selva stood on the edge of the forest. She could go no farther, nor escape from what she was.

Peter, whom she did not yet love, but whom she felt she might one day truly love and who had come to represent to her all that she might have been, had gone farther and gone higher. He had gone where he had no right to go. Clay, coming into her bedroom in the chalet, had said, "Maybe he thinks we don't believe he ever climbed a mountain." How did she know, Selva asked herself, whether or not he had climbed before? True, he wore the clothes. He spoke of the Weisshorn in Switzlerland. But he had not climbed to the top of the Weisshorn. He had come running back to his mother. Still, he was young then. Now he was a grown man. For all that, recalling their times together, their going to the beaver meadow and what had happened since, Selva, warming her hands over the fire, stamping her feet, wondered. Their association had been like a weird dancing class. Peter came forward. She retreated. She advanced and he drew back. An old word used by her mother came to mind. An elderly woman on a nearby ranch had died, it was said, of age. Selva's mother had given a little snort. "She could have got out of bed if she had tried," she said. "She was fey. She wanted to die." "Fey" — that was the word.

Selva looked up again to the ridge and its blue shadow creeping lower on the snow. Peter was up there. She was up there for Peter was part of herself. He was that part of her which had climbed the highest — and now he must return to her again. She would go to him, cradle his head in her arms. She would love him as woman had never loved a man before. She would bind him to her with desire and shackle him with need. She would love him as the forest loves the mountain and as the river loves the valley. She would at once enfold him and flow through him. She would be the wind on his cheek, the breath from his lips. For him she would be today, tomorrow and all the days that came after.

She swung about. With her wet moccasined foot she kicked the wood and embers from the fire, scattered them sizzling on the snow. Here the snow was deeper and well above her ankles. She turned from where the fire had been and commenced to run up the steepening slope. "Peter!" she called. "Peter, dear, dear Peter." She slipped. She fell and rising to one knee, halted, for above her she saw a movement. A man stood a moment against the skyline. One man or two? She could not be sure, he had dropped so quickly from her sight. Was it Peter, was it Clay?

She waited, still upon her knee, her teeth, unheeded, chattering in the cold. Her breath wheezed. The man dwarfed by height and distance, appeared again, arms outstretched, as though crucified, face against the wall of rock, inching along the slippery ledge. Snow fell from where he set his feet, making furrows in the slope beneath him. Carefully, carefully, he felt his way along the ledge. Off the ledge he turned, began to run. His footing failed. He slid fifty feet and vanished in a flurry of snow dust.

With a cry, Selva rose to her feet. Yet, eyes glued to the dark rock from which the man's sliding body had brushed the snow, she moved no farther, immobile, a statue planted in a weary land.

Then, a thousand feet above, the figure appeared again, full-bodied and proportioned now, riffling blue shadowed snow, face showing white against it. Clay descended in long, leaping strides.

Clay was alone, coming down the slope towards her. As he came nearer and she saw the whites of his eyes, the grey breath from nostril and lips, Selva's limbs trembled. Her body shook as with a chill. She put her finger in her mouth, clenched her teeth upon it and did not feel the hurt.

Then Clay was before her. He asked no questions, expressed no surprise at her being where she was. He had lost his hat. His nut brown hair was tight against his scalp. Against the cold he wore only his grey woollen shirt. Steam rose from his chest and shoulders. Elbows bent, his hands hung clenched and helpless. He gasped. He tried to speak. He spat, but no spittle came from his mouth in whose lip corners saliva had caked. The skin of his cheeks was yellow, old and tired.

Like a man pursued and arrested in flight, he stared at Selva, stared beyond, stepped from side to side as though he would find a way around her, leave her deserted on the slope.

"My God! Selva!" he uttered in a croak at last, "Great, Almighty God!"

He raised his head, looked about at the mountains and

in his neck below his ear, she saw his pulse beat. Confronting her again, he said, "God Almighty, Selva, he's hurt."

"Who's hurt?" She would not believe him so long as belief could be eluded, but the soles of her feet were cold.

Clay regarded her in bewilderment. "Who?" he said. "Him. Peter. The Englishman."

He spoke earnestly. "It's not my fault, Selva. I swear it's not my fault. Look!" He held out his hands. Skin was peeled from their calloused palms and as they opened before her, blood oozed from the creases of their finger joints.

"I hung on," Clay said, "as long as I could. I hung on, but he gave up."

He rubbed the back of his hand against his brow. "Selva," he said, "I don't think that that man had ever been on a mountain in his life before, unless tied with a rope to a guide. I should have known — he wore fur lined gloves. Look, we got over all right. Twice I had to help him. We camped there last night in the timber. We started back this morning. There was this rock above the waterfall. It was slippery. It was loose. I told him, I told him not to put his weight on it. Christ! Selva, he gave no heed. He *wanted* to take hold of that rock. I tell you he wanted to. It came loose. It bounced down the ridge on the other side all the way down to Geikie Meadows. I heard it smash into the timber. He, the Englishman, slipped."

Clay bit into the knuckle of his hand. "Christ! He slipped. Not far. Ten feet, to a little ledge. I could have climbed back, but he was shaking, his lips shaking. I thought he was going to cry. I got hold of a piece of solid rock. I let my feet down to him. I told him to climb up my legs. Look!" Clay twisted his trouser leg, showed a long rent in it, and a scratch on his leg, still bleeding, where a fingernail had cut.

"He took hold of my legs," he continued. "He climbed up as far as my waist. My fingers on that cold rock were numb. They were slipping. My arms were pulled from their sockets. Five hundred feet or more were straight below us, dragging on my foot soles. I told him to hurry. For Christ's sake, I said, hurry. That was when he gave up. He let go — but he didn't fall all the way. He hit another ledge, thirty feet down in the chimney where the water was falling. I climbed back and looked down. Selva — he moved. He moved. He lifted a hand, rubbed his face, but his left leg was doubled back under his shoulder. The boot was there under his shoulder."

Clay moaned, swayed. "I called to him. I told him to hang on. I dropped my pack, my axe. I dropped everything. I made it over the ridge and down to here. He was yours. I gave him all I had."

He grasped her shoulder, shook her. "Tell me," he demanded, "are the boys there? Are they at the chalet? I've got to get Slim Conway and one of the others to come back up here with me with a rope. We can get him out with a rope.

When Selva did not answer, but instead pressed with one hand the other against her mouth as though to stifle a long pent-up cry, he shook her again so that her head wobbled on her shoulders. Yes, she remembered, the boys were there at the chalet. She had seen the horses dropping down from Crooked Pass. Of what was it they had reminded her? What was it again? It had seemed funny, out of place. That was it, they had looked like ants crawling in single file down a sheet hung upon a line. You never saw ants crawling one by one down a sheet upon the line? Never, never at all? Who ever saw ants, even a single ant, upon a sheet hanging from the line? Or was it not a sheet, but a tablecloth hanging from the line?

The fire by which Selva had stood had given the shape and colour, but not the reality, of heat. Making the fire, she had been sweating from her climb. Having made it, she had stamped her wet feet, swung her arms as the sweat cooled upon her. Then, scattering the fire, she had run up the slope towards where she thought Peter might be and halted when she saw Clay coming down it towards her. Now, beside him, listening as he spoke, the chill had not left her. She had a cold, perhaps a fever. Shivers coursed her body. Goose flesh formed until the nipples of her breasts were aching. The wind blew, searched craftily beneath her garments with an old man's icy fingers. The light on the snow around her dimmed and Clay's voice became no more than a distant memory of speech until, seeing again the vision of the ants crawling down the sheet upon the clothesline, Selva giggled against her hand. Her shoulders shook. Whoever heard of ants upon a sheet hanging from the line? She laughed, choking against the hand. In a moment, she was sobbing and pounding her doubled fists upon Clay's chest — pounding, pounding, arms swinging even as he held her off. Her shoulders began to shake again. Her whole body shook, her teeth chattered. Finally, her knees gave way and Clay caught her as she fell.

He picked her up in his arms. After a few steps, he shouldered her as he would a sack of grain and walked down the mountain side, forded the creek and followed the trail to the chalet. The world to Selva at times was red and whirling. Then again, it would be black and still, and once or twice aroused by the agony of breathing, she opened her eyes and saw a dark heel, moustached with snow, seeming to pause, to be there without movement beneath her.

After a while, through the redness and the whirling, she felt warm blankets around her and heard Rosie's voice in the bedroom. "I told her," Rosie was saying, "I told her not to go. I told her she would get a chill and now she may have pneumonia."

For a time Selva felt peace about her. She was alone in a white world, walking towards a snow covered mountain. Peter stood on the peak of the mountain waving to her, but as she walked towards him, the mountain moved, always moved as she walked towards it. Again, Peter was in a deep chasm or pit. Falling water hissed behind him. He was wet, curly hair plastered to his scalp with the spray. She had a rope in her hand and was letting it down to him. Peter took hold of the rope, but the rope was wet with the water and his fingers slipped from it. Again and again she tried and again his fingers slipped.

Then, it might have been a day, or a week, or months later — for time and all timely things had gone from her — she was being helped into a saddle. A hole had been cut in a blue blanket and the blanket slipped over her head. A horse moved beneath her. Whenever she was about to fall from the saddle, an arm came about her, held her once more erect. She felt the jolt of hooves and heard voices behind her and before her. Someone said, "Sam's gone on ahead for the doctor." Peter was there with her. She knew that he was there. Clay and Slim had gone up the ridge with a rope to bring Peter back. Peter who was her very own now, her most precious part. They had put a rope around Peter, her very dear Peter, and pulled him up from where he lay with his leg doubled under his shoulder. Clay had promised that they would. Peter was there on the trail, up ahead. He was on a litter made with canvas and poles, strung between two old and steady pack ponies. This she had seen without apprehending and had apprehended without seeing. Slim rode ahead of him. Clay rode just behind. Sometimes Clay dropped back to hold her in the saddle. Slim and Clay were bringing Peter, her Peter, down from the mountains, down out of the snow into the lower valley where summer still lingered and poplar trees were medalled in yellow. Peter, even to his head, was wrapped in red blankets. Crossing the pass, the wind lifted the top blanket, folded it back, to give him a last glimpse of the mountains into which he had so bravely walked, ruck-sack on his back, ice-axe in his hand. His right eye, with the long lashes — straight and thick and long as those of a buffalo — as he lay on the litter, was open. Snowflakes fell upon it. They did not melt. Peter, though his eye was open, slept. He was asleep and all his dreams slept with him. Peter was going home, home to a house too large for walls. It had been cold through the night up there on Thunder Ridge. But Peter was warm now, wrapped in the red blankets.

Then somewhere far above her — he was so high above that he was sitting on a dark cloud — Selva saw Mr. Branchflower. Mr. Branchflower was sitting on the cloud. He did not wear his heavy climbing boots. No, he was barefoot in the cold. His bare feet hung down below the cloud. Mr. Branchflower had climbed Mount Erebus. Later, he had invited her to his cabin. And now, thrusting his stubby pipe's stem towards her, he spoke again about climbing the peak. "Experience," he said. "Remember I told you, not too difficult at all — that is, if you had had experience." But Peter, she thought, as the wind, or merely a branch which touched her cheek, brushed Mr. Branchflower aside, Peter had not attempted to climb Mount Erebus. Peter had avoided the heights, the great heights. He had gone between them with Clay on the ridge. Thunder Ridge was no more than a threshold into another valley. She tried to explain this to Mr. Branchflower, to shout to him, rising weakly in her stirrups. He was so far away now, so very, very far away on his cloud, being borne beyond the horizon, that he did not seem to hear her. He tamped his pipe, once more began to smoke it.

Then there was a camp and it seemed to Selva that the doctor, Dr. Ormsby, from Yellowhead was there. He had been sent for and had ridden in to meet them. She heard his voice, she was sure that she heard his voice and that she felt his hand upon her brow — the spry little doctor whose twinkling eyes made her think of chipped pieces of ice and who, someone had said, moved about here and there, always on the jump, like a squirrel with a nut in its mouth.

After that, there was a whiteness. There were white sheets and white walls and nurses in white about the bed, and the mornings, Dr. Ormsby taking her pulse, patting her shoulder. As through the days she grew stronger, Selva could turn on her side and look out the window and watch the town going about its business — in the morning, Mr. Peckharin, the storekeeper, passing with quick little steps, almost running, to get behind his counter, or a locomotive engineer with wide hips walking down to the roundhouse, and at night, sometimes, the call-boy — Jimmie Bright, who had done the chores at the chalet — hurrying by with his lantern. In daylight, horsemen rode proudly by the window. Down the street Selva could see the back door of the Wamboldt house where new people lived and a new maid worked. She saw the maid, who was tall and had black hair — she could distinguish no more at the distance — come out the door to shake a mop and on Monday mornings she watched her as she hung up the clothes to dry. On Sunday afternoons a man, wearing a white, high crowned Stetson, knocked upon the door and went into the kitchen. Later, they came out to go for a walk.

At night, locomotives whistled loudly in the valley.

One morning, when the late September sun slanted through the curtained window, Dr. Ormsby, who walked as though he had little springs within his shoes, came in rubbing his hands together. He wore a grey suit and had a small red rose in its buttonhole.

Sitting on the bedside chair, leaning forward, elbows on his knees, he said, "You had a bad time, my girl, a very bad time. It was a virus pneumonia. Nothing could help you but your constitution. You wanted to live and you lived."

He repeated, "A virus pneumonia. You were tired. Your feet were wet. Mentally, you were disturbed. And the germ — anyone coming in from outside might have carried it to you."

A tear rolled slowly down Selva's cheek. "I don't want to live." she whispered.

He took her hand, patted its back. "You do," he said. "You will. I think I understand. A fine young man. He's gone on before us. No one was to blame. They held an inquest. The men did everything they could, Clay Mulloy and all the rest. It was the cold and shock — and that leg. If he had lived he would have been a cripple."

He paused a moment, looked steadily at Selva. He said, "His mother came out, took the body back with her." Peter had not gone back to his mother. This time she had had to come to him. "She wanted to see you," the doctor said. "But you were too weak for visitors."

Selva turned from the doctor. Dry-eyed, she caught the pillow slip between her teeth. The doctor rose. He stroked her hair with a gentle hand. "It was no one's fault," he said again. "These things are so because they have to be." It was the last and only mention made of Peter.

Others beside the doctor now came to visit Selva. Mr. Wilkins came, his great gnarled hands holding a dozen of carnations and told her that she had been a most capable hostess at the chalet in the High Valley, assured her that she could have the same job again the next summer and in the winter, if she wished, she could take charge of the ski lodge he was building up at the ice fields. Lastly, he told her not to worry about the hospital or doctor bills. They would be taken care of.

Mrs. Weaver called. She stood by the head of the bed and brushed Selva's hair flat out against the pillow. "You have such lovely hair," she said, "but, poor dear, your cheeks are so pale and you're so thin compared to what you used to be." She added hastily, "Not that you were ever stout or even plump for that matter."

As she brushed life back into the thick and glowing hair, she retailed to Selva bits of small gossip from around the town. Mr. Winnie, the undertaker, was to marry a girl from Moose Jaw. His mother was angry and threatening to leave him and telling everyone who would listen that it was she and her money that had made him what he was today. Also, it was reported that the Wamboldts, who had moved into Edmonton, were separating. Mr. Wamboldt had been surprised in the room of a very second rate hotel on 101st Street. As for the new people in the Wamboldt house, Mrs. Weaver knew nothing about them — yet. It would take a little time. They kept to themselves. It was thought that they had private means. Mail came to them from New York, and one letter had been posted in Bermuda. Also Mr. Hamilton — that was the name, "Hamilton," and they had no children — had received a wire from Vancouver, B.C., saying, "No cause to worry. Everything quite all right with us." The wire had been unsigned.

Rosie came in to see Selva, wearing a new yellow jacket and pink woollen skirt, carrying a bunch of violets which she arranged in a water glass by the bed. The second time she came, she said, looking towards the door, "Someone's out there who wants to see you."

"Who?"

"Slim. He wants to come in, but he's not sure you'll speak to him."

Selva's eyes opened wider. "You mean, you . . . and Slim?" she asked. Rosie nodded.

"He's really quite nice," she said, "when you get to know him better."

Slim came in, coughed, pawed the floor, ran the brim of his hat through his fingers. After a few words, he left, Rosie clinging to his arm as if, by a strange mischance, he might go away without it. Her voice, piping in the hallway beyond the door, played a tune to their going.

Selva, though she did not leave her bed, went with them down the corridor and out the door to the street. She was a part of Rosie now, as Rosie was a part of her. She had become diffuse and was a part of all the people whom during the summer she had met. In cities in the East and in California, they would from time to time, recalling their holidays in the Rockies, speak her name, speak the name of Selva Williams who had been the hostess in the chalet in the High Valley, the tall girl with the Titian hair.

Clay Mulloy — he had given up a fall hunting trip into the

Smokey to stay in town — was consant in his attention. Twice a week his red roses were delivered until Selva at last in a room overflowing with flowers, in despair of checking this petalled growth which threatened to consume her, asked the nurse to distribute them among the other patients. Each day, punctually at four, Clay appeared in the doorway. Hair slicked back with water, he wore a blue serge suit, sleeves and trousers too short, the trousers tight about his muscled thighs. A black knitted tie was knotted in the part of the stiff white collar which encircled his thick, brown neck. Above it, his cheeks were flushed, his eyes seemed to protrude, as though while he stood there, he were slowly and deter- minedly choking. On his feet — narrow, high arched — he still wore unbeaded moosehide moccasins and he would move, lithe as a cougar, to the chair beside the bed.

Often they were silent, Clay, stiffly upright in the chair, elbows spread, hands upon his thighs, staring at the wall. Selva lay looking upward to the ceiling, cheeks pale upon the pillow, a little bow of blue in her hair which glinted as though flecked with copper in the light of afternoon. They did not speak because Peter was there with them in the room. They could not speak of Peter.

At other times, Clay would talk of horses, of the outfit, of what he had said to Bill Wilkins and what Bill Wilkins had said to him. And one afternoon he talked unreservedly and without cessation of the ranch on the Little Hay where the next spring he would commence to raise mountain horses.

When Selva was able, he called for her in Wilkins' Ford truck and took her to Mrs. Weaver's rooming-house where for a while she would stay. Later, he went with her to the new Hudson's Bay store next to the pool-hall. There, behind a partition, she tried on and then bought a grey flannel suit, its narrow, tapering lapels trimmed with a dark blue facing. Clay nodded to a black, cadet shaped hat with a white feather. Selva put it on before the mirror. It would go with her new black shoes with the flat bows and she told the clerk that she would have it as well. She paid for the whole with a cheque on her summer's earnings, the first cheque in her life that she had drawn.

Then, on the second Sunday in October, she felt well and in the afternoon she and Clay went walking, he in his blue suit and stiff collar, she in her new grey suit with the dark blue facings, the black, high heeled shoes, the pointed hat with the short, sloping white feather. It was a day of warm sunshine without wind and the poplar trees along the street, shorn of their leaves, stood still as if they listened. In late May when Selva had passed along the same street with Slim Conway, the poplars had freshly budded and people had been sitting on their porches in the twilight and robins had called and squirrels had chattered from the pine trees. Now, in October, the poplars were bare, the people indoors, the squirrels silent and the robins gone.

Today she did not wish to climb a hill nor to go far, yet she and Clay found themselves passing the house of Mr. Winnie, the undertaker, and passing beyond it and, inevitable as doom, beyond the poplar lined street into the gloom of pines at its end. Here, Clay stepped ahead and preceded her down the trail which led to the railroad trestle and across the trestle bridge to the park-like flats below the mountain where beaver had dammed a stream into a pool. Once with Slim, having gone down to the beaver meadow, Selva had seen a pair of swans floating on the pool's dark waters and there in the spring she had gone to pick an early crocus to put in the blue bowl on her dresser-top in the Wamboldts' house.

Crossing the railroad trestle, she held to Clay's arm for on her high heels she was unsteady. Clay's hand helped her down the gravel embankment beyond the trestle and was beneath her elbow as she climbed the slope into the trees. With him now behind her, she followed the trail by the mottled birch and turned down from it where the big fir tree grew. Then, in a moment, she and Clay were standing side by side in the beaver meadow before the pool and beneath the school-marm tree, its arms upheld to the sky.

Selva, looking about her, thought, as she had once thought before, that this beaver meadow, this vale of grass among the trees beside the water pooled behind its dam, with long shadows of afternoon now upon it, had been hers. It could be hers no more. She had come back to it, but she had not returned. Here with Slim she had listened to the small waters, heard the distant owl, seen the stars come out and felt above her in the twilight the night hawk's swoop. She had stood here with Peter and his arm had been around her, his hand had stroked her hair and she had yearned towards him. Now Slim was with Rosie. Peter was with the years.

Instead of Slim, instead of Peter, Clay Mulloy stood beside her. Clay had a place on the Little Hay between the foothills and the mountains. There he intended to raise horses to be used on the trail, deep-chested, short-barrelled horses. Now Clay was speaking to her. What he said, she did not know. She was conscious of his arm about her waist, drawing her to him.

"Don't," she protested. "I'm not strong yet. You know that."

He made no answer. Hs grip relaxed, but he continued to hold her to him.

Up the valley towards the pass a locomotive howled. It was early for the passenger, Selva thought. Still, it might be the passenger now running on the new winter schedule. In the sleepers, in the observation car, would be people from the Coast, possibly from California. They would be going east to Montreal, to the big cities. On the train might be the same conductor, the same brakeman, the same engineer who had brought Peter back from California. Peter had heard, perhaps had lifted up his head from a book when he had heard that same lament of the locomotive. It would be a book of poems. "I have trod softly, Peter," she thought. There had been a time when the locomotive might have taken her to him, to his house where his mother waited in Montreal. Instead, on his last journey it had taken him away forever. Always the locomotive whistle would call to her of whence it came, of where it went.

"Clay," she asked, putting her hands on his shoulders, drawing back her head, looking up to him, "this ranch of yours on the Little Hay . . ."

"Yes?" he asked.

"I was wondering. Can you hear the locomotives' whistle from it?"

He smiled. He said, the skin about his eyes crinkling, "I've camped there many times. Only a trail leads in. We'll have to build a road. It's about forty miles back from the railroad . . ."

"Yes, but about the whistle," Selva said.

"I'm coming to that. It's about forty miles back. There's a big slab of mountain right behind it. Tombstone mountain, it's called. I've stood there below the rock and heard the echo of a whistle from the railroad. Especially in the winter when it's clear and cold you can hear it. It's sort of this way — you can hear the whistle if you want to, if you go to just the right place at just the right time, but there's no reason why you *have* to hear it."

On the ranch on the Little Hay, with the aroma of the corrals about her, with men coming and going, stamping their boots, laughing, talking, riding away in the summer, walking off on snowshoes in the winter, dropping a pattern of lace from their feet, just as they had come and gone when she was a girl on the homestead in the foothills — there on the Little Hay, opening the door at the proper moment, seeing her breath rise in the cold moonlight, she would be able to hear the locomotive's whistle far, far away in the winter night, telling her of streets where lights shone, of bright windows and of women who passed wearing furs and fur-trimmed overshoes, of a salon where people in evening dress gathered to speak in voices assured and soft under twinkling chandeliers and into that salon, in a black dress, green earrings showing below the sweep of her tawny hair, she would be forever about to enter.

As she paused in the doorway, voices were stilled, heads were lifted. She looked back, over a bare, polished shoulder. A man came out of the dimness. He too wore full evening dress, for later, they were to attend the opera. He was a little older now and his black hair, though still full and curly, carried a hint of grey on the temples. His eyes were deep and blue, the lashes straight and thick. His cheeks were flushed. He held out his arm. She put her right hand in the crook of the elbow. He set his far hand firmly upon the back of her own. The touch was cold, icy cold. She shuddered. "Selva," Peter said, "you are late. I have been waiting. You passed me there in the shadows. I stepped back so that I might see you once more coming towards me. Let us go now into the room. Let us go into the room and meet the people." But as they turned to go into the room where the tall people in evening dress had been waiting under the giant and twinkling chandeliers, Selva saw that the people had departed, that the chairs were empty, that the room was deserted and that the light of the chandeliers above her was slowly but surely dimming. A chill breeze, scuttling along the floor, touched her ankle. It was the same breeze which now, in the beaver meadow, with the mist of autumn rising from the nearby waters, moved among the pale grasses, causing her, under her hat with its sloping white feather, to turn quickly to Clay and with a shiver of living flesh to grasp his arm, solid with muscle. For an instant, she was unable to speak. Then, she said hoarsely, "Take me, Clay, take me. Take me, hold me. I'm cold and I am afraid." And, on tiptoe, she reached for his lips to suck from them the breath that was mortal.

TALONBOOKS — FICTION IN PRINT 1977